CW01507044

# THE
# WINTER
# MYSTERY

An absolutely gripping cozy mystery
for all crime thriller fans

# FAITH MARTIN

*Travelling Cook Mysteries Book 2*

**Previously published as**
***A Fatal Fall of Snow***

JOFFE BOOKS

Revised edition 2024
Joffe Books, London
www.joffebooks.com

First published by Robert Hale in Great Britain
in 2011 as *A Fatal Fall of Snow* by Joyce Cato

This paperback edition was first published
in Great Britain in 2024

Cover art by Nick Castle


ISBN: 978-1-83526-405-8

# PROLOGUE

An old woman toddled up the freezing aisle, a glorious Christmas cactus clutched in one gnarled hand, a knotty hazel walking stick grasped in the other. From the pulpit, the equally ancient vicar smiled benignly at her as she placed it on an old crumbling window shelf, and felt himself shiver in his robes. In spite of global warming, it was an unusually viciously cold and frosty morning, and the church felt like a freezer.

Overhead, the church bells pealed, echoing sharply across the rural Oxfordshire valley. It was the last Sunday before Christmas and perhaps because of that, the church actually had a few worshippers in it for a change. Two old men, bachelor twins of the parish, coughed and sneezed in the front row, victims of the latest flu virus, and the vicar sighed in sympathy. He now had three other churches to cover in his extended parish, and actual snow was forecast! It was many years since this part of the country had seen any significant snowfall, and the man of the cloth, to be frank, could have done without it.

Ah well. The children loved it so.

Reverend Adam Clode had come to the parish of Westcott Barton just over forty years ago. A small village in the heart of Oxfordshire, it had undergone the usual changes over that period of time. It had seen two cul-de-sacs of council houses built on a patch of wasteland, and had lost the village school and post office. And, of course, the rise in house prices had forced out many of the long-standing families, as incomers with money bought up the homes needed by the local youngsters. For all that, it still remained a largely close-knit farming community.

The vicar watched as several young boys dashed in, looking irreverent, but carrying great boughs of holly. The vicar winced at the sight of the roughly broken stalks, and gave up a brief prayer that the children had combed the woods for them, and not raided the gardens of any of his parishioners.

He met the eyes of the richest farmer in the county, Stanley Kelton, beneath their fiercely bushy brows, and quickly looked away. He prayed even harder that the boys had not wandered into Kelton woods for the holly. If Stanley now came across denuded holly bushes on his land he would soon be back to church, but not for morning worship. Adam Clode could almost hear the farmer's imagined but withering tirade now.

By his side, Stanley's daughter Delia sighed in boredom, her two brothers staring absently at the hymn numbers on the wall. Given the choice, the vicar knew that none of the Kelton offspring would come to church at all. Like the rest of the country nowadays, he suspected they were at best indifferent, if not downright atheists. But Stanley Kelton must have insisted, and what Stanley Kelton wanted, Stanley Kelton got.

A moment later, the vicar found himself meeting the very different gaze of Sidney Kelton, Stanley's older brother. His blue eyes were gentle, and when he smiled at the vicar (almost as if he could read that reverend gentleman's unease and wanted to offer some comfort), Adam smiled back automatically, feeling unaccountably better.

Mrs Jarvis, the Keltons' cleaner and a long-time member of the church's unofficial care-taking committee, carefully lit the long white candles. Their flames flickered quickly, casting shadows across the sixteenth-century walls. Soon the smell of candle wax scented the air, and the holly, now placed along the alcoves by one of the sneezing bachelor twins, glinted in dark green glory.

The bells continued to peal joyfully and echo across the crisp air, and suddenly, without warning, the *real* spirit of Christmas seemed to settle magically over the church and its tiny congregation. In these times of commercialization, and over-hyped advertising urging you to spend, spend, spend, Westcott Barton, for a few minutes at least, seemed to retain a little of the spirit of Christmas past.

The old vicar straightened up as his arthritis was forgotten and the bitterly cold air in the church became irrelevant, and looked down at the pinched, cold white faces and red noses of his congregation. They waited for the sermon with patient resignation. Impulsively, the vicar reached for his songbook and called out for the carol 'God Rest Ye Merry, Gentlemen' and the congregation caught the mood in an instant.

The organist, nodding and shivering over the battered organ, sprang into life like the enthusiastic schoolteacher that he was, and voices, hoarse with colds, out of tune but gutsy, rang around the church. It was the Sunday before Christmas; there was going to be snow for the children, mulled wine for the adults and a rousing carol to lift the heart.

The season of peace and goodwill was truly upon them. And yet, in the seemingly blameless congregation, amid the holly and the singing, silently, carefully, *purposefully*, someone was plotting cold-blooded murder.

# CHAPTER ONE

The bone-shaking tractor pulled to a somewhat coughing halt as the driver peered out of his snow-frosted side window. 'There's the road to Westcott Barton, missus. Not much of one is it? And I doubt it'll be cleared any time soon either. Think you can manage it? I'd offer to take you down there, but I've promised a smallholder in the next village I'll help him move his sheep before it gets dark.'

By his side, perched precariously and distinctly uncomfortably on a rusted wheel arch, an impressively Junoesque woman with beautiful blue eyes squinted through the glass.

As the farmer had said, the lane wouldn't be much of a thoroughfare even in good weather. A single track, it was hemmed in on all sides by straggling blackthorns, and burdened with a recent and spectacular snowfall of nearly two feet, it resembled nothing so much as an obstacle course.

Jenny Starling, travelling cook, sighed deeply, hefted her holdall past the rear of the driver's seat and half rose. The farmer, a middle-aged man with a hooked nose and curious eyes, took one appreciative glance at her generous curves and decided she would most definitely need a helping hand down. He quickly opened his door and slid out, sinking into a snowdrift which came over the top of his wellingtons and promptly turned his shins numb.

He cursed mildly, but watched with bemused respect as the attractive twenty-something woman climbed out of the cramped tractor with unexpected ease and grace. Her coat was a bulky padded blue, matching the knitted bobble hat that hid a glossy array of dark brown curls. On her feet were sturdy leather boots that sensibly fitted far more snugly than his own wellingtons. She was already hoisting her holdall down after her, before the farmer could offer to reach up for it.

And he *had* been about to offer. Although he'd come across his unexpected and unusual hitchhiker on a deserted winter road — and his mother had always maintained that only riff-raff thumbed rides — there had been something about the woman that had instantly screamed 'class' at him.

In fact, Jenny usually travelled everywhere in her trusted cherry-red catering van, but not even her gallant and stalwart steed would have been able to handle the snow-packed roads, so she'd been forced, very reluctantly, to leave it under cover in a long-term car park not far from Burford. Unfortunately, all the local buses had been cancelled due to the previous day's snowstorm, leaving her with no other choice but to hoof it unless she wanted to let her clients down.

Which she most definitely didn't. Jenny had her reputation for reliability to maintain.

Luckily, she hadn't gone far when the tractor had rumbled up behind her and she'd raised a hopeful thumb.

Now the farmer watched her as she negotiated around the snowdrifts and stood by a drunkenly leaning signpost, rubbing her gloved hands briskly together for some much-needed warmth in the crisp morning air.

England hadn't had a really bad winter to speak of for some time, and Jenny hoped the snow would soon go. Still, she couldn't help but be thrilled by the sudden blanket of white that had descended on the countryside. Everywhere children were tobogganing, making snowmen and laying in ambush for the postmen with a stock of snowballs. At first, it had made her feel like singing 'Winter Wonderland' over and over again.

Until the novelty of it all wore off, that is. The thing was, she'd forgotten how damned *inconvenient* snow could be!

Ivy grew darkly in the hedgerows around her, and by the side of the road mysterious animal tracks dotted the snow. She could see the unmistakable track of a fox, the paw prints placed in a single straight line, and the light feathery trail of his brush where it had dragged along the ground. Any number of birds had left little clawed trails, but nothing much moved now — only a single crow overhead, cawing raucously as it headed for a bare sycamore.

Her eyes turned to the only sign of habitation for miles around and roved thoughtfully over the rooftops and chimneys of the village that nestled about a mile down in the valley.

'It's not actually the village itself I want, but Kelton Farm. Do you know it?' she asked, turning back to the farmer, thankful that there was no wind to drop the temperature even further.

At the mention of the farm, however, the tractor driver visibly stiffened. His eyes, which had been both speculative and friendly, suddenly turned hostile. Despite the all-pervading freezing cold, Jenny felt the temperature drop yet another notch, and her heart fell.

'Sure, I know it. You want to take this lane for half a mile or so and then take the first path on the left — if you can see it in all this,' he waved his hand at the blanketing snow. 'I doubt old man Kelton has had the track cleared just to make life easier for visitors, mind. He would have better use for the few tractors he's got, I reckon, and he certainly wouldn't want to get his precious cart horses out just for that.'

There was unmistakable contempt in his tone now, and Jenny arched one eyebrow delicately into her fringe of dark hair. 'Horses?' she almost squeaked in surprise. 'You mean proper cart horses?' she asked quietly, feeling a thrill of romanticism ripple through her.

'That's right,' he snorted. 'He uses mostly horses, and charges a fortune for folks to come and watch what he calls "traditional farming" being done. He gets all sorts out here — school trips and tourists and whatnot, and all of them paying good money for the privilege. He sells his produce to them organic people who go crazy for it, plus he rakes off all the grants he can get from the government for being so "green." That's not to mention the half-baked hippies who pay a fortune to live in his run-down cottages and get a taste of the "real thing." They think because they have to pump water out of a well by hand and live by gas lamps and candlelight, that they're experiencing something special. Truth is, the canny old sod doesn't have to pay for the upkeep or maintenance of the cottages and he can still make a tidy profit out of 'em.'

'But surely, in this day and age he has to meet certain standards?' Jenny objected.

Her knight of the road snorted disdainfully. 'Not him! Besides, nobody complains do they? Like I said, they think they're getting a taste of the good old days — growing their own veg and raising rabbits or whatever. He even set up a fancy petting zoo for kiddies in the summer — charges nearly five quid for entry. Can you believe it? Five bleeding quid!'

Jenny shrugged, wondering if it was just jealousy talking. Nowadays, she knew that many farmers had to subsidize their incomes. Maybe Stanley Kelton was one of those wise and heart-warming souls who bred rare species in an effort to save them from extinction. She knew a lot of the UK's oldest and more rural breeds of farming animals were in danger of dying out, in which case he would need the extra capital for their upkeep.

'You ask me, he likes to think he's some kind of lord of the manor still living in Victorian times. And what's to stop him? He's got all his family too scared to stand up to him. And Kelton Farm's the biggest around here,' the farmer finally admitted, grudging every syllable. 'His farmhands have got no choice but to play along with him, if they want to work that is. Even though it's bloody back-breaking work doing things the old-fashioned way. You ask me, he's just too tight-fisted to pay good money on modern equipment. There's a saying around here. You can always trust a Kelton to get blood out of a stone.'

And he gave a gurgling laugh.

Jenny sighed deeply. It was going to be one of those Christmases. She could just feel it. The farmer, noting her gloom and unable to contain his curiosity any longer, gave an artificial cough. 'You, er . . . going to work there yourself, then?'

Jenny smiled rather grimly. 'I'm afraid so. But just for the two weeks over Christmas. I'm their cook.'

'Their *cook*!' the farmer echoed, too stunned to remember his good manners. When he found those disconcertingly lovely blue eyes centred on him once more, he felt himself blush; at forty-two, it was something he hadn't done since his teen years. 'Sorry, missus. It's just that it's not like Stan to hire somebody he didn't have to. Not when he's got a daughter, like, to do all the drudgery and cooking for him.' A glint of mischievous glee suddenly lightened his dour face. 'Oh, I get it! Joanne, that's my wife, she told me that she'd heard young Delia was threatening to stop work over the Christmas season. Looks like she got up the gumption to stick by it too. Good on her, I say. But I said to Jo at the time, I couldn't see Stan going without his mince pies and turkey.' Crow's feet appeared at the corners of his eyes as he grinned at some private or local joke that Jenny fervently hoped wasn't going to backfire on *her*.

Whatever the family tensions were at Kelton Farm, the last thing she wanted to do was stand on anybody's toes. She sighed again, more deeply than ever.

Yes, it was definitely going to be one of those Christmases. 'Well, I suppose I'd better be off,' she muttered, never one to falter in the face of adversity. She glanced at the leaden skies all around her and frowned. 'There's more snow up there,' she added quietly, her words rousing the farmer from his musings.

'I reckon you're right there,' he agreed briskly. 'You mind them ditches then. Stick to the middle of the road,' he advised, climbing back into the cabin of his shuddering tractor and continuing on down the road with a blithe wave of farewell in her direction.

Jenny looked all around her at the snow and sighed. Wonderful! How was she to tell what *was* the middle of the road amongst all this blanketing whiteness? She gave a mental shrug and hoisted her tough nylon holdall firmly over one shoulder and set off.

If she suddenly found herself knee-high in a foot or so of frozen water, she supposed that she could safely assume she'd come across a ditch.

It was Christmas Eve tomorrow, and who knew what sort of welcome awaited her at her new place of work? Still, things could be worse, she told herself philosophically. At least she had a job — well, for the next two weeks at any rate.

She'd been staying in Oxford where she was hoping to secure a position in one of the many college kitchens, once the next term started. Although she'd secured a little bedsit near Keble College, her kitchen in the converted Victorian house consisted of a single gas ring, and the thought of spending Christmas alone had been a depressing one, her father still in France and her activist mother off on some crusade or other about Christmas trees. So when she'd seen the two-week job as cook at Kelton Farm advertised in the local paper, it had roused her interest immediately. And not even the derisory wages on offer had put her off. She cooked for the love of it, as well as for money. And the thought of spending a good old traditional Christmas on an English farm, cooking all those good old traditional dishes, seemed almost too good to be true.

Now, as she trudged her way through the snowdrifts, she told herself that the next time mawkish sentiment reared its seductive head, she'd look the other way!

Stan Kelton hardly sounded like a maiden's dream of an employer, and a rebellious daughter could cause her no end of problems. She only hoped there'd be no funny business this time. Through no fault of her own, she had, in the past, had to sort out some very nasty murders. People nowadays had no self-control, she thought crossly.

After a while she stopped walking, both to catch her breath and because something else had caught her attention: to her left, two rows of wooden stakes, standing a few feet apart and about a foot above the ground, led off over the crest of a hill. She put her holdall down and looked back down the road, thinking. Had she come half a mile? Straight on, the tower of the village church certainly looked closer. And that row of posts signified to her a set of fences running alongside a road. And, looking more closely still, the snow there did seem to be a few inches lower than the surrounding mass, as if, a few days ago, someone or something had passed along, flattening the first layer of snow tight. The new snowfall, however, looked ominously pristine.

'Oh, wonderful,' Jenny muttered. Above her, a flock of jackdaws rose noisily from a bare oak tree, scuffling and arguing. For a moment she watched them, envying their ease of movement as they set off towards the village. Then with a somewhat self-pitying sigh, she resumed her trudging. She only hoped the farm was just over the hill. Snow looked pretty, but it was hard going on the legs. Her calf muscles were already begging for mercy and her toes had long since said bye-bye to the rest of her.

But if the farm turns out to be three or four miles over the hill, she thought resentfully, I hope someone finds my frozen body and gives me a decent burial.

A lone jackdaw came to roost on one of the posts, and called out a cheery greeting to her as she went past. 'Jack!'

'Oh, shut up,' Jenny snarled at it, and hefted her holdall just a little higher under her armpit.

Since there'd been no telephone number attached to the advertisement, she'd written a letter, citing her previous experience and employers, and had been accepted by return of post. In that letter, Mr Stanley Kelton had specified this morning as her time of arrival. The least he could have done was have one of his horses plough a path up this blasted track, she thought, feeling more and more put upon with every plodding step.

At last, she crested the small rise and looked down, thankfully, onto a large, square Cotswold-stone farmhouse spread out below her. Although it was nearly eleven o'clock in the morning, the sky was so overcast it felt almost dark. In several windows, orange light spilled cheerfully onto the snowy courtyard surrounding it. From the set of stables off to the left, and attached to the house by a makeshift corrugated iron passageway, she could see steam gently rising into the air, although no horse, very wisely, hung his head over the half-doors into the frigid air beyond.

As she looked, a black and white shape trotted across the cleared courtyard and scratched at the door to the house. The sheepdog was evidently out of luck, for as the cook thankfully picked up a little speed, the prospect of hot tea and an even hotter kitchen fire spurring her on, the dog trotted back disconsolately and disappeared into one of the stables. There, at least, the body heat of the animals would help to raise the temperature a little.

She was out of breath but in a much happier frame of mind when she finally reached the door and banged on it sharply. At the sound, the sheepdog sped across the yard and comically skidded to a halt at the sight of a stranger in his domain. Guiltily, not to mention rather belatedly, he started to bark. Jenny glanced at him, not in the least intimidated.

'Shut up, Pooch,' a young and attractive voice said, right in her left ear, and Jenny quickly turned around.

'Hello. Are you Miss Kelton?' she asked with a bright smile. She believed in making a good first impression.

'Yes?'

Delia Kelton looked to be about eighteen or so. She had shoulder-length blond hair, the colour of ripening wheat, and deep chocolate-brown eyes. She was in a red woollen dress that was well-worn and far too small for her. The effect showed off too much leg, and pulled too tightly across her rather well-developed breasts. No doubt her strike over Christmas was probably the least of her father's worries, Jenny thought wryly.

'I'm Jenny Starling,' Jenny said, to no effect. 'I'm the cook?' Still no reaction. Delia continued to look at her, a puzzled frown pulling at her brows. 'Mr Kelton has hired me for two weeks. To help out with the Christmas dinner and so on . . .' she trailed off, dismayed to see a look of petulant fury fill the girl's otherwise pretty face.

It was at once obvious that her father had not told her what he'd done. No doubt, Jenny thought with intuitive accuracy, Delia had hoped that her threat to stop work over Christmas was going to win her some concession or other. And Jenny's untimely arrival was living proof that she had failed.

'Oh hell,' Jenny said glumly.

Delia glanced at her sharply, her eyes narrowing. 'You'd better come in,' she said at last, grudgingly.

And as the unexpected visitor passed by, her well-padded figure such a striking contrast to her own slim frame, Delia frowned. She had the uncanny feeling that the other woman had understood far more than she should have done, just from a few simple words. It left her feeling oddly vulnerable, and wrong-footed.

'I suppose I'd better show you to the kitchen then,' she said, with more hostility than she'd meant. 'I daresay you're cold after that walk,' she added quickly, by way of shamefaced recompense.

Jenny nodded gratefully, and followed her hostess into the most pitiful kitchen it had ever been her misfortune to come across.

Although the room itself was perfectly adequate — large, square and well equipped — everything else was a sight. The floor was a picture of muddy footsteps, thawing into little pools of water. Obviously, the men of the house just tramped through with muddy, snow-covered wellingtons whenever they pleased. The fire in the Aga was low, and untended; the sink was full of unwashed dishes. On the table were a few crusts of bread and a piece of uncovered, hard-looking cheese. No kettle boiled. No smell of delicious baking permeated the air.

And surely — she glanced at her watch; yes, it was now almost eleven thirty — wouldn't the men be coming in for their lunch soon? In weather like this, they'd need something hot.

Delia watched the stranger's eyes narrow.

Jenny quickly pulled off her bobble hat, revealing a cascade of surprisingly pretty, glossy dark hair. When the big cook looked once more her way, Delia found herself looking into piercing blue eyes that seemed to cut right through her.

Jenny didn't say a word. She didn't have to.

'I've refused to have anything to do with the place,' Delia said, instantly on the defensive. 'I told Father so, but he thought I was bluffing. Well, he knows differently now.' Her chin angled up as her voice rose into semi-hysterical defiance.

Still Jenny made no comment, but she wearily shrugged off her coat. Beneath it she wore a heavy ivory-coloured woollen sweater and a longish brown skirt. Her ample but sexy hourglass shape made the girl's eyes widen.

'How long is it since the men have eaten a cooked meal?' she asked briskly, instantly the consummate professional.

Delia pouted. 'They make themselves poached egg on toast. Stuff like that. Oh, all right! Four days,' she finished in a burst, her pout going into overdrive.

Jenny shuddered. Food was the great love of her life, and the thought of anyone going without a proper quantity of it for so long was horrendous! 'I see. How many will I be cooking for?'

Delia met the unwavering blue gaze, and was the first to look away. The kitchen had somehow taken on an air of sudden animation, as if it were magically aware of the presence of a maestro. Delia herself was becoming aware of the force of the other woman's personality, and felt an uprising of panic.

'Well, there's my dad and Uncle Sid. Bert, my older brother, and his son Jeremy, and Bill. Bill's my other brother. And myself of course, and Mrs Jarvis. She's our daily. Part of her wages is a cooked meal. She's a widow, lives on her own. She's late in today. I daresay with the snow and everything . . . anyway, that's all. Bert's wife left him, and Bill isn't married. Nobody stays around here unless they have to,' she finished her somewhat rambling inventory with a bitter grimace.

'Humph,' Jenny grunted, and began a thorough check of the kitchen, noting utensils and supplies as she went. Delia watched her, clearly fascinated: the cook missed nothing.

After ten minutes, she'd assembled a pile of leeks and potatoes from the cold cellar, and extracted some ham from the fridge. Herbs from the herb closet followed, and when, later, two men walked in, a blast of frigid air accompanying them, the room was filled with the smell of potato and leek soup and freshly baking bread.

Bert and Bill Kelton both moved cautiously into the middle of the kitchen, staring first at the nearly six-foot-tall figure of the unknown cook, then at their sister, then at each other.

Jenny, noticing both their caution and lack of words, frowned over her saucepan. This would never do. She turned, looked them over and nodded. 'Gentlemen, I'm Jenny Starling. Your father hired me to cook for you over the Christmas season. There's ham, potato and leek soup for lunch, with bread fresh from the oven. Sit down, and I'll lay the table.'

Bert, who was obviously the elder, slouched wordlessly at the table. He was, Jenny would learn later, forty-six years old, and his thick brown hair had begun to turn grey. He watched the world through such sad brown eyes that he reminded Jenny of a bullock about to go to the slaughter. He seemed utterly defeated, but quite by what, she couldn't tell.

Bill, younger by ten years, still moved like a man in his prime. His hair was fair, like that of his sister, but his eyes were a soft grey-blue. 'Smells good,' he said, and gave Jenny a smile that would just have to do as her official welcome. She accepted both his compliment and greeting with a bow of her head then looked up as one of the inner doors opened.

The man who came through shuffled, as though raising his slipper-shod feet to take individual steps was beyond him. In fact, everything looked beyond him. He was tall, but stoop-shouldered. Consequently, the old grey cardigan that he wore hung almost to his knees. His hair was white and sparse, and on his skull, age spots showed like giant freckles. His chest looked caved in, and as he moved he wheezed. His eyes, however, were the same grey-blue as his younger nephew, and Jenny instantly knew that this could not be the Stan Kelton who had produced such contempt in the knight of the road who'd given her the much-needed lift that morning.

No, this could only be Uncle Sid.

'Hello there, and who's this?' Sid Kelton asked amiably. 'And what's that delicious smell?' he added, his voice as paper-dry as a desert wind. His smile, though, was warm and sunny, and Jenny found herself rapidly moving forward and drawing a chair out for him to collapse into.

'Good morning, Mr Kelton. Your brother hired me to cook for the family.'

'Oh?' Sid Kelton looked troubled and glanced sympathetically at his niece.

'Just for the Christmas season,' Jenny added quickly, wanting to ease the old man's anxiety. She was rewarded by a look of relief, and nodded to herself, returning to her stove to make sure her soup wasn't sticking to the bottom. It was a thick, nourishing soup, the way any good soup should be. But as she stirred, she made a mental note: whatever the reason behind Delia's rebellion, it was obvious that her uncle was on her side.

And Jenny couldn't help but feel that any side Sid Kelton was on was the side she wanted to be on too.

'You managed to clear off Spokeswain Bridge then, you two?' Sid was asking behind her, and both men were halfway through a humorous account of trying to find the river and the small bridge that crossed it in the blanket of snow, when the outer door was flung open and a blast of snow-washed air came in.

Jenny turned, frowning fiercely as yet another pair of dirty, snow-encrusted boots came into view. With a very audible 'tut' of annoyance, she went straight to the cupboard where she'd noticed a mop, and brought it out. She began to mop the floor with quick and efficient strokes and only when she'd finished, and put the mop away, did she look up.

She'd been aware of total silence throughout her endeavours. She'd also been aware of how the atmosphere of the room had compressed. It was as if all the previous warmth she had put into it, the stoking of the fire and the smells of good food, had somehow been brought to nothing.

And when she looked up and met Stanley Kelton face to face, she understood why. Fierce brown eyes glinted from beneath bushy brows, but there was no touch of animal softness in these orbs. Stan Kelton was a bullish-looking man, from the width of his shoulders to the thickness of his waist. His large, beefy hands were chapped and reddened by the coldness outside, but he seemed oblivious to physical discomfort. His eyes ran over her, but there was no curiosity in them.

'You're the cook then?' he said flatly, and it came as no surprise that his voice was loud and dominating.

Jenny felt her backbone stiffen. 'I am,' she said, in a decibel above that she'd normally use. 'And I'd appreciate it if you men would remove your boots before coming in here. The floor is a disgrace.'

Behind her somebody gasped. Or rather, several people gasped. Jenny had the feeling that nobody, but *nobody*, spoke to the old man like that. But Stan Kelton did not, as she had half expected, explode into a show of temper. For a long moment he simply considered her in silence. Then he walked over to the stove, lifted the lid off the saucepan, reached for a spoon and took a taste.

Now everyone seemed to hold their breath except for Jenny. Jenny Starling already knew that the soup was excellent.

Stan Kelton turned back to her. 'Good soup,' he said. 'But nobody takes their boots off before coming in here, especially not in weather like this. There's no porch out there, and I ain't going to stand around in the cold, trying to prise my wellies off just to suit you. Get used to the mop.' And with that he walked to the table, took the chair that was positioned at the top, and sat down.

Head of the table. Head of the house. His power was so obvious it was almost farcical. 'Is that bread ready yet?' he asked.

Jenny regarded him steadily. Quickly, she measured the trouble of an argument against any possible gains, and shrugged philosophically. 'In a few minutes. Then it must cool. Eating hot bread is bad for the digestion.'

She waited, as if expecting him to comment. Her gaze never wavered.

'Aye,' he finally said, and leaned back, stretching his cramped muscles. 'I expect you're right. You seem to know what you're about, right enough. I don't have to tell you what I expect, food wise, do I?'

'No,' Jenny said coolly. 'You don't. I'll make the mince pies tomorrow. Will it be turkey or goose, Christmas Day?'

'Goose, woman,' Stan Kelton said firmly.

Jenny nodded. 'Goose it is. Christmas pudding then, to follow?' She didn't wait for his assent. They already understood one another perfectly. Wordlessly, she turned back to the stove.

Sid Kelton looked at his brother thoughtfully, then glanced across at the two boys. He frowned. Delia watched the cook, playing nervously with the buttons on her red dress. Jenny stirred her soup and sighed.

Well, this was a cheerful place and no mistake!

As she took the bread out of the oven and laid it on a tray to cool, she began to wish that she were back at her bedsit in Oxford. One small gas ring or not.

Merry Christmas, Jenny, she told herself wryly!

## CHAPTER TWO

The last drop of soup had gone (and she'd made six pints) and the last crumb of bread had been devoured (hard luck on any birds hanging around in the courtyard hoping for some crumbs). And the kitchen floor was once again muddy, where the men had left the table and tramped back *out* again.

Jenny surveyed the sink full of washing up and the dirty floor and sighed heavily. At the table, only Delia remained. She stayed stubbornly seated, arms folded firmly across her chest, her expression mutinous. Not that Jenny had expected any help from that quarter.

'Has your uncle gone for a nap?' she asked instead, returning to the mop, which was already beginning to feel as familiar as a lifelong friend, and setting to on the floor. Although it wasn't technically part of her duties to be a cleaner, she simply couldn't abide a kitchen that wasn't clean. No doubt her celebrity-chef father would have minions to see to his every whim, but his travelling-cook daughter had to make shift for herself.

When the younger girl didn't answer, Jenny smiled. 'After a meal it does a man good to sleep for a while,' she offered pleasantly, which would be her one and only attempt at friendship. Should it be rebuffed, she could quite happily leave the petulant little madam to her own sulky devices. She was here to cook, not to be popular.

Delia eventually shrugged. 'For an *invalid* to take a nap you mean?' she corrected her. But there was no malice in her voice, and she half turned to look affectionately at the door to the hall, where Sid, no doubt, probably *was* already dozing by the fire. 'It was a wicked bout of pneumonia and an asthma attack that did it, you know,' she said sadly.

Jenny, with the floor once more looking respectable, stopped mopping and looked up. 'Ah,' she said softly, in immediate and sympathetic understanding. 'His chest is weak?'

'Yes,' Delia confirmed. 'He was in hospital for nearly six months, back in the seventies. When he came back to the farm, he just couldn't pick up where he left off. Didn't have the physical stamina anymore, y'know? And he was still youngish then, I suppose,' she mused doubtfully. 'Lucky for him, Dad was here,' she added, her voice so suddenly loaded with vitriol that Jenny, caught in the act of adding washing-up liquid to the dishes, quickly turned her head.

'What do you mean?' she asked sharply, not sure why her own curiosity was so firmly aroused. She didn't really want to learn any more about the intricacies of the Kelton family, after all. She just wanted to keep her head down, work out the two weeks, and hotfoot it back to Oxford before any funny business (or downright *unfunny* business) took place.

Yet there was something so incredibly desperate in the girl's voice that, before she could stop herself, she'd already asked the question.

'Uncle Sid's the oldest, you see,' Delia said. 'It wasn't just his illness that made him look years older than Dad.'

'I don't follow,' Jenny said, giving up the fight and turning from the sink. She took the chair opposite the girl and looked at her frankly. Delia didn't seem to mind. In fact, she looked only too happy to dish the family dirt.

'When the farm was first built, about three hundred years ago, the original owner was, well, a bit of a rogue, as

Mrs Jarvis would say. He was rich; he didn't have a title, but he was wild and crafty and used to getting his own way,' Delia began, although quite why she chose to start her story so far back in history Jenny, for the moment, had no idea.

'His name was Greenslade. A gambler and womanizer, he lived a right old life of Riley,' Delia continued, her brown eyes coming alive. 'I daresay he saw a bit of the world,' she added, so wistfully that the cook almost winced. The girl's desire to do the same was so palpable, it almost throbbed in the air between them.

'Anyway,' Delia shrugged off her daydreams and got back to the story. 'He married some local woman who was rich and all that, but apparently they didn't get on so well. She didn't like his womanizing I expect,' Delia opined with a shrug of her shoulders, as if to say that all men were the same, and what else could she have expected? 'He certainly had a few children on the wrong side of the blanket, anyway,' she continued. 'Eventually, things got so bad between them, that the wife moved out of their newly built farm and went back home to her mother. Greenslade was livid, apparently, since she took the children, their children that is, with him. So he hunted around for all his other offspring, the illegitimate ones I mean, and had them come to live with him!' Delia grinned widely. 'Imagine the scandal that caused! But not content with that, he had his lawyers draw up an entailment for the farm in perpetuity, stating that the oldest son, no matter whether he was legitimate or not, *had* to inherit the farm. That really was one in the eye for his wife,' Delia laughed, obviously applauding Greenslade's revenge.

Jenny pursed her lips. It was, she had to admit, very racy stuff. 'I expect that curbed a lot of your ancestors' more, er, rampant behaviour,' she mused, a twinkle in her eye. 'Knowing that your peccadilloes with the milkmaid might turn out to be sons that'll inherit the family manor, I mean.'

Delia giggled. 'I'll bet it did. Perhaps that's why Dad's such a hypocrite. He can't stand going to church, but his father attended regularly, and made him go, so now we all have to toe the line as well. I daresay the Kelton men had it hammered into them right from the start to stay on the straight and narrow, or else.'

Jenny nodded, but her eyes were thoughtful. 'You really don't like your father very much, do you?' she asked quietly. 'And I don't mean you just don't get on. Lots of daughters and fathers, I expect, don't get on. But you seem to actively *dislike* him.' There was no judgement in her voice, no spurious nosiness, but even so, Delia's pretty face filled with colour.

'I hate him,' she confirmed vehemently, and raised a shaking hand to brush a lock of fair hair from her forehead. 'But then, so do Bill and Bert. So does Mrs Jarvis, if it comes to that. As does everyone who even remotely knows him, in fact,' she finished, with a forced and unconvincing laugh. She met the cook's eyes defiantly, and tossed her head. Her young voice rang with passionate conviction. 'I daresay even Uncle Sid hates him, deep down. He's every right to, when all's said and done. Dad even got his way with him.'

Jenny gave herself a mental shake. It had given her quite a turn, finding out the real depths of Delia's feelings. Even though she herself had already felt a fair bit of antipathy towards Stanley Kelton, and considered him a sorry excuse for a human being, she couldn't help but feel that it seemed somehow unnatural for a daughter to feel the same way.

Even so, she believed instinctively that the reason, and the fault, lay firmly at Stan Kelton's own doorstep, so perhaps it was not so unnatural after all. Love had to be earned, in Jenny's experience, every bit as much as respect.

Now, with Delia's last observation, she turned her thoughts back to more practical matters. 'What do you mean by that? Your Uncle Sid doesn't seem the sort of man to hate anyone,' she chided, but only gently. The girl was obviously very highly strung, and it probably wouldn't do to get her too heated.

Delia hung her head and sighed. 'No. You're probably right. Sid's a dear old thing. But don't you see? It's doubly

21

important for the Keltons that the oldest son should inherit. And by rights, that should have been Sid, and any son that Sid might have had. But Dad got his own way yet again. It must have really enraged him, being born the second son. But he never let that stop him. He's always wanted the farm for his own.'

'But it does belong to Sid, doesn't it?' Jenny asked, puzzled. 'I mean, even if your father does most of the physical labour that your uncle can't, surely the farm still belongs to Sid? Legally and all?'

'Oh, technically, I suppose it does,' Delia said, and then stood up angrily. 'But who was the one who married, and had the next son to inherit the precious farm? Who sits at the head of the table, hmm?' She tossed her head, her colour high once more. 'Not Uncle Sid, is it?' she hissed. 'It's *him*! He always gets what he wants. He's like a big fat leech, feeding off everyone else.'

On a sob, Delia turned and fled the room and a moment later Jenny could hear footsteps pounding up some stairs. She sighed, and glanced at her own holdall. She hadn't even been shown to her room yet. But she was in no hurry. It would probably be freezing cold up there, and she was quite content to stay in the warmth of her kitchen.

She attacked the dishes, musing as she did so on the odd family history. At some point the farm must have changed hands through some reckless action of an inheriting son. Unless, of course, the original Greenslade's bastard son had been a Kelton. Still, it did seem a pity that Sid had not married and produced a son. It would probably have done Stanley Kelton a world of good to not get his own way for once.

She wondered if his ill health was the only reason for Sid not marrying, or if there were yet more family skeletons waiting to be discovered in the Kelton Farm cupboards.

She was just finishing the dishes when the door opened on a blast of cold air. The woman who came in paused by the fireplace to remove her sodden boots, at least sparing most of the kitchen floor, and it was this simple act that identified her. Mrs Jarvis, the daily — had to be. Only a daily would think about sparing herself the work of clearing up after her own muddy footprints. As she turned and caught sight of the cook, she froze comically, her mouth falling open in stunned surprise.

She glanced around quickly, almost as if to check she had come to the right house.

'Hello, I'm Jenny Starling. Mr Kelton hired me to cook over the festive season. You must be Mrs Jarvis?' She beamed at her amiably.

Mrs Jarvis slowly removed her headscarf, revealing tired grey curls in need of a new perm. Her face was heavily lined, her eyes sunken in her head. Jenny wondered, with a concerned pang, what had made the woman look so ill and defeated.

'Is young Delia around?' the daily asked, her voice sounding as tired as the rest of her looked, and making no attempt to even acknowledge the introduction.

'Upstairs I think,' Jenny said, and watched as the older woman walked through into the hall. There she heard her shouting up that the footpath to The Dell was now open again. When she came back she took in the newly mopped floor and sniffed the air, still redolent of soup. She looked like a wary old cat that had come home to find a new kitten installed.

'My cottage and Cordelia Bray's place lie just over the hill,' she said, by way of explanation for her shouting up to Delia. 'Delia's great pals with Sissy Bray, Cordelia's girl. Bill and Bert have just now managed to clear a path through. Otherwise I'd have been in just as early as always,' she continued defensively. 'But you have to cross the bridge over the river, and in this snow, I didn't dare try and find it until—'

Jenny, suddenly understanding the reason for this wave of nervous chatter, waved her hand airily. 'Oh, that's all right. No need to explain to me. I'm just here for a couple of weeks to cook, that's all, then I'll be on my way again.'

Mrs Jarvis looked infinitely relieved. And, most oddly, at the same time she also looked fiercely resentful. 'Oh. I thought the devil was up to one of his tricks again.'

Jenny blinked and wondered, once again, what had turned Mrs Jarvis's world on its head. And whether or not it might have affected her mental processes. Having to work with a mad housemaid on top of everything else would really put the cherry on top of the Christmas cake! Unless, of course, she was one of these profoundly religious people.

Catching the look on her face, Mrs Jarvis managed a smile. It looked pitiful, but it was definitely a smile. 'Don't worry, I'm not mad. I was talking about Stan Kelton. I call him the devil, because that's what he is.'

Jenny couldn't help frowning. As Delia had foretold, here was yet somebody else who hated Stan Kelton. But to call him the devil was surely a bit over the top, wasn't it?

'I've only just met Mr Kelton,' she said cautiously and turned back to the stove, where she had lamb chops ready for dinner. Some dried rosemary mixed with flour and lots of breadcrumbs and some salt would make a nice crust for the tender meat. Mashed potatoes (mashed with real butter and the cream from the top of the milk) would do just nicely. And there was diced carrot and swede for vegetables. She nodded. Good, filling, tasty food. That was what concerned her. She doubted that farm workers would be impressed by cordon bleu proportions and experimental cuisine. Hot and filling, that's what was obviously required around here.

She definitely did *not* want to know why Stan Kelton was the devil, or what tricks he might have played on poor Mrs Jarvis. It was none of her business. But even as she told herself this, Jenny Starling was painfully aware that it might well turn out to be her business after all. Things had a way of happening around her.

Her father, a chef over in France, had recently begun mentioning in his letters a medium known for relieving people who were jinxed. Jenny had very politely told her beloved daddy what to do with his medium. Still, she was bound to admit that things did have a nasty habit of happening around her. But she preferred to think of it as fate, as if some obscure destiny had allotted to her the role of Nemesis, and was determined to wait for her to be in just the right place, at just the wrong time, in order to bring about the tragedies it had in store.

And you're getting way too fanciful, Jenny, old girl, she told herself stoutly. It was Christmas Eve tomorrow, and what could possibly go wrong on Christmas Eve?

Delia came down, muffled from head to toe in a long coat, scarf and gloves and rushed out the door without a word. Mrs Jarvis watched her, and shook her head.

'Poor girl. She's so desperate to get away from here, it fair breaks the heart to watch her. And Sissy is just as desperate to get away from her poor mum. Cordelia's a self-made invalid, you know,' she said chattily to Jenny, but without any obvious rancour. 'You know the type. Her husband was killed in a car crash last year, and she took to her bed and never left. She could leave it if she wanted to, of course, at any time, but why bother? Her Sissy's about the same age as Delia, and they spend all their time together plotting their escape to London. I know, I've heard 'em, chattering like two excited magpies.' Mrs Jarvis paused, but only for breath. 'Of course, they'll never get away. Cordelia could make a stone feel guilty, and she'll never let her Sissy escape. She'd have to face up to life if that happened, wouldn't she? And that devil will never let Delia go either. He keeps her penniless you know. No wonder she finally snapped and said she wasn't going to cook a thing this Christmas. He never even pays her a pittance of a wage for all the work she does around here. Too scared she'd hoard it and be off, I expect. Slave labour is what the devil demands from all the family. And all she'd need is the price of a train ticket and she could be gone. Poor kid doesn't even get new clothes, not unless the devil buys them for her.'

Jenny, who'd been busy making the crust for the meat, finally gave a great sigh and swilled her hands under the sink.

So that was why Delia had been wearing a dress that was far too small for her. And Mrs Jarvis was determined to make sure that everyone knew it too. But what was she supposed to do about it? Delia could find herself a job in Oxford or Cheltenham if she really wanted to. But breaking free took courage. And courage was something nobody else could give you.

'I daresay you want to get on,' Jenny said firmly. 'I don't know if you used to help out in the kitchen, but I think I can manage it all on my own. That'll take some of the load off, I expect,' she added pointedly.

Mrs Jarvis met the younger woman's level stare, and sighed. She was obviously not going to be drawn, and that was all there was to it. 'Fine, I'll start in the parlour,' she said flatly. 'The fire there always needs raking out. But,' she half turned and gave the cook a toe-curling look of contempt, 'you can thank your lucky stars, young missy, that you're only going to be around here for a few weeks. Stay any longer, and you'll become just like the rest of us. No matter how much you think you wouldn't. That Kelton devil can destroy the spirit of anyone he wants. You included,' she jabbed a finger in the air.

Jenny almost expected her to spit, as well. But with that rather bone-chilling prophecy, she swung around and shuffled out of the room.

Despite herself, Jenny shivered. 'Well, honestly, it's like living in an episode of a soap,' she muttered, more for the comfort of hearing her own voice than anything else. 'Or like something out of one of those Gothic novels,' she carried on crossly. 'An old farmhouse, cut off by snow, a dour old servant, going around prophesying doom and despair . . . and stop talking to yourself,' she admonished herself briskly, suddenly realizing what she was doing.

From behind her came a dry chuckle. 'Good idea. Folks around here might get the wrong idea, finding their cook muttering to herself over the custard. The thought of a loopy cook tends to make most folk nervous.'

Sid Kelton slowly made his way to the table, his twinkling eyes and wide smile belying his words. Jenny found herself chuckling.

*Chuckling!*

This would never do. She stopped at once, and reached for the kettle. 'A cup of tea, I think,' she said firmly, and Sid, about to sink into a chair, looked up, ears cocked at the sound of scratching at the door. 'The pooch,' he said anxiously. He looked at the distance to the door, then down at the comfortable chair, so close, and sighed. But by the time he'd looked back up, Jenny was already on her way to the door. She opened it, a blast of icy air hit her, and a black and white streak shot past her and vanished. Jenny closed the door, blinked, and looked around the kitchen. No sign of it. She moved to the sink, put the kettle on, and gave a quick check under the table.

No pooch.

She walked over to the cupboard to extract the sugar and glanced behind the dresser. A narrow space, but no pooch. She moved to the fridge, got out the milk and checked under the claw-footed Welsh dresser. No pooch.

From the table, Sid watched her surreptitious search, his eyes shimmering with unshed tears of mirth.

Don't tell me, Jenny thought grimly. We're back to the Gothic novel again, and the pooch is going to turn out to be a ghost dog. Saved his master from drowning fifty years ago, but died valiantly himself in the village duck pond. Now he haunts the farm, fooling visitors into thinking he's a real, live, flesh-and-blood mutt.

She glanced at the shut door that led out to the hall. No doubt the dour Mrs Jarvis had chased poor Sid from his place by the fire, but he'd shut the door behind him when he'd first come in. So where in the world had the mutt disappeared to? She'd never seen an animal move so fast.

She made the tea, returned to the table, handed Sid his mug and sat down. She took a sip. Sid watched her thinking about it, sipped his own brew and wondered what she'd do next.

Jenny, after having thought it through, lifted the table-cloth, ducked down and checked the chairs. And there, sat next to Sid and curled up tightly on the chair so that his tail didn't droop and give away his position, was the dog. One of Sid's hands rested on his head and fondled one floppy ear. The mutt, alerted to movement, turned doleful eyes in her direction.

His expression was perfectly pathetic. It was clear that he expected to be evicted once more into the snow, and was doing that heart-melting don't-hurt-me, big-brown-eyed thing that a variety of animals did so well.

Jenny straightened up, glanced at Sid and sighed. 'I suppose I shall have to get used to keeping a lookout for dog hairs,' she said mildly.

Sid smiled. 'We knew we could trust you the moment we set eyes on you. Didn't we, Pooch?'

From beneath the table came a whine. It didn't sound so sure. 'The thing is,' Sid said, his dry, laboured breathing breaking into a choking laugh, 'Pooch doesn't like sheep. He'll do anything to avoid going out with the boys. And Stan won't have the dog indoors. Says it ruins a good sheepdog.'

Jenny met Sid's eyes and began to chuckle again. A sheepdog that didn't like sheep! Now she'd heard it all. She shut off the laughter abruptly in mid-gurgle as the door opened and Mrs Jarvis came in, took one hurt look at the teapot and went out again.

Jenny sighed. 'I suppose I should have called to her that we were having tea,' she said, feeling instantly guilty. 'I was going to offer to make her one as soon as she came in. She looked frozen. But . . .' she trailed off quickly.

'But I bet she never gave you the chance, hmm?' Sid said, his smile going, the twinkle in his eyes fading, leaving them looking dull and cloudy.

Jenny felt her own good mood vaporize. 'She looks ill,' she said, by way of explanation as well as excuse. Not for anything would she tell Sid about Mrs Jarvis's tirade against his brother. For one thing, she'd never betray another woman like that. Besides, it would hardly be diplomatic.

But Sid didn't need telling. Instead, he reached for his spoon and began, unnecessarily, to stir his tea. For a long moment, the only sound was that of his laboured breathing. Once more, Jenny felt herself being drawn into the drama of the Kelton family saga, and opened her mouth to tell Sid that she really didn't want to know.

But she'd left it too late.

'Mrs Jarvis was widowed recently. A few months back, in fact. Her husband, Tom, had a smallholding just over in The Dell. A fair few acres, some sheep, goats, free-range chickens and eggs, that sort of thing.'

'Oh, I see,' Jenny said sadly. It was not illness, as such, that had drawn the lines of defeat on Mrs Jarvis's face, or scored the wounds deep in her soul.

'The thing is,' Sid continued diffidently, 'she blames Stan.' He sighed heavily, and shrugged his painfully thin shoulders. 'So does everyone else, for that matter,' he added, with determined truthfulness.

Jenny felt a cold hand snake up her back. 'Oh?' she asked warily. 'Why's that?'

Sid looked up and met her eyes. He looked pretty defeated himself. 'Because he *was* to blame, I expect,' he admitted quietly. 'The Dell adjoins Kelton land. It's good grazing, and the big barn Tom Jarvis had built near the spinney was ideal for an over-winter feeding place and shelter for our own flocks. But Tom Jarvis didn't want to sell. And,' Sid sighed, forcing himself to face up to facts, 'I daresay Stan wouldn't really have offered him a fair price.'

So Delia was right, Jenny thought glumly. Stan Kelton *did* own the farm in all but name. He did the buying, the selling, and no doubt everything else as well.

Sid stopped stirring his tea and looked up. 'Things began to happen after that.' His voice was flat and curiously lifeless. 'The river got mysteriously dammed and flooded the lower pasture of The Dell — Tom lost his whole flock of sheep. Then, at market, Stan began to undercut him, selling at a loss to himself just to ensure Jarvis, too, lost money. He was forced to take out a bank loan . . . and they foreclosed on him,' Sid continued grimly. That he felt guilt and remorse over what had happened to his neighbour was obvious, even though it was none of his own doing. That his brother Stan felt neither was a foregone conclusion, lying heavily between them. 'There was a rumour that Stan was threatening to take Tom to court over every little thing, knowing that Tom wasn't much for forms and letters and such, and couldn't afford a solicitor anyhow.' He shook his head sadly. 'It was probably true,' he acknowledged, his papery voice little more than a whisper now. 'It's just the sort of thing he'd do. But, whatever was said or not said, the result was that Tom Jarvis died of a heart attack brought on by all the stress, and Stan got the land cheap from the bank, just like he wanted.'

Delia's impassioned speech of less than an hour ago suddenly flooded back into Jenny's mind. Stan Kelton always got what he wanted. A leech, living off the blood of others . . .

'But why on earth is Mrs Jarvis working here?' she asked, instead of asking why Sid Kelton let his younger brother get away with such things. For she already knew the answer, as must everyone else: Sid was simply no match for Stan. He probably never had been. And yet, she couldn't find it in her heart to think less of Sid. Instead, she found herself despising Stanley Kelton all the more.

Sid shook his head, his skin stretched tight across his face, his eyes seeming to sink ever deeper into his head.

'Their cottage went with the land,' he explained. 'Poor Gladys was facing eviction. But my brother didn't really need the cottage — our shepherds and farmhands all live in estate cottages already. Plus we own a fair few properties in the village itself. And, I daresay, not even Stan had the nerve to throw a widow out onto the streets. He may not care what people think of him, but even Stan knows he has to live in these parts. And there are some limits, even for him.'

He sighed and drained his mug of tea. He didn't look any the better for it.

'Besides,' he continued, 'Stan has an eye for a bargain. He let Gladys stay on at the house, provided she came and worked here. Delia never was much of a housekeeper, and of course, he doesn't have to pay Gladys anything like a decent wage. He takes half her pay before she even gets it, as rent for the cottage. Yep, always had an eye for a bargain has Stan.'

When he finished, he looked and sounded exhausted. In silence, Jenny collected their mugs and took them to the sink. What could she say? What could she possibly say?

The devil, poor Gladys Jarvis had called him. Playing evil tricks.

How right she was, it seemed.

## CHAPTER THREE

The dog had stayed on in the kitchen when Sid returned to his place by the fire in the living room. Obviously the mutt knew better than to enter the inner sanctum of the house, even with Sid for protection. Now he lifted his head and shot to his feet. His ears, which had been flopped lazily over his nose, sprang to quivering attention. In a flash he shot like a black and white streak of lightning to the big Welsh-style dresser, which stood about four inches off the floor on sturdy square legs.

There, before her astonished eyes, the dog did a trick worthy of any stage magician (or octopus) and flattened his flanks and rear end enough to sidle into the tiny space. Even so, his spine scraped along the top of the wood, making her wince in empathy. His shining eyes disappeared into the gloom and the last bit of all to disappear was his plumy tail, withdrawn into the cavity like a mouse going down a hole.

Jenny fought the sudden urge to applaud and quickly turned away from the dresser. After a performance like that, she was not about to give the animal's position away. She'd just picked up a spoon with which to stir the gravy when the door opened on the now-familiar blast of snow-chilled wind. She was already reaching resignedly for the mop by the time the last of them had straggled in.

Bill, the younger of the sons, gave her a guilty look as she quickly eradicated his soggy and muddy footprints from the floor, along with all the rest. Bert, she noticed, headed straight for the table and sat with the quick and grateful slump of a truly exhausted man. Yet he looked fit enough. It was not the actual work, she thought wisely, that was sapping his energy.

Like a king ascending his rightful throne, Stan Kelton sat in the head chair and unbuttoned his coat. His hands were huge and dirty, and Jenny wondered how many sheep he had dug out of the snowdrifts that day.

She came and stood by the table. 'Are you going to wash your hands?' she asked him bluntly, and what little desultory conversation there had been, mostly Delia asking Bill if the road to the village was cleared yet, stopped abruptly.

Stan Kelton met her eyes, then glanced down at his hands. 'Later, perhaps,' he growled, bristling at her challenge. 'Why?' He thrust his whiskered chin forward, brows beetling in anticipation of her defiance.

Jenny pursed her lips. 'You can eat straight after you've been rolling about in manure and clearing out the chicken pens for all I care,' she conceded loftily. Her voice was now as cold as the snow outside, 'So long as neither I nor my food are blamed for it if you come down later with the galloping gut-rot.'

She straightened her back and met his eye, which was not easy since she stood at six feet one inch tall. She didn't even so much as blink. One way or another, she'd had a lot of practice at this sort of thing. She'd once had a lot of trouble over just this issue, concerning a canal engineer she'd once cooked for, and his very inquisitive pet rat. That unfortunate alliance had resulted in a truly lamentable incident that had left a rather queasy feeling in her stomach for quite a few weeks afterwards.

She had learned from that very hard lesson to get things straight about matters of hygiene right from the start.

Stan held her gaze for a moment, then grunted. She took that to mean an acknowledgement, nodded once and

33

returned to the oven. Once there, she dished up the meal in silence, served it, and in silence it was eaten. After a few tentative bites, Bill, Delia and young Jeremy, Bert's son, dug in heartily, the young nearly always being the most ravenous. It did her heart good to see such sturdy appetites.

Bert ate with a stolid resignation that was painful on the eye. Jenny hated to see anybody eat and not thoroughly enjoy the experience. Indeed, it was so totally unnatural it gave her goosebumps. She eyed him thoughtfully over the mashed potatoes.

Stan Kelton himself ate everything with gusto, in painful contrast to his older brother, who could only manage a small portion of his food. This Jenny also found distressing, but forgivable, since poor Sid looked physically incapable of eating a hearty meal.

She found the silence oppressive, but knew better than to break it. Only after the last plate had been pushed away did someone speak, and then, predictably, it was the tyrant himself.

'Well, that was all right, Miss . . . er. . . ?'

'Starling.'

'Right. Starling. But a bit plain. I expected something fancier from a professional cook.'

Sid coughed. 'I thought it was delicious, my dear. I only wish I could have eaten more. I do like my potatoes like that. Parsley and herbs sprinkled on them before they go into the pan, yes?'

'Yeah, nice grub,' Bill suddenly said, his shoulders hunching, as if expecting a blow. His eyes, however, blazed defiance, and when they met the gaze of his father, they refused to drop.

'And what would you know?' Stan sneered at him, his large body stiffening at this unexpected show of rebellion. 'You're as green as a cabbage, boy. And about as useless.'

Jenny stared at him in astonishment. For a start, she couldn't believe that Stan Kelton felt the need to even reply. It was such a small thing to get riled about. Surely the man wasn't such a megalomaniac that a mere comment about food would need to be trampled on so thoroughly?

No, she was sure that wasn't the issue. As Bill glowered and turned red, she suddenly understood that this argument had nothing to do with her food. Which was a relief, to be sure. No, this had been brewing for some time by the looks of it. It had only needed Bill to work up the nerve to go against his father, even in so small a way, for the floodgates to open.

As Sid reached out and laid a warning hand on Bill's arm, Stan Kelton got to his feet. His fists, Jenny noticed, were clenched at his sides. He looked ready to explode.

'I've made an apple and cinnamon tart for pudding. With custard, of course. Who wants some?' she asked quickly. She hated scenes. People, she thought grimly, really should have more sense than to go out of their way to create them. Especially at mealtimes!

'I do,' Bill said quickly, his ruddy, handsome face darkening still more as he continued the pointless defiance. 'I can't think of anything else I want more,' he added, just in case he hadn't made it plain enough.

Stan Kelton laughed. It was as dismissive and derisive a laugh as the cook had ever heard. It made even her teeth clench together, as if someone had just scraped a long hard nail against a blackboard — and she wasn't even the recipient of it.

'Have your apple pie, lad,' Stan sneered, relegating Bill from thirty-six to sixteen with contemptuous ease. 'It might put some lead in your pencil, though I doubt it.'

Bill at once reared to his feet like an angry lion. 'And what's that supposed to mean?' he challenged, blue eyes blazing.

His father's implacable brown eyes stared back at him. 'I mean, boy, that it's Bert who's had to be careful. And he was, more praise to him. He had young Jeremy there in proper wedlock.'

Jeremy, a young lad who seemed to have the ability to disappear into the wallpaper, since Jenny had hardly noticed him at all, blushed like a beetroot, and ducked his head. He was a handsome boy, with rich brown hair and the dark gentle eyes of a deer. His natural shyness would have made him easy cannon fodder for his grandfather, Jenny guessed, with real pity. But, fortunately for him, it was his uncle Bill who was standing against the firing squad wall at this particular moment in time.

'You were always free to go about and sow your wild oats where you liked,' Stan continued, his sneering voice grating on everyone's nerves. And under the dresser, even the mutt shivered. 'But I don't see much evidence of oats around here. What's the matter, lad? Not capable?'

'Enough of that!'

The voice was weak, for it came from Sid, but the tone was surprisingly forceful. It stopped both Stan and Bill in surprised mid-threat.

'Aye, enough,' Stan said quickly, before Bill, who was staring at his uncle in astonishment, could respond. 'Let's sit down and all have some of this here tart. It's what I've paid hard-earned cash for, anyways.'

Jenny turned to her oven, lips pursed. Paid for, indeed. Anyone would think he'd forked out a fortune instead of just the going wage. She had a good mind to give him mince tomorrow — and as greasy as she could make it. But pride forbade it. She wouldn't serve greasy mince to the sheepdog let alone a human being — even if said *Homo sapiens* was named Stan Kelton.

She took the huge jug of creamy and steaming custard, flavoured with rum, to the table, and cut the large tart into generous portions.

Delia, she noticed, had the grace to blush as she met the cook's eyes. But, like her brother, she too seemed hell-bent on rebellion, and Jenny still couldn't see Stanley getting any cooked meals from his daughter when her own two weeks here were up.

Now wasn't that a shame?

* * *

'You'd better come with me and pick out the goose,' Bert said to her an hour or so later. The kitchen was cleared of both debris and inhabitants, and his unexpected presence just behind her left shoulder made her jump in surprise.

'Sorry,' he mumbled, taking a shuffling step back. Close up, he looked even more tired than before. His skin was striving to match his greying hair.

'Goose?' she echoed blankly, then nodded. 'Oh, goose. I didn't see any as I came in this morning.'

'They're probably still in the barn. Delia's supposed to let them out first thing, but I daresay she forgot.' He walked towards the door, pausing by the dresser as he did so. 'Come on, out of it.'

No movement.

'Pooch!' he growled, his no-nonsense tone causing one white paw to emerge, followed by a black nose. Like a snake, the dog wriggled out into the open and gave Bert his most impressively pathetic look. 'Come on, out,' Bert said, but managed a bare tilt of his lips.

'I've never seen a dog get into such a small space before,' Jenny said, unaccountably moved by the man's smile. She wondered how long it had been since he'd smiled last.

'You'd be surprised,' Bert said, glancing down at the droop-eared, droop-tailed dog. 'He hates sheep, you see, that's his problem. He'll do anything to get out of coming into the fields with us. Never known a sheepdog like him. Oh, he can do the job, but you can almost hear him muttering and complaining about it under his breath as he rounds them up. And he hates sleeping in the barn at night. I've had to search the house many a night to find his hiding place. If Dad catches him in the house, even once . . .' he let the sentence trail off, but frowned down at the dog.

The mutt wagged a hopeful tail.

'Stupid hound,' Bert muttered, but absently stroked the dog's silky head before turning back to look at the cook. 'I should get your coat, if I were you,' he advised her. 'It's perishing out there. More snow to come, I reckon,' he added.

And as he looked at her, his eyes seemed to focus on her properly for the first time. And he was not the first man to realize that the Amazonian cook was surprisingly attractive.

Jenny agreed with his assessment of the weather a few moments later, as she stepped out into the dark courtyard and shuddered in the cold. The dog slouched by Bert's side as they headed across the yard, their boots crunching deep in the snow, the light from the kitchen window giving the night a lovely orange glow. Running alongside one wall of the house was the ramshackle corridor that led to the stables. It was probably bitterly cold in there as well, but at least it gave anybody going from the house into the stable block shelter from the elements.

As soon as Bert pushed open the door to the barn, something flew out of the darkness from within — something white, spectral and honking.

The dog gave a yelp of alarm and shot off into the gloomy interior, haunches a bare few inches off the ground, tongue lolling from his mouth in silent terror, the honking spectre fast on his heels.

By her side, Bert gave a low chuckle. 'That gander hates Pooch with a vengeance. Mind you, that gander hates everybody. The geese are further on in.' He turned and lit a small old-fashioned paraffin lamp that had been hanging on the doorjamb. 'Just point out the bird you want, and I'll see to it for you.'

Jenny wondered if the Keltons were so hard up that they couldn't afford to have electric light laid on in the outbuildings, then decided that it was far more likely that Stan Kelton was so mean that he didn't see why he should bother when sixty-year-old lamps still worked. And worker safety or risk of a fire be damned.

Jenny sighed and followed Bert inside. From somewhere came an outraged, terrified yelp that indicated the gander had scored a direct peck on Pooch's posterior. Off to her left, the mutt quickly scrambled up a wide wooden ladder that led to the loft above, and for a moment the thwarted gander paced at the bottom, honking angrily.

No doubt he did so every night, frustrated by his inability to climb. Bert, or whoever was in charge of the geese, must keep their wings clipped, thus preventing flight. How annoying it must be for him, Jenny thought sympathetically, and turned to peruse the geese, her experienced eye picking out a young, tender-breasted bird.

She pointed it out, and Bert nodded. She turned away as he caught and casually dispatched the bird with a single, humane twist to the neck with his big strong hands. City slickers would have fainted on the spot.

It made even Jenny feel slightly sick.

Finally sensing another alien presence in his barn, the gander left the cowardly mutt to his hayloft and came hissing out of the night, wings stretched out to an impressive length either side of him. Jenny turned and watched his approach, not in the least put out. As the gander gained the last five yards, she moved rapidly to one side, and put her hands on her hips. The surprised gander slid past her, skidded to a halt and turned around, neck extended, beady eye trained on her shin.

Before it could give even one honk, she said quietly, 'I'm here to pick out the Christmas goose.' She leaned down, looked the bird in his gimlet eye and said even more quietly, 'But I could always make it a Christmas gander.'

The bird blinked. He took a step back, then another, then blinked again.

Jenny nodded.

She'd always had a way with animals.

* * *

It was Bert who showed her to her room that night, apologizing as he did so for nobody thinking to see to her comfort earlier. 'Think nothing of it,' Jenny said airily, following his solid frame up the stairs.

Her room, as she'd expected, was as cold as sorbet but spacious enough, with plenty of blankets on a fair-sized bed.

Bert rubbed his hands and blew on them, for perhaps the first time playing the part of host, and running head first into the fact that Kelton Farm was not the most hospitable of places.

'There should be a fire lit in here,' he muttered, and stared at the empty grate as if he'd never seen it before. He never even seemed to question the fact that there should have been central heating installed years ago. 'I'm surprised Uncle Sid didn't light one. He's usually the thoughtful one around here,' he added, with a twist of his lips. 'After Janice left . . .' he began, then abruptly cut off the sentence, as if expecting a reprimand.

Janice was probably his absentee wife, Jenny guessed, and no doubt mention of her around here was strictly taboo. Stan Kelton would have made sure of that. He wouldn't have taken kindly to one of his minions escaping from under his very nose, of that Jenny was convinced.

So when the new cook made no comment, but merely looked at him curiously, Bert sighed and shook his head. 'My wife,' he said unnecessarily. 'She walked out on us. But if she'd still been here, you would have had a fire in your room.'

He said nothing more, but turned and left, just a little greyer, just a little more tired, than before. Yet those few simple words of his said more about Janice, and Bert's feelings towards Janice, than anything else could have done. She wondered, sadly, how Jeremy had felt about his mother's leaving and why the boy hadn't gone with her. He looked to be about eighteen now. How long had Janice been gone exactly? Not long, she would have thought, not with Bert still pining so strongly for her.

She did not ask herself why Janice had left. That was obvious, and could be summed up in two words: Stan Kelton.

\* \* \*

She awoke around six. It was still dark outside, and snowing lightly. She rose and dressed in a hurry, the cold nipping at her skin like tiny pincers. And she had a lot of skin on her large frame to be nipped.

In the kitchen she quickly got the fire going and the stove lit with the plentiful supply of logs kept by the grate. Without a thought she went to the door, unlocked it and opened it. The dog shot in and vanished. He no doubt had a secret gander-free exit from the top of the hayloft. Besides, any dog would rather jump for his life than risk the pecking beak of the white wonder.

Jenny made herself a cup of tea, and decided on porridge. Just because, she was sure, Stan Kelton was a bacon-and-eggs kind of man.

It was still practically dark when Mrs Jarvis arrived, the chip on her shoulder accompanied by a mass of snowflakes. Without a word, Jenny made the woman a cup of tea, and rose to see to the porridge. The men would be down soon, she was sure, and anxious to make the most of the meagre winter light.

'I see you've got the goose then,' Mrs Jarvis said, nodding to the bird that was hung up just inside the open larder door.

'Bert reminded me last night,' Jenny agreed, and hefted a milk churn from the cold cellar.

'Ah, Bert's a good lad,' Mrs Jarvis agreed, shucking off her coat and curling her cold hands thankfully around the mug. 'And I notice the devil is beginning to realize the same thing. Last year, when I first came to this hellhole, he was all for young Bill. Young Bill was the brains, the one with the get-go.' Mrs Jarvis frowned down into her mug. 'And I suppose he is, really. Poor Bert's never been the same since Janice left. Poor lass could stick it no more. Can't say as I blame her. Twenty years in this place is more than any flesh and blood can stand.'

Jenny measured out the oats, and recalled last night's ugly little scene. 'Bill doesn't seem to be in favour anymore,' she commented thoughtfully.

'Oh, he's all for Bert now, and takes every opportunity to jump down Bill's throat,' Mrs Jarvis agreed. 'He does it on purpose, of course. Keeps them at loggerheads, I mean.

41

All for one of them one moment, then cosying on up to the other the next. I reckon he wants his two sons fighting each other, instead of teaming up against himself.'

Jenny staunchly ignored the paranoia that was building up all around her, and concentrated on her porridge.

'The road's clear to the village now at any rate,' Mrs Jarvis carried on chattering, but the relief in her voice was obvious. 'It'll mean I can get to the shop for my Christmas stores. You don't mind if I take an hour off a little later on, do you?'

Jenny had just assured her that of course she didn't mind — and besides which, it was none of her business anyway — when, from outside, came a sudden cacophony of sound that was a mixture of honk, yell, thud and swearing.

'That'll be the postman,' Mrs Jarvis said matter-of-factly. 'The gander gets him every time.'

From above came the sound of feet clumping down the stairs, quickly followed by a lighter set of feet. Stan Kelton came in, the post in one hand, a pipe in the other. Behind him, Delia sulked her way into the kitchen, her eyes fixed on the post.

As they all watched, Stan Kelton sorted through the mixture of Christmas cards and bills and then paused, his eyes narrowing on one envelope, which was obviously a personal letter. He tossed the rest of the mail on the table and then tore the envelope, unopened, in half, then in quarters. He turned to the fire and threw them into the flames, waiting to see them curl up and turn to ashes.

When he turned, Bert was stood in the doorway. 'What was that?' he asked, his face a pasty white.

'Nothing that concerns you, lad,' Stan Kelton said. 'Sit down and have some breakfast.'

At the mention of breakfast, Jenny rushed to her porridge, but it was simmering nicely. As if it'd dare do anything else.

'That was from Janice, wasn't it?' Bert persisted, as Bill sidled around him.

Bill's face tightened. 'What was?' he asked, coming to his brother's aid, as if Bert was the younger, and he, Bill, owed him the protection of an older sibling.

'Dad threw an envelope on the fire,' Delia piped up, all three Kelton children united in their mutual dislike for the man who was their father.

Jenny hastily reached for some brown sugar. Porridge needed brown sugar. She did not, most definitely did *not,* want to get mixed up in any more Kelton dramas.

'Was it from Janice?' Bill asked, and stiffened as his father gave him a sneering look.

'Nothing to do with you, boy. Keep your nose out.'

'If it was from Janice it had nothing to do with you, either,' Bert said, his hands clenching and unclenching into fists by his side. 'Was it from her? *Was it?'* he roared, goaded beyond endurance.

Stan Kelton shrugged and turned to the table, ignoring Bert's pain. 'Who's to say now?' He sat down and then frowned. 'Hey, you, cook. What's that you're doing?'

Sid came into the room, the last down, and sniffed appreciatively. No doubt he would be able to manage porridge much better than a fried breakfast, and she smiled at him widely as she returned to the table with a huge saucepan of porridge in her hands. She placed it carefully onto the wooden mat she'd put in the centre of the table. 'Porridge,' she said, with satisfaction. 'Creamy and a little sweet, with plump sultanas and piping hot. Just what you need on a morning like this.'

'Porridge?' Stan echoed, his eyes narrowing. 'We have bacon and eggs for breakfast round here.'

'Oh really?' Jenny said, her eyes widening innocently. 'Sorry.'

'Janice always liked porridge,' Bert said, his eyes still on the fire. 'She must have bought some oats before she left.'

With that, he turned and headed for the door, going out into the cold of the day with not so much as a cup of tea to warm him up. Bill and Delia looked at one another helplessly, then joined their father at the table. Jenny, lips pressed into a grim line, dished out the porridge.

Stan Kelton would just have to like it or lump it.

# CHAPTER FOUR

Jeremy was the last to finish his breakfast, since he'd asked for a third bowl of the delicious porridge, and when he glanced up, still licking his lips, it was to meet his father's fond eyes. For Bert had returned after about ten minutes' absence, sat down at the table and without a word helped himself to porridge, all the while carefully avoiding his own father's eyes.

Now Jeremy grinned shyly. 'Going down to the pub tonight, Dad? Seeing it's Christmas Eve and all,' he added hopefully, his brown eyes shining in anticipation. A night out was obviously a rare treat for him, and Jenny marvelled anew at the restricted lives that all the younger Keltons seemed to lead. Did they not realize that it was the twenty-first century, and that serfdom had gone out in the middle ages?

Bert smiled and nodded, and started to say, 'Why not?' when Stan Kelton, in the process of selecting his wellingtons from the line-up of similar footwear by the door, turned sharply.

'There'll be no pub crawling for you tonight, my lad,' he said coldly, and thrust one foot into a depth of smelly welly. His eyes glittered as they turned on his crestfallen grandson. 'Don't think I don't know why you're in such a lather to get to the Lamb and Dog, boy,' he carried on, thrusting his other foot into the other wellington before turning back into the room, one solid mass of implacable bulk.

His face, Jenny noticed curiously, was just slightly flushed.

She glanced back at Jeremy, who, in contrast, was a stark, chalky white. Hastily, she began to inspect the porridge dregs in the saucepan, relieved for once that porridge could set like concrete and required a lot of hard work and attention to remove it. She reached for the scrubbing brush and set to. Vigorously. She managed to make a lot of noise as she did so, hoping that they would take the hint and leave her to work in peace.

No such luck.

'Leave the boy be,' Bert said, but his voice was tired and limp, as if all the fight had gone out of him. Although she didn't turn to see, Jenny could just imagine the stricken, unhappy look his son must have cast his way. Obviously, there was to be no protection or help from his father. The cook wondered briefly what the lad had done to earn his grandfather's displeasure, then shook her head. What business was it of hers?

Besides, as far as she could see, it didn't take much to rile Stan Kelton into making sure that you fell into line. That line being right under his thumb of course.

She began to hum, loudly, something from Abba. She'd been to see *Mamma Mia* at the theatre last month and the tunes were sticking, maddeningly, in her head.

'That flighty daughter of Jack Grantly's ain't for you, boy, I've told you that before,' Stan continued gruffly. 'Liz Ashcroft's been making eyes at you since you went to school — and she'll inherit her dad's farm one day, what with that useless wife of his never having had any boys. If you had any sense in that head of yours, you'd make your way over there tonight and give her a Christmas present, along with a kiss. You do know how to kiss, boy, don't you?' he taunted.

Jeremy's head sank lower. 'I ain't got her a present,' he mumbled.

'Well, go into town and get her one,' Stan roared, running out of his meagre supply of patience. 'A proper one, mind. Something a gal would like. I happen to know that she brought yours over a week ago.'

Jeremy flushed. Though naturally timid, he seemed reluctant to cower totally before his grandfather's intimidating authority, even though Stan had moved back to the table and was now towering over him.

'I want to see Mandy tonight,' he mumbled insistently, but even more quietly, his voice so soft it was almost inaudible.

'Forget Mandy Grantly!' Stan Kelton's voice on the other hand echoed around the stone-flagged kitchen with all the drama of a Zeus-like thunderbolt accompanied by a lightning strike.

Jeremy's neck had disappeared into his shoulders altogether when Jenny eventually turned around. Her saucepan was immaculately clean, and the table needed clearing. She thrust out her chin and walked determinedly forward. As she did so, she saw Sid reach out and pat his nephew's arm.

'You go to the pub tonight, lad. If the road was clear, I'd even come with you.'

Stan Kelton glanced at his older brother, shook his head in contemptuous dismissal and tramped to the door.

Bert stood up heavily. 'Go to the pub,' he agreed briefly, and followed his father silently out of the door. There were pregnant sheep to be seen to; he'd just spent another sleepless night, and those few, brief words of encouragement for his beleaguered son were all that he could muster. If Janice had been here, then together, the two of them could have protected Jeremy from his father's manipulations. But Bert knew that he lacked the strength on his own.

He lacked everything, it seemed.

As he left the room, tears were streaming down his face, but nobody saw them. And once outside, they quickly froze onto his face and dropped away into the snow.

No doubt Delia would have echoed the same sentiments to her nephew, had she not already fled the family farm for her friend's house in The Dell. Jenny had watched her go. Delia's colour had been high and her eyes were unnaturally bright. She'd wondered, briefly, if today was going to be the day when Delia and her other trapped friend would finally flee to London. Perhaps, Jenny had thought hopefully, watching her go from the kitchen window, today was finally the day when Delia would not return home.

She'd certainly looked excited enough, and was far more tense and twitchy than usual. Something was definitely in the air, and Jenny felt herself tensing up, in the hopes that nothing went wrong for her. She'd only been there a day and a night, and already she couldn't wait to get away herself.

But even as she gave up a little prayer for Delia, Jenny felt the onset of a deep feeling of unease. In her heart, she couldn't see any of the Keltons getting out from under the yoke of the farm and the man who ran it. They were too brainwashed, too beaten down, like flies trapped in a particularly viscous form of amber.

Jenny sighed.

Suddenly, someone thumped the table with a hard walloping whack. She jumped and watched Bill push his chair away and spring to his feet. 'That old sod won't be happy until we're all as miserable as he is,' he gritted, his teeth clenched in fury.

Sid looked up at him in alarm. 'Take it easy, lad. Things will work out, you'll see. Things will start changing around here soon, I promise you.'

But Bill wasn't in the mood to listen to such platitudes. Instead he threw on his coat as if he hated it, as if he hated the whole world in fact, and stormed out of the farm, slamming the door behind him with a vicious bang. Jenny winced as yet another blow thundered through the kitchen, then let out her breath in a wavering sigh.

Forcing all thoughts of the Keltons and their problems from her mind, she set to clearing the table, giving it a good hard therapeutic scrub, and set about assembling the ingredients for her mince pies. She'd already made and thoroughly mixed her mincemeat last night, since she'd added a fair amount of brandy, which needed an overnight period to really soak into the raisins, sultanas, currants, orange peel and suet.

Jeremy was the last to slouch out, watched openly and anxiously by his uncle, and surreptitiously by the cook. Both of them hoped that the lad would go and see his Mandy tonight, but both of them secretly doubted that he would.

When the door closed behind him, Sid sighed sadly. Jenny met his glance and raised one eyebrow, and Sid shrugged tiredly. He rubbed a hand across his forehead and leaned back in his chair, exhausted by all the various family tensions. 'Stan wants Jeremy to marry Liz Ashcroft because her father owns the farm that joins our land out on the west border. Ashcroft has a fair few acres, of course, but to be fair, I suppose Liz is far more likely to make a good farmer's wife than the pub landlord's daughter anyway,' Sid explained, trying to be scrupulously fair to his brother but failing miserably.

Jenny put down a large empty glass mixing bowl. 'Mandy is pretty, is she?' she asked bluntly, and Sid began to chuckle softly.

'Like a picture.'

Jenny put down her wooden spoon. 'Whereas Liz . . . ?' she trailed off, one eyebrow raised in an invitation for him to finish the sentence.

'Has a good heart,' Sid obliged sadly and tellingly.

The two looked at one another for a moment, then Sid sighed and rose to leave. 'I'd better get on with the books. That's my job around here — all the admin. I do the form filling, and apply for the grant applications, pay the bills and order supplies and so on. It's something I can do in the warm by the fire, see. Besides, accountancy isn't our Stan's strong point.'

Jenny could well imagine.

Minutes later, she jumped when, from the shadows by the sink, Mrs Jarvis came into view, her face creased into a spiteful smile. Jenny had forgotten all about her presence. She'd kept herself very quiet and unobtrusive during the breakfast entertainment. No doubt, though, she'd been lapping it all up.

'Looks like the devil's family is turning against him at last,' she said, nodding her head in acute satisfaction. 'You mark my words, they'll all leave him eventually. Just needs one to get up the nerve, and the rest will go, like a line of dominoes toppling over. And serve him right, too,' she gloated.

Jenny sighed. Mrs Jarvis, with her tales of doom and gloom, she could do without.

'Mrs Jarvis, weren't you going to go into the village to do some shopping today?' she reminded her, and none too diplomatically at that. But if the daily felt any shame, she hid it well. Instead her hands flew up to her cheeks in remembrance.

'Lumme, yes, so I was. Oh, blast and damnation, I left my purse and shopping bag back home.' She sighed angrily. 'I'd best go back and get it. You won't mind if I take the morning off, then?' she reiterated, as if desperate for reassurance or permission. But she was already walking to the door, donning her coat and muttering evilly to herself about her bad memory and the fate of devils.

Jenny watched her go, and hoped she didn't run into Stan Kelton on the way back to The Dell. With the foul mood they were both in, one or the other of them was unlikely to survive the encounter!

* * *

The first batch of twenty mince pies was in the oven by the time Stan Kelton came back. It had stopped snowing, but his hands were red and raw with the cold, and when he passed by her to check on something in the cellar, she could feel the cold coming off his clothes in shiver-making waves.

She reached automatically for the mop, which she now kept *outside* the cupboard. Why bother keeping it inside, when she was perpetually using it, she wondered peevishly, grumbling to herself as she worked.

'I'm just off to the tack room.' Stan's comment stopped her in mid-mop, and she watched, totally exasperated, as he walked back across the floor in his muddy wellies. She looked at the floor, and its single track of new, muddy footprints, and leaned on her mop, slowly counting to twenty. She balefully watched him walk to a side door she'd never seen used before, and there he took off his wellingtons and slipped on a waiting pair of old, cracked-but-dry work boots. She supposed he liked to keep the stables as dry and mud-free as he could. He obviously cared more about his carthorses than he did his own home.

As he disappeared into the corridor beyond, she breathed a sigh of relief. At least he was now out from under her feet, so once she'd mopped the floor *again* it should be all right for a few hours at least, until everyone piled back in for lunch.

Wielding the mop, she set to once more, muttering colourful curses under her breath that she'd learned from an old admiral she'd once cooked for. The range of swear words would have turned a Pimlico prostitute pink.

She had prepared baked potatoes with a cheese and onion topping for lunch, and after Stan's cutting remark about her plain food yesterday, had decided to make good use of four of the rabbits hanging in the cold cellar to make savoury rabbit with tarragon sauce for dinner. To go with it, she'd prepare some duchess potatoes and braised baby vegetables.

For dessert, she'd decided on apricot and ratafia tartlets, which was very posh fare indeed. Let him talk about plain food when he had that feast set before him! Although, Jenny fumed silently, he'd probably then complain that the food was too fancy.

At last, she could finally put away the hated mop, and fetch the rabbits. When she came back, Sid had returned from the living room and his books, and was brewing a pot of tea.

'Just what the doctor ordered,' Jenny said, giving him a wide grin. Lifting a crock dish and finding only two eggs inside, however, wiped the grin right off her face. 'No eggs?'

'They're kept in the chicken house, in the little lean-to leading off it,' Sid told her. 'You can't miss it. They're next door to where the geese are kept.'

Jenny thought of trekking across the bare arctic of the exposed farmyard and groaned.

'Don't worry. I'll have a steaming cuppa ready for you when you get back.' He gave her a sympathetic grin.

Jenny, once more muttering some of the admiral's more choice epithets under her breath, donned her coat and boots and left via the front door. She was not, definitely *not* going to go out the back way and be forced to make her *own* wet and muddy footprints on the floor when she came back. She'd be having nightmares about that damned mop if she did!

She crossed the courtyard, glad to see that one of the boys had shovelled most of the snow out of the way and piled it up against the surrounding walls. She made her way quickly past the goose shed, shivering in the icy wind and giving the gander the evil eye as he came out hissing at her, promptly sending him hissing back again.

The chickens, she saw with pleased satisfaction, were tried and true black leghorns, with a few Light Sussex hens thrown in for good measure, with a handsome Light Sussex cockerel to rule the roost. But to get to them she had to battle her way through three feet of snow, and it was heavy going. Once in the spacious henhouse, however, she tossed them some grain from the sack, to save Delia the trouble when (or if) she returned from her visit to her friend.

Inside the lean-to, she paused to get her breath back and give her arms a good thumping. She stamped her feet vigorously, but her circulation was loath to return. Good grief, it was cold. But that same cold weather, she was sure, had kept the eggs reasonably fresh. Nevertheless, as she found the store of stacked eggs, she carefully weighed each one. They felt cold and solid, and the shells were a good deep colour.

She carefully re-latched the chicken-house door behind her and trudged her way back to the farm's front door, taking off her boots in the dry shelter of the porch and standing them next to the door once she was inside the hall.

She was glad to get out of her coat and hustle back into the warmth of her kitchen. Sid was sat with his back to her at the table, and the kettle was bubbling merrily away on the stove.

'So much for having my cuppa waiting for me,' she said cheerfully to him as she passed. Her mood was gradually lifting into something lighter, even happier. The tastebud-arousing smell of cheese and onion permeated the room, and she had the prospect of a lavish meal to cook ahead of her. That alone was always guaranteed to make her beam. Besides it *was* Christmas Eve, after all.

She began to hum 'Jingle Bells.'

She walked to the stove and removed the kettle, checked that Sid had spooned a good amount of tea into the teapot — he had — and reached for the sugar. The tea made, she checked her mince pies, saw that they were nicely browned on the top and took them out. The next batch of pies was ushered in, and Jenny quickly shut the stove door, anxious to let none of the precious heat escape.

Unable, ever, to resist steaming-hot mince pies fresh from the oven, she took down a plate and with much 'oohing' and 'ouching,' transferred four of the piping-hot mince pies onto it with her bare hands. After all, who would want to eat only *one* mince pie?

She turned, the teapot in one hand, the plate of mince pies in the other, and carried them triumphantly to the table and set them down. 'Now, Sid, what do you make of those?' she asked with a grin and looked up.

And her smile froze on her face. She felt her eyes widen and begin to ache, and an instant later, she felt her knees start to buckle under her. Luckily, the chair next to her was already pulled out, and she quickly clutched the table as she sank down onto the seat with a hard 'whump.' The table rocked a little as she did so, for she was still clinging onto it, her knuckles white with the intensity of her grip.

It made Sid, whose arms were both lying limply across the tabletop, tremble just slightly.

But Sid didn't feel it.

Sid wasn't feeling anything at all.

Jenny, her mouth as dry as the Sahara, took a deep steadying breath, and held it.

She did not cry. She did not scream.

For a long, long moment, she merely sat and stared at Sid, as if unable to believe what she was seeing.

Like a nightmare, her mind played back the last few minutes. When she'd walked in, Sid had been sat with his back to her, his sparse hair pale in the overhead light. It had been so dark that morning, she'd never bothered to turn the kitchen light off. It had seemed to her then that he'd been sitting there naturally enough.

Jenny swallowed hard, fighting back nausea as she replayed in her mind the making of the tea, the transference of the mince pies and her walk back to the table.

Only to confront this monstrosity.

Jenny blinked, and took another, even deeper, steadying breath.

Sid continued to sit silently opposite her. He even seemed to be watching her, and patiently waiting. Although waiting for what, she could not have said. His eyes were open, she noticed. His mouth shut. He looked, in fact, like he always did. The teapot and mince pies steamed on the table in front of him, ready to be served.

And still Sid just sat there, a long, thick-bladed knife embedded in his chest.

So still. So quiet.

Vaguely, through a curtain of shock, Jenny recognized the knife as one belonging to the set in the drawer by the sink.

Suddenly she shuddered, her mind finally engaging into a proper gear instead of just spinning around uselessly. What was she doing wondering about a vegetable knife when she had to . . . to . . .

Jenny Starling took the last of her deep steadying breaths, closed her eyes for a moment, and then opened them once more.

She now felt perfectly calm.

She had to get help, of course. Oh, not an ambulance or the doctor. Sid was gone far beyond all of that. But the police. Yes. She needed the police.

She stood up, and blinked. If there was a telephone here at Kelton Farm, she had never seen it. She suspected that Stan had probably refused to have one installed. But surely, in this day and age, somebody must have a mobile? Although, in this house, she wouldn't have bet on it. For a start, she doubted that the wages Stan Kelton paid would allow anybody to be able to afford even such a minor luxury.

Then she realized that even if one of the others did have a mobile, she had no idea whereabouts on the farm they were in order to find them and ask them to use it. Then with a mental head-slap, she ran to her bag and delved inside for her own phone. Shock was definitely making her woolly-minded!

To her dismay, however, there was no signal, which meant she'd have to walk into the village.

Feeling stiff and disjointed, she walked to the hall, re-donned her boots and coat, this time putting on her scarf and gloves, and left the farm. She still felt gloriously numb — calm and numb. Once out of the courtyard and onto the lane, she was again in the grip of winter's chilly hand.

It never once occurred to her to seek out Stan Kelton and ask for his help.

The snow banks on either side of her were high and intimidating, covering hedge and fences alike. It was frosty, the air nipping at her nose and ears. Luckily, there was no wind, for she'd forgotten her hat. Funny, the things you think when the world has suddenly turned topsy-turvy on you.

She had gone a little way up to the road before she realized that she'd automatically been plodding in the footsteps she'd made in the snow on the way up to the farm yesterday. Then, of course, she'd been coming up to the farm, instead of leaving it, so she was putting the toe of her boot where her heel had once been.

She began to slow down as her mind insisted there was something important she had to do. Think, damn it, she thought grimly to herself. *Think*. What was it? What was wrong? And suddenly, without warning, the numbness left her, and her mind, bright, clear and sharp, suddenly came up with the answer.

It had snowed lightly in the night, and so *should have obliterated the tracks made by the bottom of her boots*. But in that case . . .

Jenny stopped dead in the middle of the snowy landscape. She bent and peered more closely into the tracks she'd made yesterday. And there, clearly defined, were the ridges of another boot, one that was longer and wider than her own had been.

Someone else had come to the farm since yesterday, stepping into the footprints she herself had made. Someone who'd walked up the farm road and stabbed Sid. Then, just as quickly as the thought leapt into her mind, it leapt out again. Of course someone had come that way this very morning. Had, in fact, delivered the mail and duly been attacked by the gander: the postman! And Sid had been alive and well long after the postman had delivered his mail and left. Plus, of course, Mrs Jarvis had been going to and fro.

She knew she was only trying desperately to keep her mind off what had happened back at the farm. But surely that was excusable? She didn't *want* to think of Sid sitting there, with that obscene black-handled blade in his chest. His blood staining his shirt. His eyes open and patiently waiting . . . waiting . . .

No, far better to think of other things.

She knew she wasn't operating at her best; shock was slowing down her thinking. The way she'd panicked over the phones before remembering to try her own mobile was proof of that. It was not like her to be so incompetent.

Although she was unaware that she'd walked on a fair way as she'd been thinking things through, she found herself stopping again and staring once more at the other tracks before her. The snow all around was pristine, except for the tracks left by first herself and then the postman.

But what if someone had used these tracks *after* the postman had been and gone? If someone *had* come from the village to murder Sid, then she herself was eradicating the marks of their footprints with her own! And the police would certainly want to be able to take photographs of the boot prints, just to make sure.

Guiltily, she took a quick step sideways out of the tracks, and sank her feet into nearly three feet of virgin snow. From now on she would just have to wade her way through the snow and leave the tracks well alone. Anxiously, she looked up, gauging the sky. It didn't look as if it was about to snow any time soon. But if it did, it would eradicate the tracks for sure.

Carefully, and still feeling about a hundred years old, she took off her scarf, selected the clearest set of boot prints she could see, and covered them with her scarf, anchoring it down in the snow so that any wind coming up wouldn't easily blow it away. It wasn't ideal, but it was the best she could do to preserve a section of the tracks.

That done, she straightened painfully and began once more to plough her way stoically through the snow, stumbling now and then, mindful that there were ditches near the hedge. But even as she trudged grimly on and at last emerged onto the main road to the village, she knew, deep in her heart, that the police would find those boot prints *had* been left by the postman after all; that no one from the village, or a stranger from outside the village, had made his way to Kelton Farm and killed poor Sid.

A tractor had flattened the snow down on the road to the village, which meant she could walk faster. She quickly spotted the cheerful bright-red splash of an old-fashioned telephone box that BT hadn't yet got around to upgrading, and made her way towards it, her breath harsh and loud in her ears.

The telephone booth was flanked on one side of the road by a row of cottages, but apart from smoke pouring from their chimneys, there was no other sign of life. No doubt people were inside, doing their own Christmas baking, or were down in the centre of the village, buying their last-minute groceries from the tiny village shop.

She was glad to be spared the curious glances and prying questions of the locals. She stepped inside the ice-cold glass booth, and lifted the receiver. But even as she did so, she was already grimly convinced that whoever had killed Sid must have come to the farm from the field, or from the direction of The Dell.

There was simply no getting away from it.

Someone who lived or worked at Kelton Farm had killed Sid. But why? *Why?*

# CHAPTER FIVE

Jenny watched the car as it pulled to a careful halt in front of her, the front wheels sliding a little on the compacted snow still covering the road. She'd left the shelter of the telephone kiosk the moment she'd seen the car appear in the distance, and now she shivered forlornly.

It had *looked* like a police car, even though it was a common model with no markings on it at all. The man who climbed out of the passenger seat was one of the greyest men she had ever seen. His hair, his eyes and his coat were all grey. He was tall, lean, and so totally unremarkable that Jenny couldn't help but feel a deep pang of misgiving. Let it just be a policeman's disguise, she thought desperately. Then told herself not to be such a muffin. The man was probably as brusque, lively and efficient as any other officer of the law. First impressions, after all, were not always right.

The man who emerged from behind the driver's wheel was a startling contrast. He was at least a foot shorter than his superior, and had a head of deeply ginger, riotously curly hair. Over the roof of the car his blue eyes shone like tiny blue lamps as they quickly ran over her, assessing and missing nothing. He reminded Jenny of a Jack Russell terrier spotting a rat.

Yet another policeman emerged from the back, this one a mere lad in uniform. His eyes widened slightly as they took in Jenny's height and rounded girth, and the beauty of her eyes.

He looked both nervous and excited at the same time. Probably his first murder case, Jenny surmised.

'Are you the woman who called a short while ago about Kelton Farm?' the tall, grey inspector was the first to speak, his voice, if possible, as grey as the rest of him. It was a flat, rather unnerving monotone.

Jenny nodded. 'I am. Yes.' She introduced herself.

'I see. I'm Inspector Moulton, this is Sergeant Ford.' He didn't bother to introduce the constable, who was doing his best not to look too impressed by the proceedings. She found that his eagerness made her want to just sit down and cry. She determinedly quashed the feeling; she could have a good cry later, in the privacy of her own room, she promised herself. Right now, she had to keep it together — for Sid's sake.

All three policemen took a step closer to her, whether by accident or design, surrounding her on all sides, as if they were expecting her to make a bolt for it — although where she could possibly bolt to in this weather, and in this remote area, she wasn't sure.

'And what can you tell me of this incident please?' the inspector asked, his eyes never leaving her face.

Frank Moulton didn't show it, but he was a worried man. Frank never showed anything of his feelings, which was probably the main reason he'd climbed as high as he had. Had his superiors the faintest idea of the extent of his own feelings of inferiority, he'd still be directing traffic. And probably feeling a lot happier than he did now.

Born and raised in a small village not two miles from Kidlington, where the Thames Valley Police Force had their headquarters, Frank was a countryman at heart. He had a simple soul, was basically honest and uninspired, and totally unsuited to his chosen profession. He'd walked a beat for years, quite happily nabbing poachers, the odd petty thief, and one or two of the more persistent housebreakers. He'd become sergeant simply because he'd had enough academic competence to pass the exam, and had become inspector ten years later, via his seniority.

He had never worked a murder case on his own before. No doubt the brass thought that someone with Frank's rural knowledge would be the most competent officer to handle a murder on a farm, so the phone call this morning concerning the murder of a farmer had come as a distinct and somewhat nasty shock to his system — and had been tinged with just a little understandable excitement and curiosity. Nevertheless, the thought of being the senior investigating officer on a real live (so to speak) murder case, was giving him a severe case of the jitters.

On the journey over, he'd half hoped to find some hysterical female who'd simply misread a nasty farming accident. But now, as he looked at the woman standing so patiently before him, he felt his hopes in that direction fading. And they evaporated altogether when she began to speak.

'I'm working as a cook, over the Christmas holidays, for a Mr Stanley Kelton and his family.' She quickly ran through all the family members and the sequence of events that morning, leaving nothing out. 'When I left to go to the chicken house for the eggs, Sidney was making the tea. When I came back, he was sitting at the kitchen table with a large knife embedded in his chest,' she finished bluntly and succinctly, but her voice took on just the faintest hint of tremor on the final words.

Sergeant Ford, who'd been taking quick and precise notes throughout, lifted his head and narrowed those laser-like eyes in her direction. She certainly sounded calm enough. Looked it, too. His eyes ran over her impressively shaped bulk, her level, quite extraordinarily beautiful blue eyes, and noted her pallor. Yes, she was upset, but hiding it very well.

Competence was written all over her. They couldn't, he thought happily, have asked for a better witness.

'And where is this farm exactly?' Inspector Moulton asked, his voice betraying none of his dismay.

'Back up this way.' She pointed in the direction they had just come from. 'The track to the farm hasn't been cleared, I'm afraid, so you won't be able to drive up there. Well, not unless you have access to a 4x4, or can get one of the other farmers to take you in his tractor. Or order the council snowplough to come out here.'

She did, however, get into the car with them (the constable in the back having to squish up in the far corner,) in order to direct them to the turnoff. Once parked, they all got out and observed the two separate tracks in the snow.

Jenny quickly told them about the tracks, her theory about the postman's boots, and what she had done about covering up two sets of prints with her scarf. As she did so, she noticed the sergeant give a very quick smile. She'd obviously done the right thing, and it made her feel a lot better. She'd half expected to be given a rocketing about tampering with evidence.

She was, however, getting distinctly bad vibes from the inspector. She hoped, very much, that Inspector Moulton was hiding his light under a bushel. But if, as she was beginning to suspect, he didn't actually have a light to hide, she was in deep trouble.

*Deep* trouble.

\* \* \*

Inspector Moulton told the constable to stay with the car to prevent anyone else calling at the farm and with orders to send for SOCO (scene of crime officers), forensics and the police doctor. Now it seemed they really did have a murder on their hands, Moulton wanted as many other officials around as possible. That way, if mistakes were made, he had someone else to blame them on.

The three of them then walked up the snow-clogged lane, stepping in the cook's second set of footprints to the point where she had left the scarf. Moulton stared at the incongruously bright blue and red scarf lying against the snow for some while, but said nothing. He was not, in spite of his inferiority complex, actually a foolish man. He just knew from experience that the less he said, the less likely he was to dig a hole for himself that he'd need to climb out of later.

They continued on until they reached the crest of the hill, at which point they paused and looked down on Kelton Farm. It looked exactly as she had remembered it from her first sight of it yesterday, Jenny realized. Which was eerie. And was it only yesterday she had first come here? It felt like years now.

But the farm shouldn't look the same, she thought resentfully. It should look different. A man had been killed there, brutally murdered. A nice old man who wouldn't hurt a fly. It had no business looking its usual, squat, square, sturdy self. It should look dark. Sad. Evil.

She shook her head and sighed deeply, telling herself not to be such a drama queen, causing Sergeant Ford to give her a quick, anxious look. But apart from the sigh she made no comment, and together they walked down to the farm, Inspector Moulton making a great show of looking around the courtyard, although to what purpose, it was hard to tell. Almost everyone from the farm, and the postman to boot, had trampled around there. Not to mention the geese and the dog.

Jenny led the way into the hall, and removed her boots. Guiltily, both Inspector Moulton and Sergeant Ford quickly did the same, and the cook gave a brief nod of satisfaction. At least their mothers or wives had trained them well.

'This way,' she said, with obvious reluctance, and they followed her across the hall to the large heavy door that opened into the kitchen. Jenny took three steps inside, and stopped dead.

A sea of Kelton faces turned her way: Bert looked haggard, and was standing the nearest to her, leaning heavily against the dresser; Bill was standing by the far door, pale and tense; Delia was sobbing quietly by the sink and Jeremy was standing by her, awkwardly patting her back. They all turned and stared at her, but it was Stan Kelton, standing just a little way from his brother's body, who reacted first.

'There she is!' he bellowed, and took several steps towards her, his meaty hands clenching and unclenching, as if in anticipation of closing around her throat. He stopped abruptly as first Moulton, then Ford, emerged on either side of her, and stood surveying the scene.

Without a word, and with not a hint of his reluctance or anxiety showing, Moulton walked forward and moved slowly around the chair to face Sid Kelton head on. His grey eyes fell to the handle of the knife sticking out of the dead man's chest, and he slowly took a carefully silent, but deep breath.

He hadn't expected the man to be so old, or look so ill and pitiful.

'Who are you lot, then?' Stan asked, but from the tone of his voice he obviously already knew.

'Sergeant Ford.' The sergeant pulled out some form of identification, which Stan barely glanced at, and then nodded in his superior's direction. 'Inspector Moulton. And you are?'

'Stan Kelton,' Stan replied, his voice at last falling to something approaching a normal decibel. But it was only temporary. 'What the hell's going on here?' he quickly added, his voice becoming aggrieved and downright threatening once more.

'I was hoping *you* could tell *us* that, sir,' Inspector Moulton said, taking the opportunity to get out of Sid Kelton's painful presence and turn his attention to the blustering younger brother.

The cook had described the family well, for he had no problems picking out the family members. Nevertheless, he went through the motions of having each of them formally identify themselves. It passed the time well, and gave him time to think. Although what he was going to do next, he had only the most general of ideas.

When Delia, the last to give her full name, age and — ridiculously — address, had finished, there was a long, cold, frightening silence. Everyone looked at everyone else. Finally, predictably, it was Stan Kelton who spoke first. 'Well? Aren't you going to arrest her?' he roared, chin thrust forward, fierce brown eyes blazing.

Moulton felt a rush of hope, but his voice was totally neutral, as he said casually, 'Arrest who, sir?'

'Well, her of course,' Stan said, pointing an imperious finger in Jenny's direction.

Ford looked at her quickly at this, and saw a look of exasperated contempt cross the cook's otherwise completely composed face.

'We come back here,' Stan Kelton continued, picking up a really good head of steam now, 'and find Sid . . . poor Sid . . .' his impressive voice choked a little, 'sitting there . . . like that . . .'

At this point, Sergeant Ford sidled around to get his first good view of the deceased, and paled slightly. As it had struck his superior a few moments before, he felt an acute wave of pity for the old man wash over him. His eyes were open, and Ford hadn't expected that. They seemed . . . not accusing, as you might expect, but more . . . Ford didn't know. He had never had to investigate a murder before.

He turned quickly away.

Jenny noticed the policeman's unease, and felt her heart sink. As time wore on, she was becoming more and more glumly certain that it was going to be left up to her, yet again, to sort out the whole sorry mess and unearth the identity of the killer.

Stan Kelton roused himself. 'As I said, we found poor Sid like that, and *she* was the only one missing!' he exclaimed impressively. 'And the knife's from the kitchen. And she's the only stranger here. It's obvious she did it.' He finished on a flourish, but his eyes, Jenny noticed, were hot and troubled, the first genuine emotion she had ever seen in him besides anger.

And in that moment, she felt genuinely sorry for Stan Kelton. It must have been a shock, even for him, finding poor Sid like that. Sid, who was his brother, his own flesh and blood, after all. Her pity quickly fled, however, when she found herself the object of all eyes.

Exasperated, she glanced at Moulton. 'Well, of course I was gone. I had to go to the village to phone you lot. The farm doesn't have a landline of its own and there's no signal around here for a mobile phone; well, not on mine anyway. What else was I supposed to do, finding poor Sid like that? Wait around here and see who might be next?' She left unsaid the fact that, with a killer on the loose, she might have been forgiven for fearing for her own skin as well.

Moulton looked back to Stan.

Stan stared at her. 'Well, none of us did it,' he challenged belligerently. 'That only leaves you.'

Moulton looked back at the cook.

'And why would I do it?' she shot back, just as bluntly. 'I've only been here one day, and I'd never met any of you before then. What reason would I have to kill any of you?'

Moulton looked back at Stan. He reminded Jenny, who was beginning to feel distinctly irritated with him, like a spectator at a tennis match.

'But you were the only one here,' Stan was all but shouting now.

Moulton looked back at the cook.

'You were only in the stables,' Jenny reminded him flatly. Moulton looked back at Stan.

Ford coughed discreetly. Stan, Moulton and Jenny all looked at him, surprised by the interruption.

'Perhaps,' Sergeant Ford said reasonably, 'it might be helpful if we establish a timeframe for this, er, incident. Miss Starling, you told us you saw Mr Kelton alive when you went to fetch some eggs. What time was that, would you say?'

Jenny, relieved that someone was making some sense at last, paused. 'I'd done the baked spuds for lunch, and they were half done. We'd had elevenses . . . I'd say it was between half eleven and twelve. You'll have a record of my phone call, though, so we can help trace it back from that,' she reminded him, and Moulton glanced at her quickly.

Now how did a simple country cook come to know so much about police procedure, he wondered.

No, Frank Moulton was not a foolish man. Just a man who knew that he was in over his head. He let the moment pass without challenging her. Time for all that later.

Ford, scribbling industriously, merely nodded, having missed completely what his superior had so quickly picked up. 'And how long did it take you to fetch the eggs? A minute?'

'Oh no, much longer than that,' Jenny said, and ignored Stan Kelton's sour grunt of disbelief. 'The path to the chicken shed hadn't been cleared of snow, so I had to walk through it to get to it. Then I had to clear a big batch of snow from in front of the door with my feet before I could open it up. Then I was very careful selecting the eggs when I was there, weighing them, you know, to make sure none of them were addled,' she added, seeing Ford's puzzled glance lifting up from the notebook. 'There's nothing worse than the smell of rotten eggs. I had to make sure none of the eggs were light, and therefore off, before I brought them back to the kitchen,' she continued the culinary lesson determinedly.

Opposite her, Stan Kelton shifted restlessly.

'Then I fed the chickens, so that Delia wouldn't have to bother, then I had to re-shut the lean-to door, come back, take off my boots and coat and come back in here. I would say I was gone at least, at the very *least*, five minutes. Much closer to ten, I would have thought.'

Sergeant Ford, whose legs were still aching after tramping through the snow to get there, thought her assessment was probably a very accurate one. It would take some time to clear three foot of snow from in front of a door. 'I see. So, what we need to know now is, where was everyone between eleven thirty and twelve thirty?' He looked up and around generally, his eyes alighting on no one in particular.

'I was with Sissy,' Delia said at once, and flushed when everyone turned to face her. 'Sissy Bray, my friend. I was at her house,' she added, suddenly aware that in her haste to clear herself she had come across as rather callous and selfish, even if it had been a perfectly natural impulse to do so. She was young and in shock, after all.

Unless she was a much cleverer actress than any of them credited.

'And at what time did you return here?' Ford asked, not giving his superior so much as a glance, apparently unaware that he was subtly usurping the inspector's authority. Moulton, though, was glad to let him get on with it and simply watch and listen.

'About, oh, I don't know. Quarter to one?' She turned about the room until she found her brother, Bill.

Bill moved from his position by the back door and nodded. 'That's right. I was here then.'

Ford turned to him. 'And what time did you get back here, sir?'

Bill shrugged. 'I can't say. I didn't think to look at the time. The first thing I saw when I walked through the door was . . .' he trailed off, unable to say the words, but he pointed a shaky finger in his uncle's direction.

'I see,' Ford said, not without sympathy. 'And where had you been all morning?'

'In the lower pasture, making sure there were no more trapped sheep.'

'Alone?'

'Aye, we split up to cover more ground,' Bert answered, picking up the thread of conversation with surprising authority. Without being asked, he gave his own whereabouts, about half a mile from that of his brother. 'I found a ewe, but she was a goner,' he added, almost to himself. 'I got back here . . . I dunno . . .'

'Not long after me,' Bill confirmed thoughtfully. 'If you remember, you asked me what I was standing around for like a spare scarecrow,' he reminded his brother.

Bert nodded. 'That's right. And then I saw Uncle Sid as well. Now I think about it, I saw you going in just as I was coming down the footpath.' Bert added quickly, 'You couldn't have been here more than a minute or two before me. I left the ewe on the side of the footpath about quarter of an hour after I heard the church clock strike twelve. It must have taken me another fifteen minutes to get here.'

'About twelve thirty then?' Sergeant Ford probed carefully. 'For both of you?'

'Aye,' Bert nodded.

'What happened then? After you arrived?'

'I went to fetch Dad,' Bill said. 'I knew he was working in the tack room; we're going to need the horses soon. A thaw's on the way,' he added, apropos of nothing.

Nobody asked why the horses would be needed, or how he knew that there was a thaw on the way. Country folk knew about weather, and nobody in the room was interested in horses just then.

'I came in through this door,' Stan picked up the story at this point, and nodded to the side door that was still standing open to the dark corridor beyond, 'just as Delia came in through the back door. I wasn't in time to stop her seeing . . .'

Delia began to cry again. In the warm, quiet room, her sobs echoed eerily. It was an ancient sound, reminding the cook of just how many women, through the ages, had cried for their menfolk, who'd been killed without reason.

'Do you want to go upstairs, Dee-Dee?' Jeremy murmured, half taking her arm in an effort to prise her away.

'And you, sir?' Sergeant Ford said quickly, realizing that Jeremy was the only one yet to give an account of himself.

'Jeremy was the last of all of us to get back here,' Bert quickly leapt to his son's defence. Perhaps *too* quickly, Jenny thought curiously. Bert had also been anxious to point out that his brother had arrived only moments before he had. Why did he feel the need to protect so many, unless he believed they needed it?

Yes, Bert Kelton for one didn't believe his father's accusations against the cook. Interesting, that, Jenny thought. Very interesting.

'And where had you been all morning?' Ford asked the youngster, with no particular emphasis, but again, before Jeremy could open his mouth, his father leapt in.

'Up at the far corner of Dingle field,' he said quickly. 'That's over near Ashcroft's place, as far from here as you can get on our property.' He made it a point to draw their attention to the fact. 'He was taking some winter feed to the yearling rams we've got up there. Need to keep them fat for market,' he added.

But again, no one was interested in the livestock.

'I see.' It was Moulton who said the words, but Jenny was beginning to wonder if he saw at all.

Ford did.

She certainly did.

Any one of them could have done it.

Bert, Bill and Jeremy were all alone. Any of them could have come back to the farm, watching and waiting for an opportunity, then observed the cook leaving for the hen house, and crept into the kitchen to kill Sid. Then it was just a question of quickly making their way back to the fields, only to return at lunch time all innocent and seemingly unknowing.

Delia might have the best alibi of all, if her friend and her friend's mother, Cordelia Bray, could assure them that Delia had been in their sight all morning.

Stan Kelton, working in the tack room, was the nearest on the spot of all of them. And, to police eyes, she herself was right on the spot as well. Nobody, nobody at all, had an alibi.

## CHAPTER SIX

Detective Chief Inspector Bryant arrived with a small army of men less than half an hour later. A small man, he had a small man's bluster, amply backed up by a large moustache and a suit that Sergeant Ford would never have been able to afford if he'd lived on bread and water for a month.

'So, Moulton,' the chief inspector said, rubbing his hands together briskly and peering carefully at Sid Kelton's body, which hadn't yet been either moved or touched. 'Looks like a pretty nasty but straightforward business.' Which was somewhat unhelpful, Jenny privately thought, but had more sense than to say.

Moulton nodded obediently, if a shade dubiously. Although he rather doubted the accuracy of his superior's summation, he was, nevertheless, the only one present to actively welcome his officious and pompous company. With the chief inspector on the scene, he felt that heat was off himself. Or so he thought.

'What's the story so far then?' Bryant asked with ghoulish relish, his little button eyes snapping around the room, resting on each member of the Kelton family in turn. He seemed to be buzzing with thought and speculation, and

Jenny felt her spirits finally lift a little. At least the man had a bit of get-up-and-go about him.

The sheepdog, which was obviously unnerved by all the activity, and on hearing yet another stranger's voice in the midst of his territory, chose that moment to decide that he really couldn't keep quiet any longer, and let out an ear-piercing bark. At the same time, he jumped down from the seat under the table and proceeded to give Bryant's ankle a thorough sniffing.

The dapper chief inspector leapt back as if he'd been shot. 'You great hairy miserable dollop,' he squeaked, although no doubt he'd meant it to come out as a leonine roar. He hopped nervously from foot to foot and scowled down at the animal ferociously.

Not a particularly dog-friendly sort of man, the chief inspector, Jenny mused, hiding a smile behind her hand and pretending to smother a cough.

The sheepdog, never having heard a human being make quite that sort of noise before, looked up at him curiously, head turned to one side, ears pricked up in interest. Perhaps he'd do it again?

Bert stepped forward without a word and grabbed the dog by the collar. The mutt tenaciously dug all four sets of claws into the flagstones as best he could, guessing — quite accurately — that he was about to be turfed out ignominiously on his ear. His claws scraped gratingly across the floor as Bert pulled him to the door and neatly ejected him.

Bryant straightened his tie and pretended his dignity had not been severely ruffled. Taking the cue, Moulton nodded at Ford. 'Sergeant Ford, read back the initial statements please,' he ordered, a past master in how to pass the buck without seeming to.

But Ford related the events without mishap, even managing to make it sound as if he'd covered much more ground than he actually had, in the half an hour or so that had been made available to him.

Inspector Moulton was not the only one who knew how to deal with the top brass.

In a corner, trying to appear as inconspicuous as possible (not an easy feat, to be sure, considering her size and visual impact), Jenny watched and listened, her heart sinking ever deeper into her boots. If Moulton had failed to fill her with confidence, Chief Inspector Bryant was now filling her with downright foreboding. Unless she was mistaken, he was showing all the signs of a rat about to desert a sinking ship. And her gloom was quickly vindicated.

'Right, well, I can see you have everything under control,' Bryant said, much to Moulton's utter dismay. 'Needless to say, we're going to keep on this till we have a result,' Bryant turned quickly, spearing his underling with a gimlet glance, checking for any sign of rebellion.

But although Moulton could have matched Jenny Starling, misery for misery, not a flicker of it showed on his face. 'Of course, sir,' he said, voice as bland as milk.

Bryant's tense little shoulders relaxed and he nodded. Good man, Moulton. He might not have many high-ranking cases under his belt, but it was clear that nothing fazed him. And clearly, the man was far more at home in this kind of environment than himself. That damned dog with its muddy paws. Another moment and it would have stuck its nose in his crotch, no doubt.

He looked at his watch. 'Right, the boys should have taken casts from those footprints by now,' he said, and mumbled, rather reluctantly, 'Good thinking, that, Moulton. The scarf. It showed initiative.'

Sergeant Ford cast a quick, guilty glance at Jenny, but Moulton was already taking the credit with a dry, 'Thank you, sir, I do my best.'

Bryant bristled out, as energetically as he'd bristled in. Stan Kelton, who'd remained narrow-eyed and stiff-lipped throughout, let out a snort as the door closed behind him. 'Fat lot of good he was,' he snarled.

Nobody, for once, disagreed with him.

The police surgeon arrived just as Bryant exited, and walked straight in to examine the body, not even glancing at the silent assembly. As he touched Sid's neck and officially proclaimed him dead, Delia made a small sound and fainted. Luckily, Jeremy was on hand to catch her.

The doctor, a fat-faced individual in his early sixties, looked up from the body and sighed, but not totally without sympathy. Delia was a pretty young girl, after all, and looked a pitiable sight, lying limply in her nephew's strong arms.

'Better take her upstairs. Sleep's the best thing for shock. Make sure you cover her with plenty of blankets, mind,' he added, and gave the young lad an encouraging smile.

'Ah, let's all get out of here,' Stan Kelton said heavily, and for once his sons were quick to comply. In the living room they huddled around the fire, each and every one of them studiously avoiding looking at the set of accountancy books that Sid had been working on just a few hours ago. They were still lying around haphazardly on the small coffee table next to his favourite armchair, as if expecting him to come back any moment and take up where he had left off. And the fact that he would now never be able to do so made a lump rise to more than one throat.

* * *

Jenny remained in the kitchen, watching everything. For one thing, it was her domain and she'd have felt out of place in the living room with the rest of the family. For another, she was curious to see if the doctor found anything abnormal during his initial examination. Although what that might be she had, as of that moment, no idea.

Apparently there was nothing to catch his attention, and within the hour the police team had bagged the knife, which the doctor had carefully removed, and had collected several small bits and pieces that would be taken away for analysis. Finally, two sturdy constables came and carried the body away. Jenny supposed they would be having trouble getting a mortuary van out to the farm. Not for the first time, she cursed the snow that was keeping the Kelton home so isolated.

Without Sid, the room seemed strangely empty.

As the last of them left, Jenny finally roused herself. 'Can I clean the floor now?' she asked, looking around the filthy floor and already reaching automatically for the mop.

Moulton jumped, having forgotten that she was there, and then looked down at the floor. He frowned. 'Ye-es,' he said, reluctantly and uncertainly, elongating the word as he did so. He'd seen for himself a team of men search the floor and pick up the odd piece of frozen mud. And there was nothing to be discovered from the muddy footprints themselves, that was for sure. The Kelton family and half the Thames Valley Police Force had trampled all over the kitchen floor that morning.

Still, he didn't like it. He didn't like making decisions at all. Not even the small ones.

Jenny picked up the mop and set to. She felt utterly depressed.

'I shall need your full name and current address . . . er . . . madam,' Ford said, for the first time realizing that he hadn't asked her for the information before. When she'd introduced herself at the telephone kiosk, she'd only referred to herself as Miss Starling, and both men had more or less promptly forgotten it, in the current excitement.

He shot Moulton a guilty look.

Jenny, her mopping finished, sighed deeply. Her parents had run true-to-type in the eccentricity of forenames for their only child.

'My name,' she said firmly, 'is Miss Jennifer Zenobia Lucretia Minerva Starling.' She added the address of her little bedsit as an afterthought. She doubted she'd be staying there for long anyway.

Both Moulton and Ford were staring at her openly now, her simple introduction more than enough to make them both gape. Moulton in particular felt like falling to his knees and kissing her feet, but thankfully restrained himself.

'Miss *Jenny* Starling?' he repeated, hardly able to believe his luck. 'You, er, are the *same* Jenny Starling who had a hand in helping to solve that nasty poisoning business at a birthday party last summer, aren't you?'

He just managed to contain a whoop of joy as she nodded reluctantly.

'And you solved that locked-room murder case the year before, right?' Sergeant Ford piped up.

Again, the cook nodded reluctantly. 'I did have the pleasure of helping some people out of a bit of a tight spot, yes,' she said, in massive understatement.

'Splendid,' Moulton said happily. He didn't add anything else, but then he didn't need to. Jenny glanced at Sergeant Ford to see if he shared his superior's unusual enthusiasm. Ford, though, was frowning. And it was a very familiar sort of frown indeed to the unhappy cook. She'd seen it on many a policeman's face in the past, which was not surprising really, since she had it on good authority that her name was now famous — or, more accurately, *infamous* — in police circles. Nobody liked a busybody around to muddle up his own investigation, even if she *did* have a very disconcerting habit of being useful at times. It all smacked too closely of popular detective fiction for most coppers to stomach.

Usually, Jenny made it her practice to avoid policemen, who in turn were very grateful for her efforts in this direction. But Moulton, it seemed, was going to prove the exception to the rule, as his very next words showed.

'So, Miss Starling, what do we do next?'

She was just about to open her mouth and say that she didn't particularly want to do anything next, when the door opened on a blast of cold air, and Mrs Jarvis bustled in.

'Oh, but that's cold out there. Mind if I have a cuppa before I go on to the . . . vill . . . age . . .' Her voice trailed off as she took in the presence of the two strangers and, for the first time, sensed the unmistakable odour of tragedy in the air.

Her appearance on the scene gave Jenny the sudden and disorientating sensation that she was in the middle of a not particularly good farce. She almost expected an unseen audience to laugh and applaud at this entrance of the light comic relief.

'Whatever's the matter?' Mrs Jarvis said in alarm, pulling off her bobble hat and her cheeks turning rosy red in the warm air of the kitchen.

'Who are you, madam, if I might ask?' Ford leapt in, notebook in hand.

'Well, I'm Mrs Jarvis, of course,' she said, as if she suspected Ford fell little short of a Toc H lamp in the brightness stakes.

'She's the daily here,' Jenny explained quietly.

'What's wrong?' Mrs Jarvis demanded sharply, her lower lip beginning to tremble. 'You're the police, ain't yah?' she challenged with her hands on her hips, her voice defying them to deny it.

'We are, madam. I'm sorry to say Mr Kelton has been murdered. Would you mind telling me where you've been this morning?' Ford tried again.

Mrs Jarvis's jaw dropped for a moment, and then her eyes began to glitter. A wide and unpleasant smile quickly curved along her face. Both policemen began to stare at her in astonishment.

'No, Mrs Jarvis, that's not it!' Jenny said sharply, understanding that smile and the meaning behind it all too well. 'It wasn't Stan,' she added quickly, than added more quietly, her voice bleak, 'It was Sid.'

Mrs Jarvis gasped once, went white, and tumbled onto a chair, one hand pressed against her skinny bosom.

'Sid?' she whispered. 'Oh no, not Sid!' she all but wailed. 'No, that can't be. It's the devil. He should have been the one killed,' she mumbled, in her state of shock and confusion seeming not to care that Sergeant Ford was writing down every incriminating word she said. She suddenly sat up straight, her nostrils flaring. 'Who did it? Which dirty dog did it?'

Suddenly she shot up to her feet again, the chair wobbling behind her and finally falling to the floor, the crash it

made sounding loud and harsh in the quietness of the room. 'It was *him*, wasn't it?' she breathed, her eyes going alarmingly round and wide. 'He did it. The devil!'

Sergeant Ford frowned over his notes. What had started out as a promisingly unusual reaction from a potential suspect looked to be turning out into nothing more than the ravings of a religious lunatic.

'We don't know who did it, Mrs Jarvis,' Jenny said warningly, but the daily was having none of it.

She turned to Moulton, instinctively picking him out as the one with superior rank. 'You must arrest him. Right now.'

Moulton coughed into his fist. 'I doubt if even the chief constable himself has the power to arrest the Devil, madam,' he responded, deadpan.

'Not the real Devil, you idiot,' Mrs Jarvis said, almost jumping up and down on the spot in frustration. 'I mean *him*! *Stanley*.'

Ford and Moulton exchanged uneasy but speculative glances. Jenny shook her head and sighed. She was getting one mother and father of a headache.

'What makes you think Mr Stanley Kelton killed his brother, Mrs Jarvis?' Ford asked, his tone so reasonable that it made Jenny's teeth grate together.

'It stands to reason, don't it?' Mrs Jarvis said, her tone getting higher and higher as she stared from policeman to policeman. 'How dense can you be?' she wailed, her Oxfordshire old-country accent becoming ever thicker as she became more and more distressed. 'That man's the devil himself. He cares about nothing and no one. He thinks he's above everyone and everything . . .'

At last, sensing that she might be making a bit of a fool of herself, Mrs Jarvis trailed off. She looked at the policemen for several minutes, breathing deeply. Then she slowly sat down once more.

Eventually, she looked across at the cook. 'Well, it has to be him,' she insisted petulantly. 'It has to be,' she repeated in a hiss, although Jenny had offered no adverse comment. 'You mark my words,' she rallied a bit, 'when all's done and dusted, it'll turn out to have been that devil what done it.' Then an astonishing look of cunning crossed her face. 'Or was responsible for it, anyhow,' she added, somewhat more cryptically.

Jenny couldn't help but feel a great deal of sympathy for her. If one of the inhabitants at Kelton Farm was the murderer (and who else could have done it?), she too hoped that it was Stan Kelton. But, she wondered bleakly, wasn't that just the ultimate in wishful thinking? At this point, there was no more reason to suspect Stan than anybody else. She'd have to be careful and not let her own dislike of the man colour her judgement, she told herself firmly. What she needed now was to keep a clear and level head. And she certainly couldn't rely on any help from Mrs Jarvis in maintaining it.

'What did you do after leaving here this morning, Mrs Jarvis?' she asked quietly instead, and from the corner of her eye, saw Sergeant Ford bristle. She was obviously trespassing on his terrain now, but it couldn't be helped; she had a better insight into the inter-relationships seething around at Kelton Farm than either policeman, which gave her an unfair advantage. Luckily, the sergeant made no comment, but duly jotted down Mrs Jarvis's story quickly and concisely, contenting himself with just the odd, fulminating look in the cook's direction.

Mrs Jarvis, it seemed, had returned home for her purse, stopped to make herself some lunch, and then decided to pop in for a cuppa at the farm before going on to the village. What she didn't admit to, but what all of them knew, was that she'd been deliberately dragging her feet, so to speak, because it was Christmas Eve, and she resented having to work it at all.

As an alibi, it was no better than anybody else's. She could have returned at any time and killed Sid.

With her story told, she seemed reluctant to leave, such was her curiosity. And it was Moulton who finally had to more or less manhandle the daily out of the kitchen and send her on her way to the village to do her postponed bit of shopping. And once she'd arrived there, they all knew that she'd make it her business to spread the gossip as quickly and as self-importantly as possible.

'I take it you've got a search party out, scouting for any footprints leading to the farm across the fields from the village?' Jenny said as the room once more fell silent.

Moulton blinked.

Jenny sighed. 'With all that snow lying around, we should make sure no one came here from the village, or from the main road. Whilst I don't think it likely that a stranger did kill Sid, it's probably a good idea to eliminate all other possibilities first,' she explained, feeling unutterably weary.

Without a word Moulton left, no doubt to give the order for a team of constables to start scouring the fields for tracks.

Ford glanced at her, something approaching respect in his eyes. He was beginning to think she might prove to be useful after all. He was used to doing Moulton's thinking for him, and he had to admit that, like his superior, he too had begun to feel a little out of his depth in this case.

It was nice to have an old hand, so to speak, hanging around — even if in a strictly unofficial capacity, of course.

'So you think it was an inside job then?' he asked, as his superior returned.

'I'm afraid so,' Jenny agreed wearily. 'Especially since the dog was here all the time. I'd forgotten about Pooch,' she admitted. 'If a stranger had done it, then surely Sid would have showed some surprise? Some alarm? The dog would have barked, at the very least. And I'm sure Pooch would have attacked any stranger that went for his master. And I heard no such rumpus.'

She thought of Sid, fondling the dog's ears. Pooch would wonder where that kind hand had got to, in the weeks to come. The thought threatened to bring tears to her eyes, and she briskly shook her head and snapped out of it. Getting maudlin, that's what it amounted to. So she'd better watch it!

She glanced up as Ford put away his notebook, the gesture reminding her of someone else. Now who . . . ? Of course! Philip Endecott.

When she'd reached the age of twenty-one her father had become convinced that his only child would die an old maid unless he did something about it. Consequently he'd hinted, bullied, cajoled and whinged until she and Philip Endecott, a turf accountant from Banbury, had finally agreed to become engaged. Philip had fallen in love with her Yorkshire puddings and jam roly-poly. Or was it her bread and butter pudding? Of course, Jenny had had no serious intention of marrying anyone at such a young age — let alone Philip Endecott. But agreeing to the pretence had kept her father quiet, and in the end, once his hysteria had worn off somewhat, it had been easy enough to convince Philip that he really *didn't* want to marry her either, divine Yorkshire puddings or not.

Funny, the last she'd heard, Philip Endecott had joined a monastery in deepest Peru. She frowned thoughtfully. Surely she hadn't scared him *that* much? Although, now she came to think of it, she had threatened to do something very physical with a spatula unless he stopped bothering her . . .

'Miss Starling!' Moulton's raised voice snapped her out of her reverie.

'Hmm?' She blinked and straightened up. 'What?' she asked briskly.

'I was saying,' Moulton explained patiently, 'that the men are searching the fields now. The body's gone, and everything's quietened down.'

'Hmm,' Jenny said flatly.

But Moulton was not a man to be easily put off. He'd found his salvation, and was going to cling to it tenaciously come what may. 'So, what do you suggest we do next?' he prodded.

The cook looked at him thoughtfully. Never before had she been called upon to take such a direct part in a murder investigation. Usually, she spent much of her time assuring the policeman in charge that she had no intention of inter-fering. Now, faced with Moulton's patiently waiting face, she felt a sudden blast of panic. What if she couldn't do it? What if Sid's murderer got away with it?

No! Such a thought was unthinkable. Jenny Starling vis-ibly stiffened her shoulders, which made Moulton, at least, feel much happier about things. 'Well,' she said practically, 'if we can't do anything positive yet, we can at least see if we can rule out Delia from the list of suspects,' she said firmly.

Moulton looked blank for a moment, then said, 'We go and see Sissy Bray and her mother?'

'Right,' Jenny said. 'And, er, Inspector? We'll all go out the front way, if you don't mind. I'd rather we got into the habit of coming and going that way. It'll save me from spending my *entire* time mopping the floor!'

# CHAPTER SEVEN

Cordelia Bray didn't *look* like much of an invalid, although Jenny had to admit that she certainly knew how to *be* one. For the cook found herself instantly agreeing with Mrs Jarvis's rather spiteful opinion of her next-door neighbour within moments of meeting her.

A well-cushioned woman, she lay on a long, comfortable sofa, and was dressed in a cosy, warm-looking dressing gown and slippers, next to a roaring log fire. By her side was a table on which rested an empty teacup, a bowl of fruit, a box of chocolates, and several popular women's magazines.

Her hair had been carefully washed and brushed, and was still more golden than grey. Her lips were coloured with a very discreet lipstick, and her face powdered to a becoming pink. Since she couldn't have been expecting visitors, and thus must repose beautifully like this all day long, it was obvious that her appearance meant even more to Cordelia than her supposed ill health.

Her voice was decidedly weak, though, as was the look in her eye, as she made a feeble attempt to sit up a little straighter. Now, was that simply play-acting or a case of genuine lethargy, Jenny wondered, with just a touch of unease. She supposed that if you played the invalid for long enough, and didn't exercise or use your muscles much, then someday you might very well discover that you'd become an invalid in reality.

The thought was rather horrific.

'Sissy, did you say these were the police?' she breathed, her eyes widening in alarm, her hands fluttering in panic. Jenny wasn't sure if the panic was real, either, or if Mrs Bray merely thought that it was the done thing to do, when your daughter ushered in such unexpected visitors to your living room.

In contrast to her mother, Sissy Bray looked the epitome of wholesome health and youth. She was Delia's age, but rather more plain and serious in her manner than her friend, and she hovered about the room as if unsure of what to do next.

Jenny could well imagine that apart from Delia, there were very few callers at their cottage. Apart from anything else, it was in such an isolated spot, with a mere footpath leading to The Dell from Kelton Farm. No car could be driven right up to the front door, and in this day and age, she cynically expected that that fact alone would put off a lot of would-be callers, anyway. She doubted that the green message — i.e. cycle or walk — counted for much in this small rural community.

As the girl, all gangly arms and legs, finally decided to settle on the arm of a huge, padded armchair, Jenny wondered with sympathy if the very isolation of her home added to the girl's obvious desperation to escape from it.

'I'm Inspector Moulton, Mrs Bray,' the inspector began gently, responding as most men would to the sight of a supposedly helpless, quite good-looking female. He even managed a smile. Ford actually blushed as Cordelia swept her eyes briefly over him.

'Please, gentlemen, do sit down. I'm afraid I can't rise . . .' Both men fell over themselves to assure her that she mustn't upset herself, and Cordelia sank graciously back against the pale mint-green cushions that complemented her colouring so well.

'Sissy, you must make some nice hot tea for our callers. The weather's so foul, isn't it? Of course, it's nice to have snow for Christmas for a change, but . . . oh, dear,' she gave a lovely little shudder that rocked her ample bosom just nicely, and then sighed deeply. 'So much of it! I swear, I think we'll be snowed in here for weeks!'

Moulton murmured, vaguely tut-tutting condolences and assurances, whilst Ford, somewhat reluctantly it seemed, reached for his notebook. Her performance over for the moment, Cordelia finally gave her female visitor a quick scrutiny.

Her eyes were faintly contemptuous as they took in her unusual height and well-endowed hourglass figure, but her gaze sharpened and then she took in a quick gasp of air as she met Jenny's eyes. Not only were they far more beautiful than her own, but they were looking at her as if they could see right through her.

Cordelia quickly looked away. She coughed gently. 'Well, gentlemen, I must say I didn't expect to ever entertain a policeman in my home. There's nothing *wrong* is there?'

At that moment Sissy returned with a tray. She had been so quick, the cook instantly surmised two things. One was obvious — the poor girl had to keep a kettle constantly on the go to have a steady supply of hot water ready; and secondly, she didn't like to be out of earshot for any longer than was strictly necessary.

That, Jenny supposed, could be put down to simple curiosity. Then again, perhaps the girl didn't trust her mother to be alone with them? And if that was the case, what was it she was afraid of that Cordelia might say?

Jenny watched the teenager closely as she stirred the tea. It had been a cold walk from Kelton Farm to The Dell, and the prospect of hot tea was more than welcome.

Sissy had none of Delia's natural poise or grace, she noted clinically, but even so she seemed to pour out the tea in jerks and nervous starts that went far beyond the fumbling of an awkward teenager. She was obviously tense and on edge about something. But that might just be put down to the alien presence of the police in her living room.

Ford helped himself to two lumps of sugar; Moulton had one. Jenny took her own cup from the girl and smiled at her encouragingly. She got absolutely no response. It was as if the girl barely knew she was there.

She's definitely nervous about something, Jenny thought uneasily, and suddenly had a very strong premonition that this interview was not going to give them the results she'd been hoping for.

'Now, Mrs Bray,' Moulton began. 'I'm afraid there's been a little trouble over at Kelton Farm,' he admitted, and Sissy's cup rattled noisily in her saucer. She quickly picked up the cup and took a sip, but nobody in the room had missed the telltale reaction.

Her mother cast her a quick, black look. It boded badly for Sissy later on, Jenny thought; Mother was going to lay down the riot act about something and no mistake. Now though, and mindful of her visitors, she merely lifted one delicately arched eyebrow and tried not to look too curious. 'Oh? Well, I've never been over there, of course. I'm completely housebound, I'm afraid. So I don't quite see . . .' as delicately as she could she urged them to get to the point.

She wants to get her daughter alone as quickly as possible, Jenny thought in quick comprehension, and felt her sympathy for the girl grow in leaps and bounds. Mrs Bray's stranglehold on her only child had to be protected at all costs. Jenny could well understand why she would deem any news, no matter how seemingly irrelevant, as a possible threat to her cosy life here in The Dell.

'Yes, well, it's Delia Kelton we actually want to talk to you about,' Moulton said. He was not about to tell the charming and unfortunate Mrs Bray all about the murder — it was hardly police policy to go about dispersing information to the general public — but he did need to get to the facts.

Cordelia shot her daughter a fulminating look. 'Yes, well, I don't think I should say much about Delia,' she began sweetly. 'You see, I don't really approve of the girl,' she carried on, fluttering her hands helplessly.

I'll just bet you don't, Jenny thought grimly. She was too much of a disruptive influence on Sissy, no doubt. And too dangerous by half, with all her ideas of running away and maybe sharing a flat together and getting a job and becoming free of their respective prisons and jailers.

'So, I wouldn't want anything I say to colour your, er, judgement, so to speak,' Cordelia was finishing, so reasonably and with such impeccable fairness that Jenny shot her a quick look. She thinks something's happened to Delia, the cook realized with sudden comprehension. Now why should she think that?

'Oh, of course not. But really, all we need to know,' Moulton rushed to assure her, 'is whether or not Delia came here this morning, and if so, how long she stayed for.'

'Oh,' Cordelia said, sounding (to Jenny's ears at least) a trifle disappointed. 'Yes, she did come this morning. About . . . what time, Sissy?' she turned to her daughter, who was staring down with intense interest into her cup.

Sissy raised and lowered her shoulders sullenly. 'I dunno. Just after breakfast. About nine.'

Ford meticulously scribbled down a note of the time. 'And what time did she leave, do you think, Miss Bray?' he prompted her softly.

Again, the teenager's shoulders rose and fell in silent misery. 'I dunno. Just before lunch.' Suddenly, Sissy lifted her eyes and stared straight at her mother. 'She's not allowed to eat here, you see. She has to go home for lunch.' Her voice, although even and steady, spoke volumes.

Cordelia flushed angrily, then, aware of her audience, half turned to the two policemen sitting opposite her, and opened her eyes piteously wide. 'The young these days don't understand about hardship, Inspector. You see, I only have my widow's pension, and with the price of food these days . . .' Her hands did a helpless butterfly act. 'I simply couldn't afford to . . . well . . . you know,' she said, her voice wavering slightly, her head dipping in very seemly humility. 'But the Keltons of course are really quite wealthy . . .'

'Oh, quite, of course,' Moulton said and cast an angry glance at Sissy. 'Children nowadays don't have much idea about the importance of money,' he agreed, his voice chilly.

'Hah!' Jenny could restrain herself no longer. She was pretty sure that Sissy Bray knew an awful lot about the hardships of life. Both men turned to stare at her, surprised by her snort of disbelief. Cordelia watched her teacup with as much industrious concentration as Sissy had previously been watching hers.

Aware that she now held centre stage, and had no one to blame for it but herself, she gave a small cough.

'I take it that Delia stayed in here most of the time, Mrs Bray?' she said, and when the woman shot her a puzzled look, nodded around the room. 'In the living room, I mean.'

'Oh. I see. No, as a matter of fact, Sissy always takes Delia upstairs to her bedroom,' she said, her voice dripping with disapproval. 'She keeps her magazines up there, you see, and her stereo, and that dreadful computer that she's always on, day and night. You know how silly girls are, with their fashion magazines and pop stars and things,' she said, not to Jenny, but to Moulton.

In Cordelia's world, it was obviously only the men that mattered.

'I see,' Jenny said, her voice droll, and turned to Sissy. 'Miss Bray, did Delia leave your room for any length of time during the morning?'

Sissy was now looking distinctly puzzled. 'Leave? No, I don't think so. Of course, I had to keep popping downstairs to see to Mum,' she said, and the cook nodded wisely. Yes, I'll just bet you did, you poor chump, she thought grimly.

'But apart from that, you were together all morning?' she persisted, beginning to feel relieved that at least one Kelton was now properly out of the running for the murder of poor Sid.

But Sissy was nodding, even as Cordelia was shaking her head.

'Don't forget my bath, darling,' she reminded, her voice sweetness itself. She didn't know why, but Delia Kelton was in some kind of trouble, and that was too good an opportunity to miss for someone like Mrs Bray.

Jenny glanced at her briefly, then turned back to her daughter as the girl sighed heavily. 'Oh yes. I had to give Mum a bath.'

'When was this?' Ford piped up, his ever-ready notebook quivering in his hand.

'Just before lunch,' Sissy said. 'I remember, because when I got back, me and Dee-Dee didn't have much time left to talk.' And the fact that Sissy had desperately wanted to talk to her friend Jenny didn't doubt, for Sissy still looked the epitome of misery. Had Delia stormed out after some kind of argument? Sissy seemed to be regretting something. But what exactly? And surely a spat between young friends could have nothing to do with Sid Kelton and his death?

'How long, do you think, did it take you to give your mother her bath?' she asked gently, and Sissy shrugged.

'I dunno. Half an hour or so I should think. It takes a while to run the water just right, and get Mum in and everything—'

'Sissy,' Cordelia said, glancing quickly at the men. 'I think that's enough.'

Moulton shifted uneasily in his chair. He, too, had no wish to go into details about poor Mrs Bray's ablutions.

'And this was just before lunch,' Jenny said. 'Say . . . one o'clock?' she asked hopefully.

But her luck was out. 'Oh no,' Sissy said quickly. 'We usually eat around twelve thirty.'

So Delia had been alone when Sid was killed. And had been alone for a good half an hour or so. Plenty of time to go to the farm and come back again. And she'd have known, from her past experiences at The Dell, roughly how long it would take Sissy to bathe her mother.

Damn!

Opposite her, both policemen were thinking much the same thing. Ford glanced at Moulton who reluctantly rose to his feet.

'And you never popped back into your bedroom for something, even once, and saw Delia?' Jenny fished, just to make sure, but Sissy was already shaking her head.

'I daren't leave Mother alone in the bath,' she said simply. Jenny nodded and sighed. And, of course, Delia would know that as well. So that was that.

Sissy rose to see them out, but once on the doorstep she quickly grabbed Jenny's arm. Moulton and Ford were already making off down the footpath, not anxious to linger on the cold doorstep. A chill wind was springing up in the east.

'I hope she makes it!' Sissy hissed, her voice rich in defiance, and Jenny met her dancing eyes with a sad look. For with those few simple words, she understood at once what Sissy was thinking, what she had been thinking all throughout the interview.

'Delia hasn't left home, Sissy,' she said quietly. 'It isn't about that.'

Sissy's small mouth fell open, her colour ebbing away. 'But I thought . . . I thought that horrible father of hers had brought the police in to find her . . .'

Jenny shook her head. 'I'm afraid not.' She looked behind her and saw Ford and Moulton had stopped, realizing that she was not following. Quickly, before one or the other of them started coming back, Jenny said quietly, 'You and she were planning to leave today, weren't you?'

Sissy automatically glanced over her shoulder back into the house, no doubt expecting her mother's accusing presence to loom over her at any moment.

Then she glanced back at the big cook and nodded miserably. 'Tell her I'm sorry, will you? But she already knows Mum found my money. I told her it was gone . . .'

From inside the house, Cordelia called her daughter's name imperiously. The girl reacted as if to a whiplash.

'I must go,' she said, and turned back. Then she hesitated. She looked back over her shoulder one last time and said quietly, 'If Dee-Dee didn't leave . . . is she in any trouble?'

Jenny nodded slowly. 'I think she may be, yes,' she said quietly.

Behind her came the crunch of feet in the snow, and Sissy quickly retreated and shut the door. When Jenny turned back, both policemen were standing in front of her, looking curious.

'Well?' Moulton said.

She shrugged. 'Delia and Sissy had planned on leaving home today,' she said quietly. 'But something went wrong.' She would rather not have given the girls away, but she'd learned before, from bitter past experience, that anything in a murder inquiry might turn out to be important, no matter how unrelated it might seem at the time. She'd also learned that it wasn't particularly clever to keep things from the police.

They tended to be just a bit touchy about it.

Moulton frowned. 'She was going to leave her mother? All alone, in the state she's in? And on Christmas Eve, of all days?' Moulton sounded shocked out of his boots.

Jenny stared at him for a moment, then sighed heavily. She said nothing however.

She was used to the stupidity of men.

* * *

Back at the farm, everyone except Delia was sitting around the kitchen table. The remains of the baked potatoes with cheese and onion topping littered the surface, though very little of it had actually been eaten. Still, she mused, it was better than leaving it in the oven to burn.

She cleared it up without comment. She had dinner to cook, which would have to be a little later than usual. Not that she expected that anyone would complain, under the circumstances.

Bill and Bert sat morosely silent, as if still unable to believe what had happened to their uncle. No doubt it was only Sid's kind and peace-keeping presence that had made life tolerable for them both at Kelton Farm. But now, with him gone, the future must look bleak indeed.

Jeremy looked nervous. He fiddled with a slice of bread, spreading crumbs around and casting his father quick, worried glances.

Stan Kelton cleared his throat. 'I know it's Christmas tomorrow,' he began, his voice gruff, 'and if you coppers want to get back to your families, you can,' he agreed magnanimously, as if he really had any say in it. 'But if you want to stay here the night, that can be arranged as well. There's two rooms you can have. Bill can light you a fire in each, if you like. If you don't, you'd best be going now. There's another snow squall on the way.'

Ford looked longingly at his superior. He was married with two kiddies under five. He *had* to get home to read them a story and later on creep into their room and fill their stockings. And for him not to be there on Christmas morning to see them open their presents filled him with a sense of gloom.

On the other hand, this *was* a murder case. And Sid Kelton had been a relatively wealthy and important man, a man of considerable property. They couldn't just take the holiday time off without someone high up back at HQ having something unflattering to say about it.

But Moulton, for once, surprised him. He hadn't missed the gloomy look his sergeant had given him, nor was he unaware of his duties. 'My sergeant will be leaving,' he said with quiet authority. 'But I myself will be staying.'

Ford smiled with relief, even as he felt a wave of guilt wash over him for all the times he'd mentally sworn at his superior, or run him down. But, truth be told, Moulton wasn't making all that much of a sacrifice. All his children had grown up, and he knew his wife could easily go to their daughter's for Christmas Day, to save being alone. He asked Ford to tell her as much, and a few minutes later the sergeant left, restraining from whistling cheerfully until he was decently out of earshot of the farm.

Jenny set to work on dinner. As she worked, though, her mind hummed. Delia had left the place that morning, expecting never to come back. No doubt she'd been smuggling out

91

the odd item of clothing, over the weeks, and leaving them with Sissy to hide. And Sissy herself had been hoarding some money, no doubt from the housekeeping.

But when Delia had arrived at The Dell, all excitement and anticipation, it was only to learn that Cordelia had discovered the stash and confiscated it, no doubt thoroughly berating and demoralizing her daughter as she'd done so.

So Delia would be on her own, if she left. And worse even than that, alone and without money. She would have had no choice but to return home in defeat. So she'd have come back to the farm feeling thoroughly enraged, miserable and totally frustrated.

And discovered her uncle, sitting at the table. Good old Sid, who was the *real* owner of the farm, but who lacked the will and backbone to stand up to her father. Sid, who must have had plenty of money of his own. Had he ever offered her any? Sid, frail and helpless, just sitting there and perhaps smiling at her, totally unaware and seemingly uncaring about the devastating blow she'd just been delivered.

Jenny sighed heavily. It was possible that Delia could have exploded in a moment of madness. But was it *likely*?

She didn't know. Not yet. She would try to get to know these people much better in the coming days. To talk to them and listen to them. And hope that one of them let something slip . . . One thing was for sure, she thought grimly, it was going to be a very strange Christmas with a police inspector as a guest, and everyone watching everyone else, and silently wondering, *Was it you?*

And for one of them, it would be the strangest Christmas of all. Watching the policeman. Waiting to see if he seemed to uncover any clue or any scrap of evidence.

Wondering if he, or she, had really got away with it . . .

# CHAPTER EIGHT

Delia awoke on Christmas morning to the sound of church bells drifting across the valley. For a long moment she lay snug and safe in her warm bed, listening to the Westcott Barton church bells tinkling joyously in the clear, frosty air, her mind, for a moment, blissfully blank.

It's Christmas, she thought then, still sluggish from sleep. And for a moment, everything was still all right. Then, like a cold wave suddenly breaking over her, she thought, *London*, and wanted to cry. Then, an even colder wave hit her, and she forgot all about her aborted dreams of escape, and she thought instead:

*Uncle Sid.*

Delia closed her pretty brown eyes for a long painful moment, and her hands curled into fists by her side. If only . . .

She groaned and sat up, and immediately began shivering in the frozen air; she had let the fire go out before going to bed. Hardly surprising in the circumstances, and not for the first time, she swore bitterly to herself about the lack of central heating. The next time she was in town, she'd buy herself an electric fire for her bedroom, no matter how much her father moaned about the cost of power nowadays. Then her spurt of defiance fizzled as she realized that the cost of such appliances was bound to be expensive, and she couldn't afford to squander even a single pound coin.

She quickly huddled into a tweed skirt that had belonged to her mother, and pulled on a blouse and a pale blue sweater which was now a shade too small for her. Goosebumps peppered her wrists as she rubbed her hands together for warmth, and to stop her fingers tingling in the cold.

She wondered yet again what sort of kink it was in her father's makeup that made him so penny-pinching when he was one of the wealthiest men around. Could he be mentally ill?

She was just about to get up and make the bed when a small white packet propped on her dressing table caught her eye. She'd missed it yesterday, being too numb and shocked to notice anything much. Now she frowned and moved cautiously around the bed, her heart suddenly hammering in her chest. She felt suddenly deeply afraid, but couldn't have said why.

She noticed her own name written on the front, and immediately recognized the handwriting.

Sid's writing.

With shaking hands she reached for the packet, which felt as cold as pity in her hands, and fumbled with the sealed flap. But, nightmarishly, it seemed to resist her probing fingers, and in the end, she angrily pulled the top off in a sudden jerk, dropping it onto the floor as the thing came apart in her hands.

An explosion of twenty-pound notes fluttered in the air and landed on the thin, faded carpet. For a long moment, Delia simply stared down at the money. Then, like a wondrous child, she bent and carefully collected them all together. There was fifteen hundred pounds' worth of them when she'd finished counting, which was more than enough to get her to London. She could even rent a little bedsit, whilst she hunted about for a job. She could also take Sissy. But why had Sid done this now?

Suddenly, feverishly, Delia grabbed for the envelope and looked inside. Then she froze as she saw a slim, singly folded piece of paper tucked inside, and licked her painfully dry lips. For a moment, a mad, near-hysterical moment, she wanted to tear the letter into shreds before she could read it. But the moment passed quickly.

She simply *had* to know.

Slowly she extracted the note and read the few brief words written on one side.

*My Dear Delia,*

*Happy Christmas, my beloved niece.*
*I hope you find the life you've always wanted, and love what you find.*

*Your loving uncle, Sidney.*

For a long moment, Delia stared at the words, as if unable to comprehend them. But, slowly, very slowly, several things became horribly clear.

Sid had known, must have always known, that she intended to leave the farm, and soon. And that he'd always intended to help her. He'd left it until Christmas Day to tell her so. Left it until she was eighteen and could legally act however she liked. He'd left it—

'Too late,' Delia whispered, and two large tears rolled down her cheeks. 'Oh, Uncle Sid,' she whispered, her words bouncing off the walls of her room and coming back to her, deepening her grief. 'Why did you leave it until it was all too late?'

\* \* \*

Bert Kelton paused as the first church bells of the morning pealed across the valley, and looked instinctively towards the village. There, through the bare skeletons of trees, he could just make out the spire of the church and a flock of rooks filling the bare branches of the ash tree beside it.

He turned his back on the sight and made off quickly in the opposite direction, ignoring the bite of fierce frost on his bare hands. He glanced down fondly at the dog trotting in resigned misery beside him. Sid's dog, really, Bert thought. Sid was the one who kept him hidden under the kitchen table. Many was the time when Bert had had to come in and hoist the dog out of the kitchen before his father got home, knowing that Stan would give the dog a kick in the ribs for daring to come inside.

He could still see Sid's eyes twinkling at him in silent gratitude, could still see his uncle's old and ill face crack into a smile as he watched Bert drag the reluctant mutt out into the yard.

'Come on, Pooch, cheer up,' he muttered. 'We have to round the sheep up out of Dingle field. If the thaw comes, the meadow's bound to flood.'

He didn't, of course, have to do it on Christmas morning. Neither did he have to do it alone. But he couldn't face his first Christmas without Janice being there to wish him a Merry Christmas with a laugh and a hug and a kiss under the mistletoe.

Beside him, the dog heaved a great shuddering sigh, as if he'd understood every word, and wasn't looking forward to it. The sound distracted Bert, who glanced down in the dog's direction once more and gave a dry, painful laugh. 'You're the only sheepdog I ever knew who didn't like sheep,' he said, and instantly felt Sid's ghost was beside him.

'Ahh, but that's what makes the hound so interesting,' Sid had said, when Bert had first told him about the young pup's aversion to farm work.

Bert almost glanced around, as if expecting to see Sid's ghost walking beside him, but resisted the impulse with gritted teeth. Instead, he frowned and put his best foot forward, intent on putting as much distance as he could between himself and the farm. He knew, one day, he simply *wouldn't* be able to go back. Every day, he had to fight an ever-stronger urge to just turn his back and walk away. Only the fact that he didn't know where Janice was stopped him. Unless he stayed, and managed to intercept any letter from her before his father got to it, he'd never know where she was.

He didn't even want to think about what he would do if she ever stopped writing. If she finally believed he didn't want to know her. Talk to her. Be with her. If that happened, he thought, he could kill—

'Damn it, Sid, it was all your fault,' he said aloud, making the dog look up at him, one ear cocked inquisitively. Bert rubbed a hard hand over his brow, and sighed deeply. 'If only you'd kicked him off the farm years ago, none of this would have happened. I'd still have Janice.'

But Sid hadn't acted. And now Sid was dead.

In the meadow, Bert surveyed the sheep, which were huddled all along one hedge, away from the wind and nestling in the lee. The snow was barely on the ground there, and they would be reluctant to plough their way through the deepening snow towards the gate.

He glanced down at the dog, which was watching the sheep with misery in his soft brown eyes.

'Off you go then,' Bert gave the command, and the dog began crossing the field obediently, forced to make his way through the snow in leaps and bounds, rather than in a straight, walking line.

Bert moved around the field to check out the spot where the wind, sweeping in from the east, had cut a shallow path in the snow. With a few sharp whistles, the dog had them heading that way.

Pooch was puzzled. He knew from past memory that the sheep had to go through the gate, so why was his master giving him commands to take them somewhere else? Then the snow under his paws became less deep, and he understood. Perhaps this wasn't going to be so bad after all. He began to pant happily, pressing his belly into the ground, watching, turning back, rounding up the silly white objects that didn't seem to have a brain in their woolly heads.

Then he heard a sharp whistled command that warned of a stray, saw one stupid ewe heading off on her own, and went after her. He nipped at her heels, never, of course, actually touching her. The stupid sheep bleated, skidded to a halt and turned.

And suddenly the world fell out from under him.

Pooch gave a single yip of surprise. He had not forgotten that there was a pond in this field, but the mutt simply hadn't known where it was, under all the whiteness that surrounded him. Now, terrifyingly, his rear end was immersed in cold, stinging water, and the dog gave a terrified yelp.

He stared at the stupid woolly-headed ewe that was trotting away and joining the others as if it hadn't a care in the world, and let out another heart-rending yelp as he felt his front paws sliding back on the ice. Desperately, he scrambled with his front paws, trying to dig them in, but he could get no purchase on the ice. His back legs doggy-paddled in the freezing water, and scrambled vainly for a foothold. He was in the pond from his back legs to halfway up his spine now, and he lifted his head and howled. The mutt could feel the heat draining out of him, and he looked across to where his master was . . .

But his master wasn't there. The dog whimpered; he hated being alone. He remembered the kind hand of his older master on his head, and wondered where he was. He wanted to be by the fire. And the big human female that had come to his home recently now regularly gave him scraps of meat. He liked her. He didn't like it when there wasn't a human around.

He howled for his master, scrambling in the ice but sinking in ever deeper. He was in almost to his shoulders now. And then, suddenly, the most wonderful sound he'd ever heard in all his canine life came from right behind him.

'All right, Pooch, hold on, boy.'

The dog turned his head and saw his master lying flat on his stomach, one large beefy hand reaching out to him. Fingers curled around the scruff of his neck, hurting him, but

Pooch didn't even whimper as Bert carefully pulled the dog from the icy pond. Pooch trustingly let go of his claw-hold on the ice, allowing himself to be totally submerged for an instant, before Bert could pull him clear.

Bert wriggled back cautiously, very much aware that he couldn't tell how far out on the pond he was. For a long while he wriggled carefully backwards, splaying his body weight as best he could and pulling the unresisting, shivering mutt with him. Only when he was sure he was clear of the pond did he sit up and drag the shaking dog onto his lap, wrapping his arms around the dog, rubbing warmth back into his quaking furry body.

He'd heard the ice crack a split second before he'd seen the dog slip in, and his heart had almost stopped. Unlike the dog, he *had* forgotten about the pond, his mind being on other things. If the dog, Sid's dog, had died because of his stupidity, he wasn't sure what he'd have done.

'I'm sorry, Sid,' Bert said, and found himself foolishly hugging the dog to his chest, crying all over it like a baby. 'Oh, Sid, I'm so sorry . . .'

Bert Kelton's shoulders shook as he sobbed like a man finally broken.

Relieved to be out of the cold, and so glad to be held in human arms again, Pooch reached up and began to lick his master's face, tasting strange, salty water. He wondered if his other master would give him a biscuit when he got home. Pooch felt as if he deserved one.

He didn't understand yet that his older master would never give him a biscuit again.

\* \* \*

At the farm, Jenny put the goose in to cook and looked up as the door from the hallway opened. The first one down this Christmas morning was not Stan, as she'd expected, but Bill. He walked in, looking like a man who'd spent the night tossing and turning. His hair was rumpled, his skin tight, and his blue eyes blazed in dry, red-rimmed anger. But it was a vague, undirected anger, and all the more debilitating for it.

'Do you want bacon and eggs?' she asked him softly, able only to offer him food, when what he so obviously needed was something far more precious. She was not surprised when he shook his head. He stood staring around him, looking lost. He was a handsome man, Jenny thought, with a slight awakening of interest, but she knew he was a way into his thirties. Why wasn't he married?

'I'll get you some tea,' she said. 'Nobody else is down yet, but I thought I heard the door go just before I got up.' She kept her voice deliberately casual, deliberately normal.

'That was Bert,' Bill said. 'I saw him leave about six.' It was still dark at six, Jenny thought, frowning. What could you do on a farm in pitch darkness?

She poured the tea, handed him a mug, heard the creaking movements of someone walking about overhead and put the bacon on to fry.

It was Inspector Moulton who put in an appearance a few moments later, his nose twitching. Still no Stan, she thought, and repressed an uneasy shiver. He'd be down in a minute. There really was no need for her to worry about a second murder, she told herself firmly. She was just being jumpy, that was all.

'I don't know what we're going to do without Sid to keep our spirits going,' Bill said at last, finally confronting his demons and ignoring the policeman altogether. But that probably had more to do with exhaustion, the cook thought charitably, than bad manners.

Moulton glanced at Bill thoughtfully. The younger son — so he wouldn't be inheriting the farm. Unmarried too, as he recalled.

'Tell me, Mr Kelton, why do you stay on here, if you dislike it so much?'

Jenny had filled him in on the family's complex and, in her opinion, downright unhealthy relationships last night, and he was frankly curious about Bill Kelton. Delia, as a young girl, might have no choice but to stay there; she had no money, and Moulton was of the firm opinion that, even in this day and age, it was better for daughters to stay in the protection of a family unit until they got married.

And Bert Kelton would one day inherit the farm, as would his son Jeremy after him, so he didn't question their allegiance to it. But Bill Kelton would not inherit. Bill Kelton worked long hours, for probably small rewards. He was also a bachelor, and yet he was a handsome enough man. Oh yes, Moulton wondered very much about Bill Kelton.

Bill looked across at him now, and gave a weary, pitying smile at how little strangers could understand. 'I'm a Kelton,' he said, as if that explained everything. 'I can't get away from here any more than Bert can. Or Delia.' He reached for his mug of tea as though it was a hefty shot of whiskey, and gulped it down. Indeed, he almost sounded like a drunken man, and yet he was terrifyingly sober. 'Merry Christmas,' he said softly, and began to laugh.

Jenny stiffened. Enough of that! Hysteria on Christmas morning was more than she had bargained for. 'Mr Kelton,' she began, her voice hard and bracing. 'I think—'

'I don't pay you to think, Miss Starling,' Stan Kelton's voice boomed across the room, making Moulton jump and spill his tea. 'I pay you to cook.' He glanced at the stove and the crisply frying bacon. He nodded, walked to the table, poured a mug of tea and sat at the head, ignoring his son, who stared blankly at the wall.

Moulton glanced at Jenny and nodded thoughtfully. He'd thought she'd been exaggerating the family tensions when she'd talked to him last night. Now, though, he could see for himself what she meant. The very air around them seemed to be bubbling. The whole place had the feel of a pressure cooker, about to explode at any moment. And yet, surely, Moulton thought with a frown, it had already done so? Sidney Kelton had been murdered, after all.

Yet Stan Kelton was a presence that nobody could ignore. Even now Sid was fading, as if he'd never been, like an old sepia photograph that had been left out too long in the sunlight. Even Moulton felt the blast of this man's powerful personality and had to stiffen his backbone against it. 'Mr Kelton,' he said firmly, 'I wondered if we might go over some old family history,' he asked, meeting Stan's eyes with his usual, deceivingly level look. 'I need to know as much about Sidney as I can learn.'

Stan scowled and shrugged. 'Don't see what good that'll do,' he grunted, but lumbered to his feet. 'I'll go look out all the family papers and the album. We can go over them after breakfast.'

\* \* \*

Delia didn't come down for breakfast, and Jeremy found the kitchen deserted when he walked in, half an hour later. There were dirty plates in the sink, so he knew that the others had been and gone, but he couldn't bring himself to care where everyone was. He felt as if he were the only one left on the face of the planet. Never had he felt so lonely. Or so guilty.

If only he hadn't quarrelled with his uncle. If only he'd listened more carefully to what he'd been trying to tell him.

He helped himself to some of the bacon in the frying pan, put it between two slices of freshly baked bread, added a dollop of brown sauce, then sat at the empty table, unable to eat it.

Instead, he found himself staring at the chair where his Uncle Sid had been sitting yesterday, a knife buried in his chest, his eyes wide open.

Looking at him accusingly . . .

\* \* \*

Bill pulled his scarf tighter around his chin as he looked out across the village. He had left the others in the living room to discuss the precious Kelton family history, mumbling some excuse about going out to find Bert. No one had objected to him leaving, although that strangely sexy-looking cook had given him a searching look.

The truth was, Bill simply could not bear to be in his father's company a moment longer than necessary. For as long as he could remember, poor Bert had been the slow one, the clumsy one, the useless one, and he, Bill, had been the brains and the firm favourite. Then, suddenly, over the last month or so, his father's ire had turned for some reason against *him*, until he was convinced that his father actively *hated* him.

Not that that wasn't fine with Bill. In fact, in many ways it was something of a relief, for Bill could not remember a time when he had ever loved his father, and now he no longer had to feel guilty about it.

As he stood out in the cold, he wondered where Bert was. He wondered how Delia was. He wondered if Jeremy would be the first Kelton to escape Stan Kelton and the curse of Kelton Farm.

He didn't wonder about Sid. He didn't even want to *think* about Sid.

\* \* \*

In the living room, Jenny, Moulton and Stan sat around the fire, the Kelton papers spread out on the table.

'So, where do I start?' Stan said, then carried on before Moulton could reply. 'Well, Sid was born in May 1940, and I was born a year later.' He sorted through the album and picked out their baby pictures. Even as chubby infants, Stan had looked the stronger, the bigger, the one who frowned, while Sid was the baby who chuckled. 'When I was twenty-two I married Eloise, when she was just sixteen,' Stan continued, and once more hunted through the album until he came to the only coloured photograph in it.

It was an expensive studio shot of a beautiful young woman with long, fair wavy hair and the deepest velvet brown eyes Jenny had ever seen. 'In 1964, we had Bert.'

'You were living here then?' Moulton put in, not bothering to point out that Stan Kelton was dwelling on *his* life, not on that of his brother's.

Stan nodded, looking surprised. 'Of course. Where else?'

Moulton nodded. 'Go on.'

'Well, Sid had a really bad bout of illness many years ago. Asthma, pleurisy, pneumonia. You name it. When he came out of hospital . . . well.' He shrugged helplessly. 'He was just buggered.' Stan paused as if about to say something else, then merely sighed. 'In '74, Bill was born, then Delia, a long while after that. Eloise died giving birth to our daughter,' he said bluntly. 'Probably had her too late in life.'

He didn't sound particularly regretful, angry, or even much interested. Not now, anyway.

Jenny's eye fell to the portrait of the beautiful Eloise and wondered. Had Stan Kelton ever loved his wife? She had certainly been lovely enough. But, somehow, she couldn't quite accept that looks alone had been reason enough for Stan to marry her. Stan, who according to his own daughter, always got what he wanted.

'Eloise,' Jenny said carefully. 'Was she a . . . did she come from a wealthy family?' she asked, as delicately as she could.

Stan looked at her, and then grunted a brief, hard laugh. 'Not particularly, no. She lived in the village. Her father owned a butcher's shop.'

'Oh,' Jenny said, genuinely surprised. Perhaps, after all, Stan Kelton had married for love. But she still somehow doubted it. Oh yes, she doubted it very much.

'And what happened to Sid, all this time,' Moulton asked, curious in spite of himself.

Stan shrugged. 'Sid came to look upon my family as his own. He treated them like his own kids.'

'He never, er,' Moulton took a breath, 'found any companionship from a lady himself?'

Stan grunted. 'Like I said, Sid came home from hospital a different man. He was always sickly. Couldn't walk far without wheezing. Couldn't do any of the heavy work.

Didn't seem to bother the ladies much, either. And over the years . . .' Stan shrugged.

Yes, Jenny thought grimly. Over the years, you just took over. And Sid let you. But why? Granted, Sid wasn't as naturally aggressive as his brother, but he had been a younger man then. Still, losing his health could have been traumatic for him. Yes, that could affect a man very badly, especially a previously fit one; a man who relied on physical strength and stamina to do his job and run the family farm. And yet . . . Jenny sighed, sure that there was more to all of this than Stan would have them believe. It just didn't make sense. Something was missing. She couldn't help feeling that a vital part of the jigsaw was being kept back from them.

Moulton thanked Stan stiffly and the farmer grunted, getting to his feet, not liking to be so obviously dismissed, but for once, disinclined to make an issue out of it. 'I suppose we'd better get together round the tree and open the presents,' he said, and shook his head. 'Don't feel much like it, though,' he muttered, then glanced quickly down at them, as if daring them to comment, as if showing even a glimmer of humanity was something to be ashamed of. Guarded against. Wisely, they said nothing, but both of them watched him thoughtfully as he walked away.

'A strange man, that,' Moulton said at last.

'Hmm,' Jenny murmured. But she was thinking not of Stan, but of Sid. And the more she thought of Sid, the more her eyes were drawn to the photograph of his lovely sister-in-law, Eloise. She of the lovely dark eyes. What secrets, Jenny wondered, had *she* taken with her to her grave?

## CHAPTER NINE

Jenny bent over the half-cooked goose and gave it a thorough basting. One of the many good things to be said about goose, she thought with immense satisfaction, was that there was always plenty of fat in the bottom of the pan. It was never going to go dry, unlike turkey, which could be a bit tricky. And goose fat made the best roast potatoes ever!

The smell of the onions roasting on either side of the bird filled the air with that particularly mouth-watering phenomenon that cooking onions always produced, but unfortunately there was no one else around to fully appreciate it with her. She checked to make sure that her stuffing of sage, onion, stewed apple, herb, sausage, celery and sweet chestnut was still firmly packed deep inside the bird, and nodded, well satisfied to see that it was.

She didn't really mind the fact that the family had been avoiding the kitchen all that morning. On the contrary, it gave her some desperately needed time to *think*. Someone had turned a radio on at breakfast, and now a church service from Oxford Cathedral, in the heart of Christ Church College, came clearly across the airwaves. A poignantly sweet rendition of 'Silent Night' by the Christ Church Choristers helped to dispel the gloom that hung over Kelton Farm.

She set to on the potatoes with gusto. It was simply impossible, in Jenny's view, to have too many roast potatoes.

She jumped when the door from the hallway opened, but it was only Moulton. 'They're all still huddled in the living room,' he said gloomily, by way of greeting.

'Humph,' the cook said enigmatically.

'That eldest lad — Bert. He came back an hour ago, soaked through and shivering fit to shift the rafters. Says he had to go in a pond after that dumb mutt of theirs.'

'Humph,' Jenny repeated.

Moulton sat down at the chair, very carefully not choosing the chair that the late Sid Kelton had frequented, and reached for the perpetually filled teapot. 'Well, I did *ask* to be filled in on the family background,' Moulton sighed, 'and I got it. In spades. I've heard all about poor old Sid's "great hospital stay," and all about how the oldest Kelton male, whether legitimate or not, has to inherit. I was even given the opportunity to go over the farm's accounts for the last two decades, if I wanted. I declined. I think they had it in their heads that I suspected the deceased of committing some sort of financial jiggery-pokery. Not that I'd be able to tell if he had, mind. We have forensic accountants for that sort of thing,' Moulton explained, with just a hint of pride. 'But from what I can tell, I think the Keltons are doing very well for themselves. Very well indeed. Which is odd, when you consider how they live. You'd think none of them had a penny to rub together.'

Jenny sighed. 'Keeping a tight hold on the purse strings is just one of the ways Stan keeps them all in line,' she explained flatly.

'You'd think at least one of them would have the gumption to stand up for themselves.'

'Humph,' Jenny said, obviously on a roll.

Moulton sighed heavily. 'I do think you could be a bit more helpful, Miss oh-so-clever-Dick Starling,' the policeman protested mildly. Then added casually, 'After all, I can't give my permission for you to leave the farm until after it's all sorted out.'

'Humph,' Jenny said, but this time with much more feeling. Moulton glanced at her, totally surprised that his none-too-veiled threat hadn't, at the very least, produced an indignant retaliation. But Jenny knew all about policemen; they tended to be a perfidious lot on the whole, in her experience.

'Well, you must have some ideas by now,' Moulton prompted, with just a hint of exasperation. 'It'll be quiet today, being Christmas Day and all, because the super will be at home with the family, but tomorrow, mark my words, he'll start leaning on Bryant, and then Bryant will start leaning on me.'

So you start leaning on me, the cook thought wryly, and reached for the horseradish to make some fresh sauce. It would make a good alternative to bread sauce. Or perhaps she should make both? Yes, she'd make both. She began to scrape the astringent root vegetable vigorously.

Behind her, Moulton heaved an enormous sigh, then nearly jumped out of his skin as it seemed to echo right back at him.

The dog, curled up in his favourite spot on the chair next to him and nicely hidden by the tablecloth, had a total affinity for any creature that could sigh as mournfully as that.

'What the hell?' Moulton said, but, perversely, Jenny decided not to enlighten him. Instead, she paused over her worktop and ran her hands across her pristine apron.

'I do have some ideas,' she acknowledged at last. 'For instance, I can tell you any number of reasons why people around here might want Stan dead,' she began, her voice thoughtful. 'Bert's wife left because of him. And Bert, if I'm not mistaken, is a man very close to the edge.'

Moulton sat up, looking distinctly happier.

'Delia is desperate to get away, and regards her father as a jailer,' she carried on inexorably. 'And desperate people can do desperate things. Bill . . .' She paused thoughtfully for a moment. 'Hmm. Bill was once the prince regent around here and is now the whipping boy for some reason, and most definitely doesn't like it.'

'Ah,' Moulton said. 'I was wondering about that lad.'

'Hmm,' the cook murmured. So was she. 'And Bill has a temper,' she mused, her voice so neutral that even Moulton, the reigning champion of neutrality, was impressed. 'Jeremy wants to marry the pub landlord's daughter, but his grandfather's pushing for a marriage to a local landowner's daughter. And that, I imagine, could drive even a relative saint into a fit of murderous frustration.' And then there was Mrs Jarvis, who perhaps had the best motive of them all. But for some reason, Jenny was loath to tell the inspector about that just yet.

Instead she frowned over the horseradish sauce. Bread sauce was more traditional. Perhaps nobody would want it? She hated to see good food going to waste.

'All good motives,' Moulton said happily.

'Hmm? Oh, yes. Only one thing wrong with them,' Jenny pointed out logically. 'It wasn't Stan who got himself murdered.'

Moulton stared at her. For a moment there, he'd allowed himself to get carried away. Now, suddenly, he slumped back. 'Damn!' he said distinctly. 'It's as if the wrong brother has been murdered. This whole setup's beginning to get on my nerves.' And Moulton hated his nerves to be bothered. It tended to upset his whole day.

He heaved another woebegone sigh.

From the depths of his paws, the sheepdog did the same. It was so good to have someone in the house who could appreciate a really good sigh.

Moulton again nearly jumped out of his skin and glanced furtively around the kitchen. The cook, who was reaching for the bread, seemed not to have heard it. He looked over his shoulder, but the door to the hallway was firmly shut. There was nobody in the kitchen but the two of them. He felt the hairs begin to rise on the back of his neck. He didn't believe in haunted places, he reminded himself staunchly. And nobody but a fool would think, for even one minute, that a murdered man hung around the scene of his demise, sighing mournfully. That was nothing more than an old wives' tale, or something out of a Victorian Gothic novel or ghost story.

'There's an echo in this place,' Moulton said uneasily.

'Humph,' Jenny took up her earlier theme, and sounded distinctly unimpressed. 'What did the forensic people find out yesterday?' she suddenly shot at him.

Glad to get back to more mundane matters, Moulton quickly told her. No footprints had led from the village to the farm, so that was out. And the footprints made by Stan, Bert, Jeremy and Bill were all consistent with them hunting for buried sheep. 'Of course, several tracks lead to the farm and back again, from several directions, but that hardly helps us. We already know the men had to come and go from the farm to the fields. And would have done so all morning, I expect.'

Jenny sighed. 'No fingerprints on the knife?'

'No,' Moulton sighed back. And waited for it.

Sure enough, a deep, mournful sigh seemed to echo from the direction of the table. And — slowly he turned his head, his neck hairs playing the last few strands of 'Colonel Bogey' — the sigh definitely *did* seem to come from Sid Kelton's chair.

The dog, who was actually sitting in his usual seat next to Sid's chair, chose that moment to let rip with another sigh just for good measure.

Moulton licked his lips. They felt distinctly cold.

'That settles it then,' Jenny said, dragging the policeman's attention back to the matter in hand. 'Nobody has a motive, nobody has an alibi and nobody left any evidence.'

Moulton's heart sank. 'You're not giving up, are you?' he asked, appalled. His first murder simply couldn't be tossed onto the 'unsolved' pile. He'd never live it down.

'Of course not,' Jenny said crossly. Give up, indeed! 'I'm merely saying that the only way to find out *who* killed Sid, is to find out *why* someone would have wanted to kill Sid.'

Moulton blinked, slowly and thoroughly thinking it over. 'You don't think somebody could have mistaken Sid for his brother?' he eventually asked. 'It would all make some sort of sense then.'

Jenny, the bread sauce made, was now in the middle of making the (very potent) brandy sauce for the Christmas pudding. One thing she abhorred was wishy-washy brandy sauce.

'Humph,' she said thoughtfully, but after a pause shook her head. 'I don't see how he could have been. Sid was a clapped-out poor old soul. Stan is a bull of a man. Besides, Sid was stabbed from the front. No, whoever did it had to have known exactly which brother it was that he or she was killing.'

Moulton sighed, then promptly wished he hadn't. He got to his feet noisily, and moved very smartly out of the room as the dog let rip with a really gusting sigh that must have started from the very pads of his paws.

Jenny watched the policeman go, her lips twitching. She promptly fished out a giblet from the giblet gravy, blew on it to cool it, and ducked under the table with it. The animal deserved a treat; that was the best entertainment she'd had in years.

'Merry Christmas, Pooch,' she said, giving the startled dog the best treat of his life. She watched him get his slavering chops around it, and nodded once, briskly, before straightening back up. She liked to reward diligence.

* * *

It was nearly one o'clock, an hour before lunch was due to be served, when someone came through the outer front door. Jenny craned her neck, and waited. Whoever the caller was, he or she was actually pausing to remove their boots. And the Junoesque cook's heart warmed: someone with thoughtful manners at last.

A few seconds later a youngish girl appeared, unwinding her long knitted scarf from around her neck to reveal a nipped red nose and large pansy eyes. Her hair was a wild nest of raven-dark curls. She would have made a perfect model for a Romany princess by one of those pre-Raphaelite masters who actually knew how to paint. The girl stopped when she saw that there was a stranger in the kitchen and gave an uncertain smile.

'Hello,' Jenny greeted her cheerfully. 'Would you like some mulled wine? I've just this second finished a batch.' She indicated a vast punchbowl, full of gently steaming wine, awash with spices, lemon and orange segments and the warming smell of melted honey.

'Oh, yes please,' the girl said, instantly winning approval. 'I wondered if . . . if . . . Jeremy was around,' she added, as Jenny, ladling out the beverage, handed her a cup. And with those few tentative words, Jenny was able to place her.

Mandy, the infamous landlord's daughter, she mused with an inner smile. No wonder young Jeremy was so smitten. 'He's with the family at the moment,' Jenny said, then paused discreetly. 'There's been a family tragedy.'

Mandy nodded. 'I know. Mrs Jarvis told my mum yesterday.' And she would tell anyone else that she could find, no doubt, Jenny thought ruefully. She glanced thoughtfully into the large, anxious eyes, and smiled.

'I'll see if I can smuggle him out for you,' she said, and was rewarded by a beaming smile of gratitude.

Jenny tapped on the parlour door and gingerly poked her head in. Her eyes fixed on Jeremy. 'I was wondering, could I borrow young Jeremy to help me bring up one of the large jugs of cider from the cellar?' she asked sweetly. She was, in fact, perfectly capable of lugging about much heavier objects, but nobody here had to know that.

Stan, who'd been staring into the fire, looked up at the interruption, and waved his hand in vague consent. The quickness with which Jeremy fled the tensely silent room was hardly surprising. Bill returned to his day-old newspaper. He'd been on the same page for the last half hour. Bert and Delia returned to playing their desultory game of cards. Neither of them knew which one was winning.

Christmas Day it wasn't. Even the presents under the tree remained unopened.

Jenny led Jeremy to the kitchen, smiling when he jerked to a halt at the sight of his sweetheart. 'Mandy!'

Mandy flew into his arms like a cooing homing pigeon and Jenny hastily turned back to her Brussels sprouts. She gave a discreet cough. 'I really do need that cider jug, young Jeremy,' she said, thinking of baked apples stuffed with mincemeat and cooked in cider for tomorrow's pudding.

Jeremy's young face flamed. 'Oh, er . . . right you are, Miss Starling,' he said, and tugged Mandy's hand. 'You can come and help me find it,' he said, his eyes speaking volumes.

Mandy followed him eagerly to the pantry door that led off down into the chilly cellar. 'Jerry, I just had to come. When I heard what had happened . . .'

'Ssshhh,' Jeremy said, glancing over his shoulder. He was not quick enough, however, to see Jenny's shoulders stiffen with suspicion. 'Come on, we'll talk down here,' he whispered, and led the way down to the dark dampness beneath.

Jenny walked slowly over to the pantry door that gave access to the underground room and nudged it open. Like most cellars, sound echoed off the thick walls, and a ghostly conversation could be clearly heard, wafting up the dark staircase.

'I don't know what to do,' she heard Mandy say, her voice, even muffled, sounding obviously upset.

'We don't have to do anything,' Jeremy said, his own voice anxious to soothe.

'But, what if people find out?' Mandy all but wailed.

'How can they find out, Mand?' At this point, Jenny felt herself becoming extremely uncomfortable, and roundly cursed Moulton. If he'd been anywhere near halfway competent, she wouldn't be forced into snooping at doorways like this. It made her feel distinctly grubby. But someone had to get justice for poor Sid.

'But there are policemen everywhere in the village,' Mandy said, her voice becoming tearful. 'They're asking everyone all sorts of questions. Did they see any strangers? Did they leave the village, and if so, did they see anyone along the roads? And you'd be surprised how many people *were* out and

113

about yesterday, Jerry, in spite of the snow and everything. Mr Dorrell was out walking to Ashcroft's place to get his turkey; Dad, as you know, was out with Fred getting in the beer. He didn't want to be left over the holidays without stocking up. Everyone was doing last-minute shopping . . .'

'Mand, Mand,' Jeremy stopped her. 'You worry too much.'

'And you don't worry enough,' Mandy shot back, her voice sharp and cross now.

Jenny nodded her head in approval. Much better. It was often far better to take the offensive.

'You don't know the police like I do,' Mandy said, suddenly sounding sixty, rather than sixteen or so. 'They dig and dig and get to the bottom of everything. What if Mr Dorrell noticed that you weren't in the far corner of Dingle field yesterday, like you said you were? He has to pass it on his way to the Ashcrofts' place, you know. People have a way of finding out about lies.'

The cook nodded in agreement. Good point, Mandy, she thought sadly. Somebody already has.

'Mand, you've got to stop this,' Jeremy said, but his own voice was less confident now. 'We don't know what time old Dorrell went to get his damned turkey. It could have been hours before or after I was supposed to be in the Dingle field. And even if it was at the same time, all I've got to say is that I must have been bent over, digging out a ewe, and old Dorrell didn't see me because I was below the hedgeline. And who's to call me a liar?'

Me, for one, Jenny thought gloomily. If it came to it. But if you weren't out and about in the fields, my lad, she mused grimly to herself, just where *were* you? And what were you up to?

'I'm scared, Jerry,' Mandy said miserably. 'If my dad finds out, or if *your grandfather* finds out . . .' she trailed off, and Jenny could see in her mind's eye the way the young girl had probably shuddered at the thought.

In fact, Jenny could well imagine that both of them were shuddering down there in the darkness, thinking about what

Stan Kelton would do if he found out — well, whatever it was that the youngsters didn't want him to know about.

'Well they won't,' Jeremy said, trying to sound very brisk, very sure and very grown up, and failing in all three departments. 'Now, let me get this cider for old cookie, and then you must get off back home. Granddad mustn't know you called in.'

Old cookie indeed, Jenny thought, lips twitching, as she smartly nipped back to her oven.

The two lovers emerged, a suspiciously long while later, both sets of eyes shining like stars. It was amazing, Jenny thought whimsically, looking at Mandy's glowing face, what a few stolen kisses could do for a girl's complexion.

* * *

At two o'clock precisely, Christmas dinner was served. In deference to the family, Jenny had arranged for her dinner and that of Inspector Moulton to be taken on trays in the parlour, whilst the family sat down at the kitchen table.

She'd done her best to eradicate the memory of Sid, and felt guilty even as she'd done so. She'd removed his chair, and placed in his setting a large holly, ivy, mistletoe and laurel table-piece that she'd made yesterday, winding pretty and festive red ribbons amongst the greenery. The range of vegetables in vast dishes and the gravy boat steamed gently. She'd lit the Christmas candles, put the goose at the head of the table for Stan to carve and stood back to watch the proceedings.

Stan was the first in, as always, and stood looking at the table. His face was unreadable. Bill and Bert smiled their thanks at her, both efforts rather strained to be sure, but a nice thought for all that.

Delia stared at the flickering candles, her eyes swimming with unshed tears as her father cut and dished the meat. Jenny and the inspector hastily helped themselves to their portions and left the family in peace.

Nobody had spoken a word.

In the parlour, the inspector dug into his dinner, his face registering his delight. The goose was cooked to perfection and the stuffing . . . he almost sighed with bliss, but restrained himself.

He'd gone off sighing.

Jenny cut through a roast potato, crisp and golden on the outside, white, piping hot and fluffy on the inside. And left it untouched on her plate. It was only the fourth time in her life that she'd failed to have an appetite.

'Not much of a Christmas for them, is it?' Moulton said, with obviously genuine sincerity, and for the first time since this whole sorry mess began, she felt herself warming to him. Just a little.

She shook her head. 'No. Not much.'

It was not much of a Christmas for any of them.

And, if she could help it, it would not be much of a New Year either for whoever had murdered Sid.

## CHAPTER TEN

Boxing Day dawned bright and sunny. Outside her window, the icicles clinging to the eaves began a noisy and annoying drip-drip-dripping that Jenny wasn't too sure that she appreciated very much. On the other hand, if it presaged a thaw, it meant that she'd have no difficulty in leaving the farm when she'd completed the time she'd agreed to cook for the Keltons.

And she'd hardly have been human if she wasn't looking forward to being able to go.

With a sigh, she rose and dressed quickly in her cold bedroom, yawning slightly as she traipsed downstairs to the kitchen. Once there, she lit the fire, let in the mutt and started breakfast. Moulton was the next down, the dark circles under his eyes mute testimony to his own sleepless night.

'Morning,' he said without enthusiasm, slumping down into the chair and managing to look even greyer than usual, a feat which, hitherto, Jenny would have thought was nigh on impossible.

She laid out the first round of sausage, bacon and eggs, and sat across from him, sipping her tea, watching him eat with automatic and instinctive approval, and thinking.

'After the others have come down, I think we should pay a visit to Mrs Jarvis,' she finally said.

Moulton, in the act of dunking his fried bread into his egg, glanced up, his eyes suddenly wide and alert. 'Oh? And why's that?'

Jenny smiled grimly. 'For the simple reason that, at the moment, she has to be our prime suspect.'

Moulton blinked. 'The domestic?' He sounded doubtful. 'Why her?' He began to wonder, on a rising tide of panic, if Miss Jenny Starling's reputation as a sleuth wouldn't, after all, turn out to be one of those modern urban legends that were more whimsical than factual. The thought was enough to send him into a funk so blue as to be very nearly black.

Jenny feloniously speared one of his sausages onto her fork and took a bite. 'Hmm, I know. I don't like it either,' she said with a sigh. 'I can't really summon up much enthusiasm for the assumption that Mrs Jarvis is our killer, but that doesn't alter the fact that she *is* the most likely. And more often than not, it is the most likely one who turns out to be the murderer. Haven't you found that?' she asked, shooting him a genuinely curious look.

Moulton, who'd only ever been involved on the fringes of a homicide case before, frowned. 'If you say so,' he said, patently unconvinced, and not about to tell her just how new he was to all of this.

Jenny leaned back in her chair, and waved her sausage casually in the air. 'First of all, you have to agree that motive is everything in this case. Right?'

Moulton thought about it for a moment cautiously and then decided that it wasn't a trick question, and nodded. 'Right,' he agreed, albeit still a little warily.

'And you have to agree that the only possible motive that seems to be going is one of resentment against Sid for not standing up to his brother. After all, if Sid had stuck to his guns, been more of a man If you like, then everyone would have had a much happier life around here. That's true to say, yes? I mean, Sid was fairly wealthy, but he had no tangled love life that we know about, and he wasn't the sort of man to make enemies that would hate him enough to want to kill him just for the pleasure of relieving him of this mortal coil. You agree?'

Moulton slowly nodded. That made sense. Life on Kelton Farm *would* have been a lot happier for everyone if Sid had been in charge. 'I still don't see how that puts Mrs Jarvis ahead of the others, though. I mean, she only worked here — she didn't have to live and breathe the bad atmosphere around here, twenty-four seven, like all the others.'

Jenny took another bite of sausage then slipped it off her fork. To the policeman's utter astonishment, she then thrust her hand under the table. He heard a distinct 'slurp' and when her hand re-emerged, minus the sausage, he finally remembered the dog. And a wave of utter relief washed over him. For a moment there he thought he was having another one of his nasty nightmares, and he was really still asleep upstairs.

'It's all a matter of degree,' Jenny said, dragging Moulton's mind back from the verge of boggling.

'Huh?'

'Bert lost his wife, but has to know, deep in his heart, that it's as much his fault as his father's. If he'd just gone with her or stood up to Stan, things might have been different. Bill is angry at being treated badly all of a sudden, but he's a grown man — he can either lump it or leave it. Delia and Jeremy are young, and can, if they can work up the courage, simply leave. It would be hard, but not impossible. And, don't forget this, because I think it's important: all those who live in this house were genuinely fond of Sid, as far as I can tell. Now Mrs Jarvis, on the other hand, has suffered the greatest and most irreparable loss of all. Her husband, the sanctity of her home, her independence and her dignity, are all gone. Of them all, she has the biggest potential grievance against Sid. And she might not have been so fond of Sid as she's always claimed. And he's not her blood relation either, is he?'

She was taking it for granted that Moulton had run a background check on all the suspects, and now knew all about the daily's tragic past. In this, she was quite right, and Moulton's eyes narrowed thoughtfully.

Now that she explained it in so many words, it all seemed so simple. In her grief, Mrs Jarvis might have got her mind all twisted up about things, brooding alone in the cottage that was hers no longer, and all because of the Kelton brothers. Yes, he could see how that could happen. Although surely it would be Stan she would try to kill, and not Sid? Except, of course, Stan was a strong bull of a man and could swat her like a fly, whereas Sid was frail and weaker, and for a woman, made a much more easy target. He found himself shivering at the thought, and reached for a piece of warm toast.

'And then there's the second thing against her,' Jenny said thoughtfully, blowing across the surface of her piping-hot tea and taking a tentative sip.

Moulton knew better than to stick his neck out for a second time. 'Which is?' he asked simply and straight to the point.

The cook smiled sadly. 'If you were going to kill someone, you'd want to blow as much smoke over it as you could. Yes?'

Moulton sighed. 'Unless you didn't care if you got caught. But no, that sounds reasonable enough.'

'Yet, on the morning of the murder, all the Kelton family came back and just stood there, well, milling around and not doing much at all in the smokescreen department. Apart from Stan accusing me, nobody said anything, or did anything that you could say was out of the ordinary.'

Moulton blinked. 'So?'

'So,' Jenny said, beginning to feel unutterably weary. 'Mrs Jarvis was the only one who went out of her way to make it plain how much she hated *Stan*. She was always drawing our attention to Stan, and away from Sid. She even went so far as to call Stan the devil. Of Sid, she said practically nothing. Now, assume for a moment she is our killer. What does she do? She comes back to the farm only when she knows that someone must have discovered the killing by now and called in the cops; and she waits until most of the initial rumpus must be over and then comes to the farm and pretends to be in total ignorance. And when we tell her that somebody's been killed, she immediately thinks — or would have us *think* that she thinks — that it is Stan who's dead, thereby distracting us yet again. And when she's told that it's not Stan but Sid, she puts on a very good performance of surprise and shock. All very dramatic, and the only one of all the suspects that stands out, just for that reason.'

'With the result that we immediately think that she didn't do it, because a killer wouldn't act so outlandishly?'

Jenny sighed. 'It all depends, you know, on how clever Mrs Jarvis really is. And how well she can act.'

Moulton grunted, not particularly interested in such details. It would simply be very handy if they could nab Mrs Jarvis for the killing. It would be a crime solved in record time, and the super would be very happy at not having to arrest a member of a wealthy and respected local family. And yet . . .

'For all that, I still can't see Mrs Jarvis sticking a knife into a harmless old man,' he said dismally.

'No, neither can I,' Jenny agreed glumly.

* * *

Mrs Jarvis's cottage was an almost exact replica of the Brays' cottage opposite. As Jenny and Moulton walked up the cleared front path, the cook saw the curtains twitch in the living room opposite and hid a small smile. No doubt Sissy was keeping an eye on things — by now she must have heard about her friend's uncle getting himself murdered. Or perhaps it was the 'invalid' herself who was intent on satisfying her curiosity? She wouldn't put much past Cordelia.

Mrs Jarvis looked surprised to see the cook, and her eyes, when they slid to the policeman beside her, widened nervously. But there was nothing in that, they both knew. Nobody liked a visit from the police, especially respectable, working-class cleaning ladies.

'May we come in, Mrs Jarvis?' Jenny asked. 'The inspector here wanted to get to know more about the Kelton family, and I told him nobody would know more than you.'

At this unashamed piece of flannel, Mrs Jarvis brightened visibly. 'Oh, right you are. Come on in then, come on in, and I'll put some mince pies out.'

Inside, the cottage was cramped with furniture and various knick-knacks, but it was cheerful enough, and Jenny gratefully took a seat on the settee in front of the fire, allowing her snow-caked boots to melt messily. Moulton chose a hard-backed chair to one side.

Mrs Jarvis quickly came back with tea and mince pies and settled herself into what was obviously her favourite, slightly sagging armchair. With her iron-grey hair escaping her untidy bun, her thick stockings wrinkling at her ankles and her flowered apron splashed with a bit of flour, she looked the least likely murder suspect you could ever hope to meet.

Jenny smiled. 'We were wondering, Mrs Jarvis, if *you* had any ideas over who would want to kill Sid,' she began, and Moulton, who'd just taken a mouthful of tea, promptly choked on it. 'You see, we just *can't* figure it out,' she added helplessly.

'Oh, I know, isn't it terrible?' Mrs Jarvis's large, rather watery eyes watered even more.

'Now if it had been Stan that died . . .' Jenny murmured, and trailed off.

As predicted, Mrs Jarvis jumped right in. 'Oh, you don't have to tell me! I know. Everyone wants that devil dead. But poor old Sid?' She shook her head. 'It fair turns my stomach. I'm telling you, I'm not sure if I can come in to work tomorrow. Being in that house . . .' she shuddered.

'Of course,' Jenny said, 'somebody might think that Sid was the real cause of all the trouble over at the farm,' she dangled the bait craftily, 'After all, Stan only got away with what he did because Sid let him. When all's said and done, Sid was the true owner of the farm.'

Mrs Jarvis's face flushed angrily. 'Now, don't you go talking such nonsense,' she snapped. 'You've only been there five minutes, young missy. What do you know about it? Eh?' Her chin jutted out pugnaciously. 'Poor old Sid never had a chance against that monster, no more than the rest of us did!' Her eyes blazed and she clanked her cup down angrily onto her saucer. 'What that poor old man suffered at his brother's hands . . .' Mrs Jarvis's bottom lip began to quiver. 'I don't know how anyone could have stood it.'

Jenny glanced across at Moulton. They were both thinking much the same thing. If Mrs Jarvis was acting, she could put Judi Dench or De Niro to shame.

'That man never drew a happy breath in his life, thanks to that brother of his.' Mrs Jarvis, having paused for breath, was more than ready to continue the battle in Sid's defence. 'My ma said, right from the time they was boys, that Stan was determined to get the farm off his brother. She always said, my ma, that Stan Kelton would stop at nothing. He hated being the younger son, positively *hated* it. He was a proper demon, even when young, to get his hands on Kelton land. And look how right she was!' Mrs Jarvis huffed impressively. 'When I think of poor Eloise, I could just cry.'

Jenny, who'd been about to admit defeat and scrub Mrs Jarvis from her mental list of suspects, suddenly stiffened. 'Eloise? You mean Stan's late wife?'

'Hah!' Mrs Jarvis all but shouted. 'She should have been Sid's wife by rights. Everyone knows that.' And she nodded sagely.

Jenny settled back against the settee, her head slightly cocked to one side. 'Oh?'

Moulton, who'd been about to suggest they leave, having arrived at the same conclusions as the cook, saw the change that came over her and found himself fascinated. Her eyes had developed the look of a cat sat waiting at a mouse hole. She languished on the settee like one of those Buddha statues that tourists came back with from India, looking slightly ridiculous and totally unthreatening. And yet, Moulton seemed to understand for the first time just how dangerous Jenny Starling actually was. Her reputation was certainly no whimsy and he was suddenly sure that if anybody could see her way through this damned case, it would be her. And with that realization, he felt a great weight lift from his shoulders.

Even though he couldn't understand why she should be so interested in old family gossip, he was willing to bet his last pay cheque that she knew what she was doing. And that whatever she learned would all be of use in the end.

So he tuned in his ears and took it all in.

'Eloise was a lovely young gal, Miss Starling,' Mrs Jarvis said, her voice softening a little now, as she cast her mind back through the years. It was amazing, Jenny thought absently and not for the first time, the power that nostalgia had over people. The good old days were always golden, it seemed. 'We went to school together. She was a little older than me, but she never looked down on us younger ones, the way you can when you're a kid. She was as sweet on the inside as she looked on the outside, and all of us kids knew that Sid Kelton was head over heels in love with her. When she was fifteen, he asked her to the church dance. They looked really good together. Old man Kelton, Sid's father, was right pleased about it too, her being a butcher's daughter, like. And then . . .' her face clouded, 'then Stan got wind of it. And that was that.'

Jenny again said, 'Oh?' and the single bland syllable was once more enough to launch Mrs Jarvis on in her tirade.

'Well, Stan couldn't have that could he? Sid would marry, have a son, and that would be that. Stan would never get his hands on the farm. So he did the most wicked thing you could ever think of.'

Jenny's eyes widened in sudden understanding, and she slowly nodded. 'He seduced Eloise,' she guessed, her voice flat and grim.

Mrs Jarvis nodded. 'I daresay you want to blame Eloise for that. After all, if she was in love with Sid, she should have had the gumption to stick with him. But you didn't know Stan in them days. He was a handsome devil, much more so than Sid. And he had, oh, I don't know how to describe it

124

really. A kind of . . . *energy* that fair took your breath away. All the girls felt it. And when he'd made up his mind, nobody could say no to him. Before anyone knew it, he'd swept her off her feet. Poor Eloise, she was such a simple-hearted gal. I don't suppose she knew what hit her. And then . . . there she was, married to the wrong brother, living at the farm with her real true love lost to her forever.'

Jenny ignored this rather over-romantic assessment. 'But didn't Sid carry on living at the farm as well?' she asked, sounding puzzled.

'Aye, he did,' Mrs Jarvis said. 'It was his home, wasn't it? Where else was he going to go? But it must have been torture for him — well, for them both really, I imagine. But it got Stan what he wanted, didn't it?' she pointed out savagely. 'Sid never did look at another woman after Eloise. And when he came back from hospital that time so . . . well . . . he was like a shell of a man. A thin, pitiful husk with no guts left in him — no gumption at all,' she shook her head sadly. 'By then Eloise had had Bert, of course. A few years later she had Bill, then finally Delia. And Stan had the farm in every way that mattered and, more importantly, he knew that Bert, his own son, would one day inherit as well. What did it matter to him that he made Eloise and Sid's life a misery? I sometimes think it was an act of mercy that Eloise died when she did, giving birth to Delia and all, I really do. It got her out from under it all, and far and away to a better place. It fair broke Sid's heart though, for all that.'

Jenny nodded. It all had such a tragic ring of truth about it. She glanced tellingly at Moulton, who took the hint and got to his feet.

'Well, thank you, Mrs Jarvis, for your time,' he said politely, and Mrs Jarvis flustered and blustered, and pressed another mince pie on them as she led them to the door, all animosity now forgotten.

Once outside, Jenny glanced across thoughtfully at the Brays' cottage, but after a pause, turned back down the little footpath.

'Well, that seems to be that,' Moulton said, his mouth still full of the mince pie he was munching.

'Yes,' Jenny agreed thoughtfully. 'But it does open up some rather interesting questions though, doesn't it?'

Does it? Moulton wondered, and glanced across at her, then promptly slipped in the snow and fell flat on his backside with a painful yelp.

'Careful!' Jenny said sharply, quickly hiding a smile. 'It's the thaw. It always makes things more slippery,' she added with unctuous sympathy.

Moulton cursed roundly and struggled to his feet. He glared at the cook, wondering why she should be as sure-footed as a mountain goat. With her hourglass bulk, she should be as precarious as an elephant on an ice rink.

'Questions?' he finally said petulantly. 'About what?'

'About Sid of course,' Jenny said impatiently. 'I think, you know, that you and I should go to the pub after lunch. Have a Boxing Day drink, what do you say?'

Moulton rubbed the cold wet snow off his derrière and scowled at her, wondering what she was up to now. And mourning the loss of his mince pie, which had landed in a particularly grey and slushy snowdrift.

\* \* \*

The Lamb and Dog was nicely crowded with lunchtime post-Christmas revellers when Jenny and Moulton walked in a few hours later. There was one of those brief, embarrassing lulls in the level of conversation as the locals assessed the newcomers, but when Jenny carefully nudged her way to the bar and ordered two brandies, the landlord happily obliged and normal talk quickly resumed.

Mandy's father was a big blond man, which meant that his daughter had to take after her mother. His eyes were as curious as those of a bird as he handed the brandies over. Jenny pushed Moulton's glass along the bar, where he'd managed to wedge himself in, between the greengrocer and a church warden. She left her own drink untouched on the bar. She rarely drank, and certainly not to excess, ever since that cringe-making incident a couple of years ago concerning herself, a couple of Trafalgar Square pigeons and a merchant seaman who went by the unfortunate name of Alphonso Font.

'You're the cook up at the farm, then?' Mandy's father asked, and she smiled at him, glad to have been given such a perfect opening.

'That's right. Although I'm wishing now I'd never answered the damned advert.' She heaved a much put-upon sigh.

The landlord nodded sympathetically. 'I can imagine. It's not what you'd expect, is it?' he added, somewhat unnecessarily, Jenny thought. Then he nodded down the bar. 'That the cop in charge then?'

Jenny, aware of the many ears that were quivering like antennae in her direction, nodded firmly. 'I'm afraid so. The poor man had to stay Christmas Day up at the farm. Today, we both needed to get out and about a bit. It's terrible up there at the moment — the atmosphere and all, you wouldn't believe it. And when I think of poor old Sid . . .' she let her voice trail off sadly.

There was a general sighing all around her. And just as she'd hoped, it broke the ice.

'I knew old Sid well,' a deep-pitched voice piped up from her right, and when she turned to look, found that it belonged to such a weathered, craggy face that the man could only be a farm worker. The years of his outdoors life were stamped all over his body. 'Known him yonks, I have.'

'I was only there a day before . . . well . . . it happened . . . but he seemed like such a nice old man,' she agreed, her voice soft and sad. There was something so homely and downright comforting about her that the villagers' natural reticence around strangers waved a collective white flag and sank beneath the waves.

'He was. There was nothing wrong with good old Sid,' somebody else said, with rather too much emphasis on the 'Sid.'

But Jenny was not here to find out how much the locals hated Stan — that much she was taking for granted. No, it was Sid's past that she wanted to ferret out.

'It seems such a shame that he never married,' she mused. 'I mean, that he never had a son to look after him. I suppose it's not my place to say this, but his brother did seem to . . . well . . . to bully him a little. I couldn't help but wonder why no woman had snapped Sid up a long time ago. In his younger days, he must have cut quite a dashing figure, I would have said.'

Not that I'd really noticed for myself, she left unsaid, but her tone left little room for doubt.

Her quaint old-fashioned words, her implied modesty and her very appearance, which so perfectly matched that of the archetypal rotund and friendly cook, soon had cautious tongues loosened, and she was the darling of the bar in next to no time. Moulton could only admire the performance in respectful silence and keep to the background, so as not to queer her pitch.

Everyone began to reminisce about Sid Kelton. She heard again the story of Eloise, and was not surprised to have Mrs Jarvis confirmed in her opinion that everyone knew that Eloise was Sid's girl, and should have been Sid's wife by rights. She heard, yet again, the sad tale of the changes in Sid when he came back from the hospital.

'Coughing something awful, he was.' One farm worker, now long since retired, finished off his account of meeting Sid in the pub a few weeks after he came out. 'Hardly recognized him. Like a man who'd had all his juice sucked out of him, leaving just a dry old stick in his place. And him then having to go back to the farm, with Eloise being there, and young Bert and all . . . I can tell you, I felt right sorry for him, so I did.'

There was a general murmur and shaking of sorrowful heads. Jenny sighed and shook her own head mournfully. 'It seems such a shame. But surely some of the village girls were interested?' she fished openly, but again there was a general murmur of regret.

'Sid didn't want no one but Eloise,' the landlord took up the tail. 'My ma tells me my own sister Fanny was fond of Sid, and would have took him on, even with his chest being like it was, but Sid . . . well, poor old Sid never did get over Eloise.'

'But surely,' Jenny said, her round face a picture of sympathetic innocence, 'before that bad spell in the hospital . . . well . . . him being a young man still, surely there were some local girls he . . . ?' She said it with such understanding, and with her wide blue eyes so lacking in disapproval, that nobody took offence.

'Young men liked to sow their oats,' someone muttered at the back, and there was a general guffaw of laughter.

'I know what you mean.' It was the church warden (who else?) who was the first to admit to his own peccadilloes. 'I was head over heels in love with Lucy Wentworth. Remember her?'

There was a general salutation to the absent Lucy Wentworth, who'd been a good-hearted (not to mention liberal-minded) woman, by all accounts.

The landlord winked at Jenny, who let the church warden ramble on. 'In the end, I never did see her again. She ran off to Liverpool with some prat from the Territorials.'

There was another loud wave of laughter, and into the companionable silence that followed, Jenny dangled her hook. 'So was there someone poor Sid turned to? With Eloise out of the picture?'

But nobody knew of any woman Sid might have turned to. At his place along the bar, having kept as silent as a mouse, Moulton finally (if belatedly) caught on to what she was doing. She was fishing to see if Sid could have had an illegitimate son. And with the Kelton farm always going to the eldest, regardless of whether or not he was a bastard, he could see how important that might be. And that it would be a possible motive for Sid's murder went without saying.

But nobody, it seemed, knew of Sid having a dalliance with anyone. And in a village of this size, everyone almost certainly knew everyone else's business. Everyone had known of the church warden and the luscious Lucy, for instance.

'But surely, after he came out of hospital then,' she continued to probe mercilessly, 'he couldn't have wanted to live all those years without a little female company?'

And she looked so charmingly curious, the way fat cooks are supposed to be, that nobody ever wondered why she should be asking them so many questions. But yet again, everybody swore that poor old Sid wasn't the type to get any lass into trouble.

And now the poor old bugger was dead.

The mood began to turn nasty. When were the coppers going to arrest somebody for it? How could anyone in the village feel safe with some lunatic going around stabbing people in the chest?

Moulton took the hint, swallowed the last of his brandy, and beat a hasty retreat.

Jenny stayed on, however, and in exchange for their gossip, fulfilled her part of their unspoken bargain by describing what had happened up at Kelton Farm on Christmas Eve from an eyewitness point of view, being careful not to get too morbid, or give out too much detail.

'It's more than I can stand, I can tell you,' she said at last, and, like a cinema when the film had come to an end, everybody parted to let her leave, fond eyes watching her go.

A nice gal, that. And a good cook too, every one of them would have sworn. It was only after she'd gone that the landlord noticed that her brandy still stood, untouched, on the bar.

# CHAPTER ELEVEN

On the way back from the village pub, Jenny turned off into the fast-melting lane that led to the farm and saw, walking just a few yards ahead of her, a familiar, cheery, carrot-topped figure.

'Sergeant Ford!' she called, and saw his head swivel around with a jerk of surprise. But the policeman's face broke into a pleased smile as he spotted her and he paused to allow her to catch up to him. As she passed the spot where she had covered some of the footprints with her scarf, she noticed that the melting snow had all but obliterated the patterns on the boots.

Everywhere, things were dripping. The trees had lost their heavy burdens of snow, and a deep ditch, either side of the land, was flooding with meltwater. In the sky above, a pale, sickly-looking sun was beginning to poke some tentative rays through the clouds. The going was fast becoming treacherous, and in more ways than one, the cook thought to herself grimly.

Unless she was very much mistaken, the killer who must still skulk undetected at Kelton Farm would be beginning to relax by now, and growing more and more confident that he or she would never be exposed. And that was usually when mistakes were made, in her experience. Or was that just wishful thinking on her part?

Ford, his cheeks reddening in the nippy air, watched as the six-foot-tall cook approached, his eyes taking in her surprisingly pleasing and shapely girth and sure-footed progress. She never seemed to trip or stumble, for she had that kind of grace with which large people were sometimes gifted. She looked so totally as he remembered her that he was half expecting her to have the puzzle already solved, and announce that he was just in time to make an arrest.

Now wouldn't that be nice, he thought, with an inward and well-concealed grin. 'Miss Starling. I hope you had a merry, well at any rate, a reasonable Christmas,' he murmured, just managing to stop himself from sounding too cheerful, whilst at the same time guiltily aware that he, himself, had had a marvellous time.

Sledging with his kids had driven all thought of murder and mayhem from his mind, at least for a day. His wife had been very appreciative over that little silk trifle of a negligee he'd given her, too!

Jenny smiled grimly, but overlooked his near gaffe. The less they said about the kind of Christmas she'd had the better, in her opinion. 'Have your people traced the owner of those footprints yet?' she huffed, glad to stop beside him and get her breath back.

'They belonged to the postman, I'm afraid,' Ford said. 'Just as we thought. We questioned him, of course, but he didn't see anybody suspicious hanging about.'

'Hmm. And he's all right too, I suppose?' she asked curiously.

'Been doing the job for nearly twenty-two years. Married, six kids and genuinely sad to hear about Sid Kelton. Apparently, Sid used to have him in for a cup of tea, whenever Stan Kelton was well out of the way. He'd put a drop of brandy in it for him too, so the postie says, when the weather was really bad.'

Jenny merely nodded. She was hardly surprised, either by the postman's undoubted innocence, or by Sid's kindness. When his brother wasn't around, that is.

'Inspector Moulton was expecting you this morning,' she warned him, and saw his already chapped face redden to an even deeper shade of beetroot. Not that she could blame him for stealing an extra morning off. But she'd heard Moulton muttering under his breath about his sergeant's absence, as he'd beat a hasty retreat from the Lamb and Dog.

Ford muttered something about having to check in at the police station first. It sounded a likely story, even to her unofficial ears. She could only hope that he would have thought of something better by the time they got back.

They set off for the farm together amicably enough, Ford subdued and rapidly losing his Christmas spirit, Jenny thoughtful and pensive. She had learned nothing much of value in the pub, except that Sid had almost certainly left behind no by-blows to queer the pitch. Not that it would have put her any further forward if she had discovered a bastard son.

Even if Sid *had* had a son to inherit and thus take away the farm from Stan Kelton, then Sid's murder still wouldn't have made any sense. Sid had been old and weak, and couldn't have been expected to live for many more years. All his unknown heir would have needed to do was wait for nature to take its course. Besides, with so many people abandoning farming nowadays, who was to say that any child of Sid's would even want to inherit the farm? No. Until she could understand the *why* of it all, she was lost.

As they approached the farmhouse, Ford slipping and sliding a little in the thawing mud and snow, the gander suddenly shot out of ambush from behind a rusting cart. Hissing mightily, his neck was elongated and bent at such an angle that his sharp beak was making straight for Sergeant Ford's most vulnerable spot. Whether this was due to luck or dastardly experience, Jenny wasn't quite sure.

'Oi!' Ford yelped, and took smartly to his heels.

Jenny watched the pair of them steam away across the cobbled yard, and looked up towards the farm. A fire was sending white-grey smoke out of the chimneys, the dog and

Bert were out in the fields at the back, and things were getting back to normal in a way that the cook didn't much like. Already it was as if Sid were fading away, forgotten and ignored, whilst the murderer breathed ever more easily. It didn't help her dour mood that the more she thought about it, the more convinced she became that Sid had been trying to tell her something, sitting there at the table, his wide blue eyes open but lifeless.

But what?

Jenny paused in the courtyard, vaguely watching as Ford ineffectively tried to safeguard his vulnerable bits from the gander's long reach and strong, uncannily accurate beak.

Once more, in her mind, she went over that terrible scene of only two mornings ago. Back from getting the eggs. Boots, scarf and coat off. Into the kitchen. Kettle boiling. Making tea. Getting the hot mince pies out. Walking back across the, for once, blissfully clean and dry floor and sitting down in her chair, looking across and . . . Sid. Dead. Blue eyes open and looking at her. Except, of course, they weren't really looking at her — they couldn't.

Now what, *what* out of all that was she missing? Something about that scene was niggling away at her, taunting her that if she could only figure out what it was that was wrong, she could have the whole thing solved. But the only aspect of it that stood out in her mind's eye were Sid's own watery blue eyes gazing back at her as if trying to tell her something. Blue eyes? Jenny frowned, wondering. There seemed to be something lurking at the back of her mind about Sid's blue eyes. Some snippet of forgotten or barely remembered information about . . . well, what exactly?

But the more she pressed her subconscious for it, the more confused she became until, annoyingly, the only thing that sprang to her mind at all about blue eyes was an old country and western song that her father had been fond of about *Blue eyes crying in the rain*. An old Willie Nelson song, wasn't it?

And a fat lot of good that did her!

134

She looked up, distracted, as a door banged shut behind a furiously cursing Ford, who'd at last managed to get into the house with little worse than a solid peck on his backside.

Jenny went back to walking, and thinking. Halfway across the courtyard, the gander, flushed and overconfident after his successful tangle with — and routing of — the law, rashly decided that the time had come to regain his badly dented ganderhood and take on the big woman interloper.

He set forth with his neck outstretched, wings outspread, and hissed with gusto. Jenny, who was far too big to be able to run (or even jog) with anything approaching dignity, merely looked up and waited for her moment.

The gander was just within beak-distance, and they had a firm eye-lock on each other, when she said firmly and quite clearly, 'I could always make goose-liver paté for a starter.'

The gander, upset by her confident tone, began to back-pedal furiously, way too late, of course, and he began to skid precariously on the icy cobbles, his webbed feet finding little purchase in all the icy slush, and within a blink of an eye he shot past her like a water-skier out of control. She heard a dull thud, and as she turned, saw a single white feather float past her. She was just in time to see the gander stagger away from the rusting wheel of the cart, into which he'd run, full pelt.

'Stupid bird,' Jenny muttered, then smiled wryly. She was hardly proving to be a shining light of intelligence herself. Blue eyes crying in the rain, indeed.

Hah!

* * *

Ford and Moulton were locked in a serious conference in the lounge when Jenny checked that her ham, leek and leftover goose pie in the oven could do with another half hour. The vegetables were done, salted and ready to be cooked, and her kitchen was in immaculate order. As usual, she had her domain to herself.

So a small unhappy sound had her lifting her head instantly, eyes wary. She relaxed and smiled briefly at Delia, who hovered in the doorway, wringing her hands together in front of her and looking totally miserable. 'Hello, Miss Starling. You're back.'

Jenny knew she wasn't required to answer, and didn't. Delia continued to wring her hands. 'Inspector Moulton says he's finished with Uncle Sid's room now. He says we can clear it out, if we like.'

The cook nodded. 'And your father asked you to see to it?' she guessed bluntly. Such indifferent heartlessness was typical of Stan, Jenny thought crossly. She doubted that it had even crossed his mind that it was a task that Delia must dread.

Delia nodded. 'I wondered if, well . . . if dinner can wait for a while if . . .'

'You want me to help?' Jenny quickly came to her rescue. Not only was she genuinely sympathetic — after all, to a teenage girl, death was not something to be born stoically — but she was curious as well. To be offered a legitimate reason to look through Sid's things was an opportunity too good to be missed. 'Of course I'll help. We'll need plenty of bags.'

Delia, wilting in relief now that the task need not be faced alone, ran ahead to fetch out from the staircase cupboard some strong, sturdy black bin bags. Then she followed the cook up the stairs. Once outside Sid's door, she would have lingered apprehensively, no doubt working herself up into a good head of skittish steam, had she not been dealt with firmly.

'Now,' Jenny pushed open the door and stepped briskly inside. 'Will anyone in your family be wanting Sid's clothes, do you think?'

Delia blinked. 'I don't know. I don't think they'll fit Dad, or Bert.'

'What about Bill? No, he's not as big as Bert I know, but still he's not skinny enough. They'll fit Jeremy though, won't they?' She raised one eyebrow questioningly. 'He's only a bit of a twig. But they might be a bit old-fashioned for a young-ster. What do you think?'

Delia, for the first time since Christmas Eve, managed to laugh. 'I don't think Jeremy will want Uncle Sid's old cardigans and baggy trousers, somehow!'

Jenny smiled, glad to see some of the terror leave the girl's dark eyes. 'No, I expect not. Right then, all his clothes should go to charity, yes?'

Delia nodded. Making that decision, for some reason, had her feeling suddenly very grown up.

'Right then. They need to be folded carefully and put into the bags.'

Delia, once guided, set to with a certain resignation. The girl had really suffered for want of a mother, the cook thought with a pang, as she watched Delia settle down by the wardrobe. It couldn't have been easy, all those formative years, growing up in a household full of men.

Jenny, having sorted out Delia to their mutual satisfaction, realized that she was now free to look around. This she did with meticulous care.

On Sid's bedside table was a pair of dark-rimmed reading glasses, a glass for his teeth, a roll of indigestion tablets and a table lamp. She moved on to the small dresser against one wall, going through the drawers and carefully putting away folded shirts and cardigans, but coming across nothing more helpful than a small battered box that, once opened, revealed a small gold locket inside.

Checking that Delia was still busy with her uncle's suits hanging in the wardrobe, Jenny prised open the locket with a sturdy thumbnail. She was hardly surprised to find a faded picture of Eloise in one side, and a very young Sid in the other. She sighed, and carefully put the box to one side. Delia should have that, of course. She'd give it to the girl later, when she was feeling a little stronger and less weepy.

The bottom drawer felt heavier the instant she went to open it, and, looking down, she quickly saw why. It was filled with magazines, some of them ancient. Her eyebrows rose for an instant, then resettled themselves. She shouldn't have been so surprised. After all, what could poor Sid have had to do all day except read? She knew the radio that played constantly had been his, and that he'd been in the habit of turning it on first thing in the morning and leaving it on — a habit that Bert seemed to have taken up where his uncle had left off. But that, Jenny suspected, had only been Sid's way of creating some noise, in an effort to make the deserted farm seem less lonely during the day.

She lifted out huge piles of *National Geographic*, science magazines and innumerable gardening magazines. Sid had obviously been a fact buff, rather than a fiction reader.

She glanced down at one magazine, not surprised to see that it was over twenty years old. He was obviously a hoarder.

'I see Sid liked to read a lot,' Jenny mused, and Delia glanced uninterestedly over her shoulder.

'Hmm. Bert always picked them up whenever he went to the doctors or dentists or whatever. Sid had piles of them, just waiting for him to get around to browsing through them. He was always trying to get me to read them,' she said, her voice a little wistful. 'He thought it was educational. "Look at this, our Del, all about this tribe in South America," he'd say. "They hunt with poisoned darts." And I'd read the article, just to keep him happy, but really, I wasn't much interested. He used to read my fashion magazines sometimes, saying how pretty I'd look in this or that. But I think he just liked to look at the pretty models.' Delia's voice ended on a wobble, and Jenny thoughtfully turned away.

She stacked the rest of the magazines at the foot of the bed, and double-bagged them into the sturdiest bags of all. They weighed a ton. 'I think the old folks' homes and day care centres should have these,' Jenny said, and Delia nodded, not even looking at them.

'Whatever you say.'

The cook turned to the bed next, carefully stripping it down and putting the sheets to one side to be washed. She was just pulling the bottom sheet out when a multicoloured object half slipped from beneath the mattress.

Jenny picked up the vintage magazine and flicked through it. It was one of those science-explained-for-the general-reader publications. It fell open at an article about genetics, and how baby rabbits with brown eyes were unlikely to produce blue-eyed bunnies and vice versa. It all sounded rather old hat to her — nowadays, surely genetics was far more advanced, post Dolly-the-sheep. She tossed it aside without much thought and sighed.

Fascinating, Jenny thought wryly, and was once more back to *Blue eyes crying in the rain*. Typically, now that she'd remembered the song again after all this time, she was beginning to wonder if she was ever going to get the tune out of her head. It had been buzzing about in the back of her mind all afternoon.

She sighed, tossed the magazine into the already bulging bag with the others, and continued her search.

A few minutes later she found a bag of mint imperials, tucked guiltily away in his sock drawer. That, a bag full of assorted change, a small but unmarked calendar and a safety pin was the sum of her haul. Which wasn't exactly helpful.

She looked at the mint imperials and smiled. He might not have felt like sharing them when alive (and every man needed a vice) but he would hardly mind now. She offered one to Delia, who looked at the white bag and burst out laughing.

The young girl took one and sucked it with a slight grimace at the astringency of it. 'Good old Sid,' she sighed, rolling the hard sweet into one cheek pouch. 'I used to get these for him from the village shop. I never fancied them much, but Dad was always guzzling them down, so Sid always kept a little stash somewhere, just for himself.'

Jenny helped her cart the bags of clothes and magazines to the hall, where they'd just have to stay until tomorrow.

'I think I heard Bert saying that he was going into Burford tomorrow,' Delia muttered. 'He can take them somewhere.'

She turned abruptly and left the pathetic bundles in the hall. No doubt it had suddenly occurred to her that it wasn't much for a man to leave behind him after his death.

Jenny returned silently to her kitchen.

There she found Ford and Moulton, tucking into a slice each of her Christmas cake, and discussing the case in desultory tones.

'Find anything of interest?' Moulton asked, perking up a little at the sight of the cook. Jenny sighed, but dutifully gave a brief but thorough rundown on her afternoon's activities and finds.

'Old magazines,' said Ford dispiritedly. 'Wonderful.'

Jenny grimaced. 'What did you expect? A letter, starting off, "In the event of my sudden death, I would like it to be known" . . .' She broke off, aware that she was being snappish with the wrong people. She sighed deeply. 'I'm sorry. It's just that I can't get it out of my head that I'm missing something. Something important.'

Sergeant Ford poured her out a cup of tea. 'Don't get in a tizzy about it, Miss S. We all have days like that.'

Jenny took a long sip and sat back with a sigh. 'Yes, but this is different. At the back of my head, a little imp is saying that it's all so simple. I've seen something or heard something or know something that makes it as clear as a pikestaff who murdered poor old Sid, and why, and I'm just not *getting* it.' She thumped an angry fist on the tabletop.

Moulton shifted uneasily in his seat. 'Have you ever had this feeling before?' he asked, trying in his own way to help her out.

Jenny heartily wished he wouldn't bother.

She smiled ruefully. 'Yes. Twice, in fact. Once at a certain birthday party, and once in a locked room.'

The two policemen looked at each other knowingly. 'But both those times . . .' Moulton trailed off delicately, not actually wanting to say out loud that both those times she'd actually unmasked the murderer, right under the nose of the attending police inspector.

Jenny grunted inelegantly. 'Oh yes, it came to me *eventually*,' she admitted. 'And both times, it was shocking how simple it all really was. And even more shocking was how clear it became just how *stupid* I'd been,' she said, somewhat ungrammatically.

Absently, she reached for a slice of cake and took a generous bite. Luckily, it would take more than embarrassing remembrances of past stupidities to put Jenny Starling off *her* food.

'No, there's no getting away from it. We've learned all we're going to learn,' she murmured. 'Nobody's going to come out of the woodwork now and say they saw X sneaking back into the farm on Christmas Eve. None of your people are going to miraculously send a message saying the forensic lads have come up with a piece of cast-iron evidence pointing to X. Nobody here's going to break down and admit what they know, or think they know. Where we are now is where we're going to stay, until one of us uses our loaf and figures out what it is that's staring us right in the face.'

The two policemen looked at each other, both fighting a growing feeling of dismay. Without saying it aloud, each acknowledged that they didn't have a clue.

'My pie!' Jenny suddenly wailed, making them both jump out of their skins, and dived for the oven. But her pie was a lovely golden brown, not daring to be anything else. She removed it to the hot plate and returned, limp with relief, to the table.

There she slumped in her favourite chair and glanced across to the space where Sid's chair had once stood.

Sid, waiting so patiently for her to bring his killer to justice. Sid with his wide blue eyes, open and staring.

And from the radio, playing somewhere in the background, the melancholy voice of Willie Nelson began to sing:

'*In the twilight glow I see her, Blue eyes cryin' in the rain . . .*'

'Oh shut up!' Jenny Starling snarled at it.

# CHAPTER TWELVE

Bert walked in from the raw wet and cold of the fields, but wished he was still out there, for all the warmth and supposed security the farmhouse kitchen had to offer him. He closed the door wearily behind him before traipsing further into the room, his boots sounding loud on the uneven tiles, his gait unsteady.

The big cook was just adding a pinch more salt to a saucepan that was spurting forth a marvellously scented steam. One quick relieved look told Bert that there was no one else around, and his shoulders slowly slumped in tiredness and relief.

Jenny gave the saucepan a good stir, and the scrumptious smell of herbs filled the air. Bert watched her in silence for a while, his shoulders beginning to ache now the tension had left him. There was something so soothing about the domestic scene being played out around him that was all the more blissful for being so unexpected. Normally Delia would be the one cooking, and feeling resentful and surly as she did so, which meant that her culinary offerings usually consisted of oven chips and pies bought from the supermarket.

He'd been dreading coming back to the farm. Or rather, to be more accurate, he'd dreaded returning to the Kelton household more than usual. Perhaps it was the lack of all the other Keltons in the room, or perhaps there was something about the cook herself that gave Bert such a welcome feeling of relief and succour. There just seemed to be something so dependable and so warmly human about the big attractive cook that instantly made Bert's heavy heart lift.

He missed his wife suddenly and ferociously, and felt utterly weary as he pulled back his chair and slumped down. Beside him, the dog slunk under the table and settled his chin on top of his new master's boot. He gave a huge sigh.

To the dog, the kitchen was heaven simply because it was sheep and gander free.

Jenny turned, glanced at the floor and the line of wet and muddy tracks, sighed heavily and reached for the mop. Bert coloured.

'Sorry.'

'What you apologizing for?' Stan, who'd been watching the scene unnoticed from the hallway door, now belligerently demanded. He moved into the room and took his usual chair. 'I keep tellin' you. A floor was made to be walked on.' He scowled at the cook, who continued to mop in dogged silence, then turned back to Bert. Not surprisingly, every scrap of well-being he'd been feeling had completely drained away.

'Where's the Old Bill, anyway?' Stan barked, at nobody in particular.

'Upstairs,' Jenny responded shortly. They'd gone into a huddle after a report had been delivered to Moulton. By the look on the inspector's face, no doubt it had also contained a sharp reminder from his superiors to get on with it and make an arrest as quickly as he could. She hadn't seen a paper in days, and wondered if the press was making a big noise about it. Murder in a snowed-in farm had probably made titillating Christmas fare for many newspaper readers.

Moulton had huffily decided on a strictly all-police conference in the privacy of their 'incident' room — also known as Moulton's ice-cold bedroom. Jenny wished them luck for their brainstorming session, but she didn't exactly have high hopes.

The outside door flew open for a second time and Bill came in, slinging his heavy-weather coat onto the chair and creating a freezing draught as he did so. He reached for the teapot. Jenny sighed heavily, and once again reached for the mop.

Bill watched her angry jerking movements as she cleaned the floor yet again, then glanced at his father's set face. He noted the beady eyes, just waiting for him to say something — anything — so that he might jump down his throat, and pressed his lips firmly together. He scraped back his chair with a loud screech and sat down. The glare he gave his father was one of pure and undiluted hatred.

Moulton, who'd very quietly crept down the stairs on hearing the return of the Kelton men, found himself shifting uneasily at the sight of it. He'd seen hate in many a man's eyes before, but none that pulsed with such burning intensity. If looks could kill, he thought grimly, they'd have a second homicide to investigate, right there and then.

'There's two more ewes dead,' Bert said flatly, apparently unaware of the antagonism raging around him. Either that, Jenny thought grimly, putting away her mop, or he was by now so totally inured to it that he didn't even acknowledge it anymore. 'And if this thaw continues, we might have problems with flooding in the lower meadow.'

'We already have,' Bill said. 'I noticed the brook is already coming over the banks.'

'We'd better tell Mrs Jarvis not to come in until we're sure the bridge is safe then.' Bert shifted his weight a little, forcing the dog to lift his chin patiently and wait for the boot to resettle itself into a proper chin-rest once more. He didn't sigh though; he'd heard Stan Kelton's voice, and knew better than to give his presence away.

'We'll see about that,' Stan said. 'I pay that woman good money.'

'You pay her a pittance,' Bill corrected, his big hands closing into fists.

Stan Kelton's head reared back. His brown eyes became as black as thunder. Bill's blue eyes stared back, as cold as ice.

'And I suppose, if the farm was yours, you'd run it into the ground, paying everyone ridiculous wages? You're soft, boy, that's your trouble. You've got to be liked, just like your uncle had to be liked. Well, what good did being so damned well-liked do for him, eh? You tell me that!' Stan roared, thumping his fist down on the table.

Moulton moved forward, taking a chair next to the cook and accepting the ubiquitous cup of tea from the always-full teapot.

Bill glanced at the policeman and sneered. Nevertheless, he subsided into his chair and contented himself with merely giving his father yet another killing look. 'I suppose you'd rather our daily try to cross the bridge and get swept away and drown, right, Dad?' he drawled, his fair hair flopping over his forehead as his chin jutted pugnaciously forward.

Bert sighed heavily. 'You just can't let it go, can you?' he asked, but whether he was talking to his brother or his father, neither Moulton nor Jenny could easily tell.

Stan leaned forward, his bullish neck straining with thumping little nerves, his face flushed an ugly, angry red. His eyes were all but popping out of his head. 'And what's that supposed to mean?' he bellowed.

Bill leaned forward also, putting the two men nearly nose-to-nose.

Jenny took a sip of tea, and watched them, the expression on her face one of mild interest.

'It means what it sounded like,' Bill snarled back. 'You all but killed her old man. Why not go for the double?'

'You jumped-up little bastard!' Stan yelled, and reached out meaty hands that went straight for his son's neck. Bill, taken by surprise, was half dragged across the table before he could get a firm grip on anything to keep his feet anchored to the floor.

Jenny hastily removed her plate of mince pies from the table and out of the fighting arena. Really, these men had no manners! It had taken her hours to make them, and she wasn't about to see them scattered and trampled underfoot in a melee.

'That's enough!' a voice roared, so loud and commanding that Jenny nearly dropped her teacup. For the sound had definitely, but definitely, come from Moulton.

*Moulton!*

Both men did a swift and comical double take. At the same time, pounding footsteps could be heard speeding across the ceiling and rapidly thumping down the stairs. Ford, reacting to the unusual sound of his superior's raised voice, rushed in panting and wild-eyed, then skidded to a stop in the middle of the kitchen, taking in at once the frozen tableau and glancing quizzically at his chief.

Bill Kelton was still half-hauled across the table, and Stan's hands were still clamped tight on the collar of his son's shirt. Both were staring at Moulton in astonishment. The policeman was sitting stiff and bristling like an insulted cockerel, his face flushed.

Jenny, who was also staring — with some admiration — at the usually meek and mild Moulton, suddenly realized her mouth was hanging open, and closed it with a decisive snap.

Ford didn't know whether to laugh, do some shouting of his own or come indignantly to his inspector's aid.

'Mr Kelton,' Moulton said, his voice once more bland enough to dry paint. 'Please release Mr Kelton.'

Stan blinked, looked across at his son, seemed to notice for the first time that he still had him by the throat, and with a growl thrust him backwards and contemptuously away. When he landed back in his chair, it rocked a little under Bill's solid weight.

'Get out,' Stan snarled at him. 'Just pack your bags and don't come back.'

Bert's head snapped up. Bill's stormy blue eyes widened with incredulity.

Jenny, under cover of the table, gave Moulton a very sharp kick in the shin. Moulton winced, but (very manfully,

146

Jenny thought) refrained from yelping. He stared at her. The cook slightly — and warningly — inclined her head towards Bill.

Moulton blinked, not getting it.

Jenny gave him another sharp kick in the shin. It was, she was later to recall, one of the more satisfying moments in her life.

Moulton winced again.

Eventually she sighed heavily. If you wanted a job done . . . 'I think, Mr Kelton, that the police will have something to say about Bill, or anyone else for that matter, leaving the premises just yet. I think Inspector Moulton will want everyone available for interview. At least until everything's settled.'

Moulton fought the desire to rub his abused shin, but caught on at last. He nodded briskly instead. 'Quite right. No one leaves here until I say,' he said forcefully. Although, in fact and in law, he had no means of enforcing that order.

And bully for you, Jenny thought wryly.

* * *

After an excellent dinner, and a superb Bakewell tart, Jenny cleared away with her usual efficiency and found, for once, that she was becoming heartily sick of her kitchen! With a final mop of the floor (she seemed to have spent the last few days doing nothing else, so why fight it?) she left her natural domain to sail forth into the sitting room.

Delia, Jeremy and Bill had all decided to go to the pub and brave the village gossip. They had to do it sometime, they reasoned, so why not tonight?

Jeremy, of course, had needed no persuading to go and see his lady-love, and Delia had already started her campaign to become Bill's favourite shadow. Ever since Bert had told her about Bill's upcoming exile, Delia had seen her chance.

Even though she now had Sid's money to help her, the thought of leaving the farm and setting off on life's great adventure on her own had clearly been daunting for the inexperienced teenager. Without her best friend to share the upheaval with her, some of her bravery had, understandably, fled. But with an older brother to look after her . . . well, that was different. They could go to London together. Set themselves up in a two-bedroomed flat. Look for work together. And Bill, seeing right through her, had smiled and been the one to make the suggestion that they all go to the Lamb and Dog and get pie-eyed.

Stan had snorted and taken off to the stables, muttering something about harnesses that needed cleaning. So Jenny had confidently expected to have the room to herself, but as she entered, someone stirred on the sofa and a moment later she saw Bert lean forward to toss a three-day-old newspaper onto the table. He looked up and saw her hovering in the doorway, and smiled wryly.

'Come on in, Miss Starling. I daresay it's a relief to get out of the kitchen for once.' He stood up to chuck another log on the fire, and leaned one arm along the mantelpiece to watch the spluttering sparks fly up the chimney. It was strangely mesmerizing, and Jenny followed the light show with interest.

'Your two companions in detection have decided to opt for an early night. The young sergeant has decided he'd better stay on here too for the time being. I rather think he suspects one of us might take a midnight stroll into Inspector Moulton's room to slit his gizzard.'

Jenny stared at his tense back thoughtfully. Once again she was struck with the feeling that Bert was very much an unknown quantity in the Kelton family. When she'd told Moulton earlier that she didn't think anyone was going to say anything that they hadn't already said, she'd been thinking mostly about Bert. For Bert, she suspected, knew far more, or at least *suspected* far more, than he was willing to say. She hadn't forgotten, on the morning they'd discovered Sid's body, how anxious Bert had been to corroborate both Jeremy's and Bill's story about when and in what order they'd returned to the farm.

Or had he just been anxious to give himself an alibi? Saying he saw Jeremy and Bill ahead of him certainly tended to deflect suspicion from his own time of arrival on the scene.

Bert, as if aware of the cogs silently turning in her mind, turned from the fireplace, his face flushed from the heat. His gentle brown eyes watched her for a moment, his eyes questioning.

Jenny nodded towards the Christmas tree. 'You should give that some water. Its needles will start shedding, else.'

Bert glanced at the tree. It seemed years, not a week, since Delia and Jeremy had decorated it, giggling over the decorations like five-year-olds. His eyes fell to the carpet beneath the tree, where a few presents still lay unopened.

'Sid's presents to us,' he said, as if she'd asked a question. 'I haven't been able to open mine. The others must feel the same way.'

Jenny nodded, and made her way to the sofa, where she sat down and reached for the paper.

Bert watched her in silence for a while, his lips bearing the ghost of a wry smile, then he walked to the tree and stooped over the presents. He quickly read the labels, and picked up his own. It was a rectangular, well-padded present. He moved back to the armchair at a right angle to the grate and sat down, absently pulling at the brightly coloured Christmas paper. His eyes strayed over the top to look at the cook.

'I've been watching you, Miss Starling,' Bert said, his tired voice so calm and without inflection that Jenny was almost alarmed.

'I know you have,' she replied just as calmly.

Bert nodded. 'The Old Bill . . . they don't treat you the same as the rest of us. At first I thought . . .' he gave a good solid rip on his parcel, and found himself holding a brown legal-looking envelope. He'd been expecting socks or handkerchiefs. That was Sid's usual offering. Now what the hell was this all about?

He glanced up, realized the cook was waiting for him to continue and struggled back to what he'd been saying. 'I thought it was because you were a stranger,' he muttered. 'Someone with no reason to kill poor old Sid. But then I began to wonder. And I noticed how you watched everybody,' he carried on, turning the envelope over and over in his hands, his restless movements at odds with his clear, calm voice.

It couldn't be easy, Jenny thought, opening a Christmas present from a dead relative. No wonder he wanted his mind on other things when he did so.

'I noticed how nothing ever escapes your attention,' Bert continued, his voice almost dreamy now. 'And then, when I got to know that ridiculous Moulton better, I realized that it was *you* who was really in charge here.' His simple, honest face creased into a frown. 'And I don't understand why.'

Jenny found herself totally unprepared, at a dangerous crossroads. Should she tell him about her past successes in the field of murderer-finding? If he was the killer, it wouldn't, perhaps, be the smartest thing she'd ever done. So should she lie? Pretend to be one of those undercover detectives, whose tales of derring-do were so popular on the telly nowadays?

No, too outlandish by far.

Bert, perhaps never expecting an answer from her, returned his interest to the envelope. With fingers that shook, he prised it open and pulled out the wedge of papers it contained, frowning in surprise.

He opened them out, and a loose-leaf note fluttered onto his lap. He picked it up and read it, and as he did so, his face transformed itself into one big picture of massive shock. His eyes rounded. His lower lip fell open, and all the colour fled from his cheeks.

Jenny quickly craned her neck and read the upside down address of one Janice Kelton. It was a Woodstock address, and after a quick bit of mental geography, gauged that it was probably no more than ten miles away from the farm.

'All this time she's been so close,' Bert mumbled, his voice as hurt as that of a child who'd just been robbed of his lollipop. 'I could have walked the distance . . .'

If only you'd known where to walk to, Jenny finished the thought for him. But — the cook suddenly straightened up. How had Sid known where Janice had taken refuge? And why had he waited until Christmas Day to tell Bert?

Jenny stared at the legal-looking document, still lying untouched in Bert's lap. She licked her lips, her fingers literally itching to reach out and take it.

'What are the other papers, Bert?' she asked at last, unable to bear the suspense a moment longer, her voice almost a whisper. She didn't want to break the suddenly fragile mood, but her curiosity was in danger of eating her alive.

Bert blinked, then looked down. He'd forgotten that there was anything else. All he'd been able to think about was finding Janice again, getting Janice back. And an escape, finally, from Kelton Farm.

Impatiently, wanting to get back to thoughts of Janice, he picked them up and started to read. The frown that came to his brows deepened the further he read, until his weather-beaten face had so many cracks and creases in it that it looked like one of his own fields after ploughing.

'I just don't understand this,' Bert said at last, after turning the last page. 'I need a lawyer.'

Jenny, for one wild moment, thought he was confessing to the killing of his uncle. Then Bert held the papers out to her, as if people confided their private family business to their cook every day. Jenny took the offering and instantly saw what he meant.

The document was written in the worst kind of legalese, with parties of the first part doing something in Latin with the party of the second part. But, even with great chunks of the document lost to red-tape mentality, she managed to grasp most of it.

Sid Kelton had not only known where Janice Kelton had escaped to, he'd also set her up in her own business. An antique shop, to be exact. And not only did Janice benefit, because the business was in Bert's name too.

She looked up to find that the elder Kelton son was back to staring at the precious address of his wife. 'An antique shop?' Bert said, dazed, having figured out as much as Jenny. 'Of course, she always loved buying old things,' he murmured thoughtfully, his voice dazed. 'She was forever dragging me off to village fetes, and those auction thingies where some old lady had died, and the contents of her house were being sold off. She bought all sorts of knick-knacks, mostly china. Dad said it was all rubbish, but—'

'But I bet she knew what she was doing,' Jenny guessed shrewdly. And, she added silently, I'll bet my last wage packet that *Sid* knew that *Janice* knew what she was doing.

'Perhaps Janice used her own collection for stock, to start her off,' she hazarded, and looked thoughtfully at the half-owner of 'The Old Duke' antique shop, West Bladon Road, Woodstock. According to the papers, the shop had started up business just a few months after Janice had first left.

But why hadn't Sid said anything about all this? Bert stared at her. 'I don't understand it,' he said at last.

'No,' Jenny said softly. 'I don't, either.' But it was time she found out.

# CHAPTER THIRTEEN

Once she'd discovered a promising new trail to follow, Jenny was loath to give it up and just retire meekly to bed. What's more, she couldn't shake off the feeling that she was being totally *dense* about something.

And in circumstances like these, action was definitely called for. Even if her brain cells refused to get in gear and come up with something useful at least she could ferret out some more information. Even if she didn't then know what to do with it!

So it was that she and Bert stayed up waiting for the others to get back from their night's carousing, long after Stan had said a grumpy goodnight and had followed Moulton and Ford up the stairs to an early bed.

It was nearing midnight when Jenny heard the dog outside give a soft, welcoming bark, and moved out into the hall with Bert not far behind her. Why they should both feel that tonight was going to be so important — for everyone — neither of them could have said, but the air of expectancy was so thick that it could almost be cut with a knife.

Jeremy was the first to come through the door, his young face flushed, not so much with the dubious merits of alcohol, but as a result of a whole evening spent openly and above board with the beauteous Mandy.

Bill, though, following him into the relative warmth of the house, was most decidedly a little the worse for wear. His nose was just beginning to sprout a nice crop of red veins, and his speech, when he greeted his older brother and the cook with cheerful gusto, was just slightly slurred. But whether he had been drinking to celebrate his unexpected release from Kelton Farm (Moulton and the Thames Valley Police Force permitting), or was mourning the loss of what was, after all, his home and livelihood, she was not so sure.

She rather suspected Bill wasn't, either.

Delia, the last in, shut the outside door quietly behind them and glanced upstairs, no doubt expecting her father to poke his head over the banisters at any moment, bellowing brimstone and curses.

Jenny had no difficulty ushering them all into the lounge, with the promise of a hot drink and a late-night snack. She left to make strong cocoa — Bill at least, needed his head clearing — and loaded a tray with fresh bread, cheese and pickles. She came back to find everyone sitting on the sofa, like peas in a pod, staring happily into the leaping flames in the fireplace.

For the first time she noticed how very much alike Bert, Jeremy and Delia all were. The dark eyes and strong Kelton features. Bill, too, had the Kelton nose and chin, but the resemblance ended there. A family united. Except for one. One, at least, was now very much an outsider.

She put the mugs down and watched, pleased, as young Jeremy reached for his cocoa with evident pleasure and sipped the strong, milky brew. Delia made a face. 'Cocoa! I can't remember the last time I had that,' but when she retrieved a mug, Jenny noticed that she sipped it with just as much juvenile appreciation as her nephew.

Bert was watching the cook closely, a war of fear and resignation waging behind his eyes. She resolutely ignored the wary, rather frightened look he sent her way; sentiment had no place in a murder inquiry. Besides, the look of fear in his eyes might well be for himself: *someone* in this house had killed Sid.

'I think your father has something to tell you, Jeremy,' Jenny said, getting straight to the point. Bill, whose head had been lolling back on the sofa, suddenly snapped upright. Delia froze, cocoa mug halfway to her lips. Jeremy flushed.

Suddenly, the feeling of well-being and comradeship fled. Eyes shifted to look at one another, then just as quickly shifted away again. Delia fought back a nervous titter. Something was in the air tonight, something that had, until recently, been a stranger at Kelton Farm. Namely: change. And she wasn't quite sure how she felt about that.

For years, time had plodded on as always, seemingly without any hope of things being different. Now, this Christmas, the Kelton world had been turned on its head. And was evidently still turning. Now, everyone turned to look at Bert to find out the latest twist. The latest shock. The latest danger.

Bert stared down at his large, calloused hands for a few moments, then sighed. 'I opened Uncle Sid's Christmas present to me today. Inside was Janice's address, and the deeds to an antique shop.'

There was a small gasp. From Delia, Jenny thought, but didn't take her eyes off Jeremy.

'A shop?' It was Bill who spoke — or rather slurred — the question, his voice raised a notch in squeaky surprise. 'What do you mean, a shop? A proper shop, with stuff in it to sell?' Obviously the alcohol he'd consumed wasn't helping his mental synapses to fire properly.

Bert nodded. 'Apparently, Sid set up Janice in the antique shop almost straight away. She's been living and working in Woodstock all this time.'

Jenny wondered, briefly, why no one had discovered Janice's new profession, but then, just as quickly, stopped wondering. When the Kelton family went to Woodstock, it was to buy groceries, hardware or farm equipment. Or, in Delia's case, check out the boutiques. Which one of them would even think of looking around yet another tourist trap of an antique shop? And which neighbour would risk Stan's ire by mentioning Janice's new venture to any other member of the Kelton family, should they have accidentally found out about it?

'I don't get it,' Jeremy finally said. 'Mum's in Woodstock?'

'With her own business,' Bert confirmed. 'Or rather, our own business. It's half mine apparently, according to the papers in Sid's present.'

'Bloody hell!' Bill said, all squeakiness gone. 'What came over old Sid? It's not like him to be so . . . surprising.'

Jenny, the only one not sat on the sofa, but facing them in the armchair, was in a perfect position to note any tiny reaction, and instantly saw that Delia had stiffened. She looked like a cat that had just spotted a very fast, very hungry-looking dog.

The cook's eyes zeroed in on her like hunting Spitfires. 'What did Sid give you, Delia?' she asked softly, catching the girl unawares and giving her no time to martial her thoughts or prepare her lies.

Delia gaped at her, wondering why the cook was picking on her all of a sudden, then belatedly noticed that she was now the centre of attention. Bert, Bill and Jeremy were staring at her in a way that she most definitely didn't like.

'Oh all right!' she snapped, but her anger was more an instinctive reaction to fear than anything else, Jenny surmised. 'The night . . . the night it happened . . . no, the next morning . . .' she fought hard to keep her voice under control and clear her head, licking her lips nervously. She had to think clearly — it was obviously important. 'I woke up and saw an envelope with my name on it on my bedside table. It was Sid's handwriting. In it was some money.'

'How much?' Bill asked, surprised by yet more evidence of Sid's largesse.

'Quite a bit, actually,' Delia said. 'All in twenty-pound notes.'

She paused, but wasn't at all convinced that she wanted to let her family know just how much Sid had given her. She needed time to think this through. After all, a girl had to look out for herself. Especially now.

'There was a letter as well,' she added quickly, anxious to find her way onto less hazardous ground. 'It said . . . well . . . it wished me luck in a life away from here.' Once again her voice was wobbling, and her eyes were flooding with tears.

Genuine grief for a lost uncle, or merely superb acting? Jenny wondered. She was beginning to suspect that the clue to this whole mess depended on the reason behind Sid's sudden generosity. For a man who didn't have much beside the farm, he'd obviously been depleting whatever savings he'd had to splash out on his nearest and dearest. But why now? Why this Christmas? What had changed? If she knew that, she thought, she would know who had killed him. And why.

She'd learned from Bert earlier on that Sid's past Christmas gifts had been of the usual variety: socks, hankies, perfume for Delia, that kind of thing.

Of course, Sid might simply have thought that Delia was now old enough to leave home, and there was nothing more sinister to it than that. Perhaps he hadn't felt able, in all good conscience, to give his niece the money to leave until he was sure that she'd become old enough, and presumably sensible enough, to put it to good use.

But what about Bert? It could have been sheer coincidence that Janice had left him at the same time that Delia had come of age, thus forcing Sid, yet again, to be more than usually generous to a member of his family. Or then again . . .

Jenny glanced quickly at Jeremy, who was staring at his aunt with puzzled eyes.

'Jeremy?' the cook said sharply, and noted out of the corner of her eye how Bert came to instant attention. 'What did your uncle give you?'

Jeremy blinked. 'I don't know. I haven't opened his present yet.'

As one person, everyone turned to look at the tree, and the two presents remaining. Wordlessly, but grim-lipped, Bert did the honours and fetched Jeremy's present.

It was tiny — a mere box, not more than three inches square. Jeremy winced as his father dropped it into his hands, and for a long moment simply sat and stared at it, too frozen by a sudden, unnamed terror to open it.

Jenny waited patiently. Delia sat forward on the sofa, fascinated to see what was inside. Bill, Jenny noticed with one quick, comprehensive glance, was sobering up fast.

Eventually, aware that there was no ducking it, Jeremy took off the wrapping paper, the smallness of the parcel and his own nervous fingers that had suddenly become all thumbs making the task a nerve-rackingly long and clumsy one. Eventually, though, he had a small, plain blue box in the palm of his hand. He lifted the lid.

Inside was a set of car keys.

He stared at them, his young face slowly draining of colour. The insignia on the keyring was for a small mid-range hatchback. Not a hugely expensive car, to be sure, but a car. Something Jeremy, from the look on his face, had not expected to be able to afford to buy for another good few years yet.

'A car.' Jeremy said the two words as if quoting from a tablet of stone.

'What about it, son?' Bert said, his voice tense and nervous. Even Bill, usually the least observant of the Kelton bunch, noticed it, and gave his elder brother a quick, curious and touchingly anxious look.

How these Kelton men liked to stick together, Jenny thought. It was touching how a tyrant could unite his enemies in a way that no other bond could. Had Stan Kelton but known it, he'd created a strong, supportive, loving family unit here. She had a good mind to tell him so, just to have the entertainment of watching him grind his teeth in frustration! But, of course, she wouldn't be so petty as to point it out to him. Well, not yet anyway.

Jeremy reverently lifted the keys into his hand, and noticed a slip of paper underneath. He seemed not to have heard his father's question. He opened it out, his eyes blank as he read the few words.

'It's an address,' he said quietly. 'Of a garage in Woodstock. The car must be there.'

'Why a car, Jeremy?' the cook asked quietly but firmly as Jeremy closed his fingers possessively around the set of keys.

He looked up at her then, not sure he wanted to answer, then glanced across at his father, and finally at all the others, patiently waiting. He felt like Delia had only minutes before. Something was in the air — something important — but he had no idea what the implications might be for himself, or for anyone else.

'Several weeks ago, the beginning of November I think it was, I was in here with Sid. He'd finished with the accounts and I was back early from collecting the horse feed from Simon. Sid called me in. At first I thought he just wanted a chat, like. You know how lonely he could get, and how he always kept you nattering just when you wanted to get off, or had work to do.'

Delia smiled and nodded. Bert shifted uneasily on his chair. 'Anyway, somehow the conversation got around to what I would do if I left the farm,' Jeremy continued, slowly feeling his way into his recital. Jenny found his carefulness with words very interesting. He might be young, but he was not rash. Interesting, that.

Bill's bleary blue eyes, the cook noticed, had shed the very last vestiges of drunkenness at his nephew's surprising statement, and she didn't need to be a mind-reader to know why. For years, the Kelton men had been all but semi-willing prisoners of Kelton Farm. Now, in the space of a day, one had been threatened with eviction and one had been sounded out on another potential escape. What the hell had been going on? For something obviously *had* been going on. And why hadn't he known about it?

Bill ran a hand across his face, and began to sweat; he could feel it starting to ooze from his pores. The room was hot. He wanted to go out and get some air but something else kept him rooted to the spot.

Bert breathed in, hard. 'And what did you say, son, when he asked you what you would do?' he asked gruffly.

Jeremy looked at his father helplessly. 'What could I say? I said I was never going to leave, so what was the use in dreaming? But Sid was insistent. Looking back now . . . I wonder . . . but at the time, I just thought he was trying to get at me. You know, force me into doing something about, well, living here.' Jeremy flushed and carefully moved his eyes away from those of his father. Bert's hands clenched into fists, then, very slowly, unclenched.

Everyone in the room knew what Jeremy had meant. Sid had been urging him not to be like his father — not to get trapped there on the farm. To break away, as Janice, his mother had done. To be his own man.

'I got rather . . . well, to be frank, I got angry,' Jeremy said, being scrupulously honest. 'I told him to shut up about what I'd do. I wouldn't do anything. I *couldn't* do anything.' The lad's voice had been getting gradually louder and more strident with remembered frustration, no doubt just as it had done back in November, when talking to his uncle. 'But Sid wouldn't back down,' Jeremy continued, his voice falling back into a more normal — and puzzled — tone. 'It wasn't like him. You all know how Sid hated to argue. He'd always back down to avoid a fuss. But this time he didn't,' Jeremy frowned. 'He kept pushing, and pushing. He said there must be something I wanted. Something I dreamed of. He said young men always dreamed of *something*. That's when I blurted it out, like. About wanting a car.'

Bert leaned forward, forcing his son to look at him. 'Why a car, son?'

Jeremy gave a slightly embarrassed, slightly defiant laugh. 'I told him if I had a car I could get away. I could pick Mandy up, and drive off into the sunset. With a car I could get a job — turn the car into a taxi, maybe. I don't know, something. I always thought if only I had wheels I could really get away. No more stupid horses playing up to the agri-tourists. No more long boring bus rides into Oxford or Burford. No more walking into the village and walking back. A car of my own somehow seemed like the answer to everything. And Sid seemed to understand when I told him. He was so kind about it all. I even confessed that sometimes, at night, I dreamed of rolling up outside the Lamb and Dog in a car, my very own car, and tooting on the horn. I imagined Mandy sticking her head out of the window, perhaps frowning at first because of the noise, and then seeing it was me.'

The lad's face was bright now, his eyes glowing and his voice full of the promise of his youth. Jenny wasn't the only one in the room who found a lump coming to her throat.

'I imagined her running out the door and dancing around the car, talking a mile a minute, the way she does. And then, when she fell quiet, I would ask her to marry me — to come away with me in the car, far, far away from Westcott Barton. We'd never have to see a farm or a village pub again . . .'

Jeremy trailed off, only now becoming aware of how much he'd bared his soul, and he suddenly blushed to the roots of his hair. His hand though, Jenny noticed with a wry smile, was still closed tightly and possessively around the car keys.

And why not, she thought. Why shouldn't a car, a simple, ordinary car, be the difference between a life of drudgery, and the hope of a whole new, shining future? Stranger things happened at sea all the time, so her grandma had always contended.

Jeremy's dream was by no means as foolish as it might sound. Mandy probably would abandon her father and the Lamb and Dog for a young man with a car in a trice! Especially when that man was Jeremy. After all, in such unique circumstances as these, a mere car was the equivalent of a maiden's dream of a big white horse that would take her far away from the drudgery of her everyday life.

And Sid had probably realized the same.

'So,' Jenny said, letting her breath out in a whoosh. 'A shop for Bert, a car for Jeremy, money for Delia . . .' She turned and looked at Bill.

Bill stared back at her, blinking quickly. It had only just begun to occur to him that all of this was hardly any of the cook's business, but now the thought simply fled; he had other things on his mind. He got to his feet, with just a residue of lightness in the head, thanks to the pub's rather potent scrumpy, and retrieved the last package from under the tree.

Quickly, almost feverishly, he yanked the cheerful paper aside. It was a deep, square box, which turned out to be a complex model of a three-masted sailing ship.

Jenny, who had noticed several models of ships scattered around the farmhouse, had already surmised that one of the Kelton men must be a model buff.

Bill stared down at the gift, his eyes bemused. 'She's a beauty,' he said absently, looking at the picture of the finished model on the lid of the box. He'd spent many happy hours making up the ships, most of which Sid had bought for him as Christmas and birthday presents.

'But it's hardly a new life, is it?' Bill spoke out loud the thought that everyone else in the room was thinking, his voice hard and flat.

First his old man had turned on him for some reason, and now Sid? Bill could almost understand his father's nastiness — Stan probably thought it was high old sport to make a fuss of him for the first half of his life, then turn against him for the second half. But *Sid*? Sid, who didn't have a mean bone in his body. Why had Sid thought that all the others deserved a new life, but not him? Bill's knuckles turned white as his grip tightened compulsively on the box, and one cardboard side slowly began to cave in. Slowly, through his pain and anger, he became aware of a great silence. He looked up sharply, meeting the cook's eyes first. Funny, he'd never noticed before how beautiful they were. They were bluer than his own, fringed by dark lashes, and quite, quite, extraordinarily lovely.

The look in them, however, was totally unreadable. It was like looking into a mirror, where he could see only his own reflection. It left him feeling oddly unnerved.

Quickly he looked across at his brother, but Bert was still frowning at Jeremy. Delia, beside him, impulsively reached out and grabbed his hand. She gave her brother's fingers a simple, comforting squeeze. For some reason, it made his heart leap.

Did they all think . . . ? Did Delia think . . . ? He swallowed hard. Oh Lord, what should he do now?

Jenny sighed deeply, and rubbed one finger against her nose. It was a habit of hers, when she was deep in thought. Had anyone pointed it out to her, of course, she would have denied it strenuously.

So, it turned out now that Sid had been behaving very strangely just before his death. For a start, he'd been spending his money as if there were no tomorrow. She felt a cold hand clutch her, somewhere deep in her throat, as she realized that, for Sid, there *had* been no tomorrow. Had he known he was going to die? Perhaps he'd had some sort of premonition? She thinned her lips angrily. Now don't start getting morbid, she told herself grimly. Or fanciful. Now is a time to be practical. And think, damn it! Think!

Stan might run the farm, but the profits, at least legally, must have belonged to Sid. And, for some reason, this year, Sid had decided to spend his money like never before, with the vast majority of it being spent on Bert. There was no getting away from that. Setting someone up in a business was a major undertaking.

Jenny looked across at the elder Kelton son, her mind whirling. Why had Sid done it? Did he have a guilty conscience about something? That was the most obvious answer. But about what? What could kind, ineffectual, good old Sid have to feel guilty about? Money for Delia; a dream come true for Jeremy; a whole new life away from the farm for Bert and his long-suffering wife, Janice.

And why nothing for Bill?

Jenny's eyes narrowed thoughtfully. Either Sid had nothing to feel guilty about in Bill's case, or . . . Sid didn't feel he owed Bill anything. The cook turned to look thoughtfully once more at the younger Kelton son.

Bill was staring blankly at the beautiful picture of a three-masted sailing ship in his hands. His face was as closed as a baker's shop window during a yeast shortage, yet something was definitely going on behind those cloudy blue eyes.

What on earth could he be feeling? Betrayal? Confusion? If he'd killed Sid, maybe even vindication? Who could say?

Jenny sighed. She'd have to inform Moulton and Ford about these latest developments before she turned in. Moulton would have a fit if she kept him in the dark for even a night.

But she doubted he'd be able to see the light, any more than she could.

Sid had definitely been up to something in those last few weeks of his life. Why did he want everyone out of Kelton Farm? Was he thinking of selling it? If so, that put Stan Kelton firmly back in the frame. Previously, she hadn't really considered him because he'd had no motive.

But even as she liked the thought of it, she somehow simply couldn't imagine Sid selling the family farm. The land was as much in his blood as it was in that of Stan or any of the other men folk.

As she climbed the stairs, hearing the others trooping up after her, all of them no doubt locked deep into thoughts of their own, she suddenly wondered what Sid had given his brother Stan for Christmas.

She'd noticed that Stan's present was the only one missing. Somehow, she didn't think Stan would be in any hurry to tell her.

# CHAPTER FOURTEEN

Jenny awoke bleary-eyed and disgruntled, and promptly discovered that a sheepdog was lying firmly across her chest. As she blinked, rather surprised by this development, the dog — with his nose a mere few inches from her face — executed a wide yawn that displayed fangs, pretty ribbed pink gums and a swinging pair of tonsils. Not to mention a case of extremely bad breath.

'Gerroff,' Jenny growled, and rolled the mutt off her chest and onto the floor. Immediately, she began to breathe easier. Literally.

She watched the dog warily as she dressed and combed her hair, wondering how it had gained access into the house. It must, she concluded, have seized the opportunity to sneak in with all the others last night. No doubt it had slunk into the shadows and hid itself somewhere in the hall. She wouldn't put it past him to be able to wriggle himself into the casing of the grandfather clock. Any dog with the abilities of this one should join a circus act, Jenny mused.

The black and white mutt leapt lithely back onto her unmade bed, turned a few circles on the still-warm blankets, and settled down with a beatific sigh.

'Gerroff,' the cook said again mildly. The dog looked at her.

Jenny looked at the dog.

The dog got off.

Together they trotted down to the kitchen to start a new day. Soon eggs, bacon and sausages were sizzling in the frying pan, tea was brewing, a cheery fire was seeing off the last of the snow's cold hold on the farm, and Jenny began to see light. Or rather, began to think that she would soon.

Stan Kelton clumped in a few minutes later — quite a feat, since he was wearing nothing more than socks on his feet — and glanced at the stove. 'I want fried bread today as well.'

No 'please' of course. No 'good morning.'

Jenny inclined her head, regal as a queen. 'Certainly.' Stan poured himself a cup of tea. 'And Christmas is over. I think you can leave now. I know you've still got a week to go, if we stick to the letter of our agreement, but I won't hold you to it. Under the circumstances.'

'Very magnanimous of you, I'm sure,' Jenny murmured, not a trace of sarcasm in her voice. 'But I think the inspector might have something to say about that.'

Stan's fiercely bushy grey eyebrows met over his eyes. He watched the cook add several slices of bread to the frying pan, his lips tight. 'Hah! You've got those cops eating out of your hand,' he said, more as a statement of fact than as a question. 'Everyone knows that.'

Jenny turned, ready to defend with her last breath the honour of the Thames Valley Police Force, then saw there was no need. Behind her, in the doorway, Moulton coughed discreetly. Stan Kelton, far from embarrassed, shot him a dirty look over his shoulder. 'You'll be wanting some grub then, I expect?' he asked bluntly. 'Eating me out of house and home. And expecting me to keep a cook on when I don't need her no more.'

Stan took his customary seat as Jenny brought the frying pan to the table, and dished out a huge breakfast for the two men, and a slightly (but only slightly) less huge breakfast for herself.

She put some bread under the grill to toast, and returned to the table.

Moulton nodded at her. 'Miss Starling is helping us with our inquiries,' he began, ignoring the way the cook winced, and enthusiastically cut into his bacon. Just as he liked it: crispy but not so crispy that it shattered under the fork. 'As a matter of fact, Miss Starling has helped a lot of policemen with their inquiries,' he added, casting Stan a sly glance from under his hooded lids.

If he was pleased to see the way Stan Kelton gaped, Jenny supposed she couldn't really blame him.

'Eh?' Stan asked, somewhat inelegantly. 'What do you mean?' He glared at his cook, who was just opening a jar of marmalade. 'She doesn't look the criminal sort to me. If she is—'

'Mr Kelton, Miss Starling is certainly not the criminal sort,' Moulton cut in, unwilling for some strange reason to sit by and let the Junoesque cook be insulted. It was not as if he liked the woman, of course. He didn't. Nor was it male gallantry. In fact, if asked, Moulton couldn't have said why it was that he was so eager to leap to her defence. He just was.

'Miss Starling happens to have been involved — strictly as an observer, of course — in a few of the most puzzling murders this country has seen in the course of the last few years.'

Stan's lower jaw literally dropped. 'Eh? She what?'

Moulton sighed but opened his mouth to continue to spread the tales of her prowess, and Jenny wondered despairingly if she really could consider herself justified in giving his shins yet another hearty, well-deserved kick. But she supposed not, and sighed.

'Miss Starling has several times, er, helped the police to ascertain the identity of the guilty party,' Moulton confessed.

Very policeman-like language, Jenny thought, her lips twisted into a grim smile as she collected the toast. He certainly wasn't going to say that the police had been baffled (that phrase so beloved of the tabloids) and that she had as good as handed the culprit to them on a silver platter. On the other hand, it was what he *didn't* say that made it so obvious that that was exactly what she *had* done.

And now, Stan Kelton would be on his guard.

Thanks a bunch, Inspector Moulton, she thought with a sigh. She glanced up as she returned to the table with a plate of steaming golden toast, and noticed Stan watching her with a new light in his eyes, and a very firm line to his lips.

Wonderful!

Moulton, perhaps aware of having upset the cook in some strange way — women could be very odd at times, he knew — had enough sense to eat his breakfast quickly, and without another word, and then took himself off to Ford's room. He was anxious to fill his sergeant in on what Miss Starling had told him last night.

When she had knocked on his door, at an hour well past midnight, and he'd awakened to see her standing over him, his heart had lurched. For one awful, yet oddly exhilarating moment, he'd thought . . . but of course, he wilted now in remembered relief, she had only had business on her mind, and what she'd told him had certainly been interesting. But for now he quickened his step, anxious to get free of the tense atmosphere in the kitchen.

Jenny watched the great big booby disappear into the hall and sighed. She glanced across at Stan, who slowly leaned back in his chair. 'So. We're in the presence of a clever-Dick amateur detective, are we? I thought those only existed in novels and on the telly.'

Jenny shrugged. 'I just happened to be in the wrong place at the wrong time, and needed to get myself taken off a suspect list. To do that . . .' she shrugged again and trailed off.

Stan's slightly sneering smile began to slide off his face. Slowly, he leaned forward, his eyes narrowing. 'You mean you really have solved murders before?'

Jenny buttered her toast, speared her fried egg with a very savage prod from her fork, and reached for the salt. 'Yes,' she admitted shortly.

Stan stared at her for a long while, but she said nothing more. Angry at not forcing her to buckle under, the farmer glanced over his shoulder, but no one else seemed to be stirring just yet. Slowly, he leaned even further forward across the table, his hands coming together to lie in a twisted knot in front of him.

When Jenny reluctantly looked up into his eyes, she didn't — but most definitely *didn't* — like the look in them.

'When you find out who killed Sid,' Stan said, his voice for once held way below its natural bellow, 'I want you to tell me before you tell the cops.' His brown eyes bored into hers; his face had lost all colour and his chest heaved, as if he were having difficulty breathing.

'Oh?' Jenny said, her voice as light as one of her sponge cakes. 'And why should I do that?'

Stan Kelton leaned back in his chair, his eyes glittering. 'You know very well why I want you to do that.'

Jenny reached for a second piece of toast, and put a slice of bacon onto it, then folded the toast over to make a sandwich. She took her own sweet time about it. When she finally looked back at him, her eyes were like mirrors.

Bill had come up against that same phenomenon only last night, and now it was his father's turn to look into the cook's eyes and see nothing else but his own reflection there.

'The murderer of Sid Kelton,' Jenny said quietly, but in a tone of voice that sounded as if it could travel to the heavens themselves, 'will go to prison for the rest of his or her life for it. We've had enough trouble in this house without adding vigilantism to it.'

Stan's hands clenched into fists in front of him.

'The state will see to justice, Mr Kelton,' she assured him quietly. 'Never you fear about that.'

* * *

Everyone was at the breakfast table (including Moulton, who'd come down to keep Sergeant Ford company) when the letterbox rattled, and for the first time since the very first fall of snow, the daily newspaper slipped through the door and thudded onto the mat.

Jenny, washing up at the sink, glanced through the window to see a young lad all but sprint for the rapidly clearing lane. No doubt it was not the gander this time that made him want to make such a hasty departure, but the desire to be as fast and as far away from Kelton Farm as possible. No doubt the villagers had been talking of nothing else but the murder since Christmas Eve. She could well imagine the paperboy's friends teasing and taunting him about having to deliver a paper to the 'death house.'

A moment later, Stan Kelton roared in outrage. The unexpected shout made everyone jump, including the cook, and it quickly became clear that the villagers of Westcott Barton had not been the only ones talking about it.

'Look at this!' Stan bellowed, his roar making the dog, currently hidden behind the cooker of all things, whimper in fright. Jenny quickly banged a pot lid to cover the tiny sound, but Stan had his mind on other things anyway.

'The bloody vultures!' Stan's face was red, his blood vessels popping spectacularly. In his hands, the local paper shook in a frenzy of rage, and Moulton glanced sourly at the big blazing headlines.

LOCAL FARMER STABBED IN THE CHEST IN HIS OWN HOME. POLICE HAVE QUARANTINED KELTON FARM.

Moulton sighed. They hadn't quarantined the farm, of course, but when had the truth ever stood in the way of a good story?

Regardless of its accuracy, one thing was for sure: once his chief saw it, he'd be given enough paperwork to paper the walls with, if Miss Starling didn't pull her finger out soon and point out the killer.

If there was one thing his chief hated, it was to be made a fool of in the press. And if there was one thing Moulton hated, it was to be on the receiving end of his chief's displeasure.

Stan indignantly began to read the article, which was by and large factual, but written in such a way as to make the very most out of innuendo and gossip. It also stressed that the police had been unable to find any evidence of a stranger having called at the farm to kill Sid, and speculated why two police officers were actually staying at the farm. And, they wondered out loud, and oh-so-innocently, how difficult it could be to unmask the killer, when there appeared to be such a limited range of suspects.

If only they knew!

Of one Jenny Starling, there was as yet no mention, and the cook felt a little guilty at feeling so relieved. But give them time, she thought grimly. Give them time.

The Kelton family listened to the recital in dour silence. Sid was described as a 'gentle, well-liked man' whilst Stan was the 'very respected source behind the Kelton wealth.' And for 'respected' everyone could read 'feared' with no difficulty.

The unnecessarily gory details of the murder were the worst, and Jenny's guilt intensified. No doubt the reporters had questioned the villagers, who'd been only too happy to pass on to them what the Keltons' cook had said. Oh well, it had always been inevitable. It only made things that much more uncomfortable.

For the killer as well, she hoped.

* * *

At just gone ten o'clock, Moulton put his head around the door, noted that the cook was at last alone, and beckoned Ford in after him. He shut the kitchen door carefully behind him, causing Jenny to look up over the mound of lamb she was washing under the tap.

'Inspector,' she said, rinsing the meat. 'Lancashire hot-pot for dinner, with plenty of onions mixed in, with cauli-flower and carrots. And I thought I'd do a raisin and—'

'I don't care what's for dinner,' Moulton said quickly, knowing how lyrical the cook could wax when it came to food. Ford, who'd been licking his lips in anticipation, stiff-ened his backbone contritely.

Jenny sighed and nodded to the table. 'Let's sit down then, shall we? Delia's off to the Brays' and Mrs Jarvis hasn't come in yet.' She wondered, privately, if Mrs Jarvis would ever come back to the farm. 'The men are all out in the sheep pen, so that's something to be grateful for. Bert muttered something about dyeing the pregnant ewes blue and the others red.'

But Moulton was even less interested in the daily running of a sheep farm than he was in what was for dinner. Well, not quite. He did have to admit that Miss Starling was a cook who could make even a fasting monk think twice, but . . .

'Look, what do you really make of all these strange Christmas presents of Sid's?' Moulton dragged his thoughts firmly back to the matter in hand. 'Ford and I were saying only just now that in quite a few murder cases, it's usually the way that the victim has behaved oddly in some way before he or she is killed. And, more often than not, it's usually the reason why they acted queerly that got them killed.' Moulton, aware that he'd been rather less than clear, grappled for an example. 'I mean, I was reading about a case last summer where a man suddenly started coming home late, smelling of perfume, and making excuses to his wife. She knew he was having an affair, and killed the poor sod with his own garden spade.'

Jenny sighed. 'Men can be very stupid sometimes.'

Moulton flushed. 'That wasn't the point I was mak-ing,' he gritted. 'I'm saying that Sid Kelton *had been* acting strangely lately.'

'Hmm,' she agreed. 'But I don't see why that would have got him killed. After all, he wasn't exactly doing any-thing nasty was he? Quite the opposite, in fact. Why would Delia want to kill the man who was giving her escape money?

Or Bert kill the man who'd been so good to the wife he obviously still adores? Do you really think Jeremy was so angered by his new car, he took the steak knife to his uncle?'

Moulton sighed, then suddenly perked up. 'But none of them knew, did they, that they were going to get such generous gifts?'

'Agreed,' Jenny said. 'But how much farther forward does that get us?'

Ford sighed. 'But it has to be significant,' he whined. 'Sid had been acting out of character. *Somebody* for *some* reason must have taken exception to it.'

'Granted, but why exactly?' she wailed in frustration.

\* \* \*

The men had returned for lunch. Jenny had happily prepared leeks stuffed with ham and cheese and baked in the oven. With it, she'd served freshly baked bread rolls, and brought out the Christmas cake for afters.

Delia, it seemed, had, for once, been invited to stay on for lunch at the Brays'. Perhaps even Cordelia felt obliged to offer the grief-stricken girl a few crumbs of comfort.

The cook was just clearing the table when her sharp hearing detected a somewhat timid knock at the front door. Since thick walls, shut doors and general conversation had kept it from the others, she wiped her hands on the towel and went out into the hall. There she opened the door to a tall, thin woman, with a very nice complexion and large, anxious eyes.

The visitor was obviously surprised by the cook's appearance and blinked in evident confusion. 'Oh. Er, hello. I was wondering . . . er . . . if my husband, Bert Kelton, was home?'

Jenny smiled widely. 'You must be Janice? I'm the cook, hired by Stan for the Christmas holidays. Please, do come in.'

Janice smiled nervously and walked in with some trepidation. And who could blame her for being unsure of her reception, Jenny thought. She took the other woman's coat, scarf and gloves and lent her much-needed support by following her into the lion's den. In the doorway Janice abruptly halted, the sight of Stan Kelton's broad back having that effect on a lot of people.

It was her son who saw her first. Jeremy leapt to his feet, his face alight with happiness, and Jenny instantly saw that the lad had inherited his slim build from his mother. His rather pretty face, too, for that matter. 'Mum!' he cried, beaming at her, and Bert instantly lifted a white face to that of his wife. It was as much movement as he could manage, for after that he sat, seemingly frozen, in his chair.

Stan Kelton reared up to his feet and spun around. Janice would have taken an instinctive step back, but Jenny had positioned herself right behind her, and a bulldozer would have something to do to shift Jenny when she'd made up her mind to do something, much less a mere willow of a woman like Janice.

'Mrs Kelton, I'd like to introduce you to Inspector Moulton and Sergeant Ford,' Jenny said, a little louder than need be, and stared tellingly at Stan as she did so.

Stan slightly subsided. Even he felt inhibited when it came to family feuding in front of a police audience.

'Hello, everyone,' Janice said, her voice small and unsure in the suddenly silent room. 'I—' She stopped, looked at her son, looked at her husband and said in a quiet, deeply pained voice, 'I read in the papers this morning about Sid. I had to come.'

That simple.

Jenny knew that, normally, the police would have been to see Janice long before now, and she wouldn't have had to read about Sid's death in the newspapers. But being Christmas, and so short-staffed, she supposed they hadn't yet got around to it. Similarly, she supposed Janice had spent a rather lonely Christmas, so wouldn't have heard any local gossip about Sid's murder.

Bert, at last, slowly rose to his feet. 'Janice,' he said, his eyes drinking her in like a man that had been crawling across the Sahara for a week, just sighting his first oasis.

Janice took a tentative step forward. 'You haven't been in touch — all my letters, my Christmas cards, my gift for Jeremy . . .' She looked hurt and confused. 'Did you not get them?'

Before Bert could explain, Stan growled, 'I thought when you left in such a high and mighty dudgeon, my girl, that you said you wouldn't ever set foot in this house again!'

'Oh for Pete's sake!' Bill roared, before anyone else could jump in. 'Janice loved Sid, just as much as the rest of us. And it's Christmas! Why shouldn't she be here?'

Moulton coughed. 'Please, sit down, Mrs Kelton,' he said politely.

And Stan was forced to watch, helpless and outmanoeuvred, as Janice Kelton walked into the room and went straight to the empty chair beside her husband. Slowly, with tears in her eyes, she reached out to take his hand. Bert, hardly able to believe his luck, squeezed his fingers around hers.

Jenny watched them, and wondered. In fact, she wondered very much.

# CHAPTER FIFTEEN

Jenny went straight to the stove to put the kettle on. If Janice Kelton could work up the courage to come back to Kelton Farm, the least, the very *least* she could expect was a good cup of tea and some warm mince pies with clotted cream.

Stan Kelton glared at his daughter-in-law, scowled at Bert, saved the most dirty of his looks for the two policemen, then very firmly sat down again. He was not about to leave Bert alone with Janice, a fact that was surely now obvious to everyone.

'Mum, Uncle Sid gave me a car for Christmas,' Jeremy broke the awkward silence first, his youthful enthusiasm making even Moulton smile. If it weren't for the fact that the lad might be a killer, Moulton wouldn't have a thing against him.

Janice half laughed, no doubt feeling overwhelmed at being with her family again, and relieved that the first awkward moments were now behind her, even if the presence of the silently fuming Stan could hardly be ignored. 'Did he? That was nice of him. But I thought, I mean the papers said that Sid died on Christmas Eve.' Her voice was puzzled, as well it might be.

'He did,' Stan said flatly.

Janice's eyes flickered in his direction, then away again. She looked at Bert, who was still holding onto her hand and not about to let go. He still looked as dazed as a bear that had stumbled into a honey factory. A slightly silly grin was beginning to spread over his face. His eyes ran over her features hungrily, and he was breathing in deep, almost panicky gulps.

Bill gave Janice a happy nudge in the ribs, and winked at her when she smiled at him.

'I opened the present yesterday,' Jeremy was forced to explain, his youthful zest becoming flatter and flatter. He looked from his mother to his father, then at his scowling-faced grandfather, and wondered, rather belatedly, if there wasn't a fresh disaster just looming on the horizon. In his joy to see his mum again he'd forgotten, for one lovely, giddying moment, just how bad things really were here.

Jenny very firmly put a mug of steaming tea down in front of the visitor, and a plate of nicely warmed mince pies. Janice helped herself to two sugar lumps from the bowl and a generous dollop of milk. 'Those look wonderful,' she said, nodding at the mince pies.

Jenny beamed. What an obviously nice and good woman Janice Kelton was.

Bill rose determinedly to his feet. 'Well, Dad, we'd better get back to them ewes. It'll be dark by four, you know, and we've still got a good three score to do.'

Stan's lower lip curled nastily. 'I know when it gets dark, boy, and I can count.' His voice was so filled with contempt that Sergeant Ford actually winced. Janice's face paled in shock. She gaped at Bill, who was red-faced and breathing hard, like a bull that had just spotted a red cape. She hastily transferred her surprised glance to Stan. Obviously, when she'd left, Bill had still been very much the blue-eyed boy. But Stan's lip curled even more in distaste. It gave his face such a hateful expression that Janice felt all her old antagonism and despair rise up to fill her throat.

'The ewes won't dye themselves,' Bill's voice gritted past his teeth, and he took a determined step towards his father.

It was almost as if he was willing to physically manhandle his father out of the room, to give Bert and his wife time on their own. Moulton, for one, was convinced that Bill was about to attempt to pluck his father from the chair right there and then.

Stan obviously thought so too, for he suddenly lurched to his feet, looking ready to kill his younger son if he tried it.

Janice's jaw dropped.

Moulton said firmly, 'If you wouldn't mind, Mr Kelton, I would like to talk to your daughter-in-law and your son, Bert, alone for a few minutes.'

Stan's murderous gaze swivelled in the policeman's direction. He glanced briefly at Bert, still sat firmly beside his wife and still holding onto her hand like a drowning man holding onto a lifejacket, and a very odd look passed over his face.

Jenny, who just caught it, thought for one insane moment that it was a look of fear, but at the same time, almost a look of love.

She immediately thought she must have imagined it, but then, after he'd stomped out, a triumphant Bill fast in his wake, she wondered. Why *wouldn't* Stan Kelton love his eldest son? Even a man such as himself could be afraid of losing yet another member of his family. It was only natural, after all. She really mustn't let her dislike for the man influence her thinking.

When the door slammed shut behind the two men, Janice turned to Bert, her face still showing her shock. 'I thought Bill was his favourite,' was the first thing she said, and Bert smiled wryly.

'He was. Now I am. Neither of us knows who's coming or going. It's Dad at his best.' There was a world of defeat and hate in his voice.

Janice blinked, then shook her head. She didn't like to see Bert, her easygoing, good-hearted Bert, like this. Quickly, she changed the subject. 'I really am sorry about Sid,' she said softly, and looked across at her son. 'I know how you both loved him. So did I.'

At that point, Moulton took over, and began a rather pompous but undeniably official interrogation, but Janice could tell him nothing new. She herself had been in her shop all day Christmas Eve, and quoted the name of an assistant who could corroborate it. She also offered the name of two regular customers whom she'd served in the shop that day, one who'd bought an eighteenth-century Toby jug at around 11:30, and one who'd bought a Victorian jet mourning ring at just before one o'clock.

Not that Moulton had seriously considered her as a suspect, of course. But it paid to be thorough.

He sighed at Ford, nodded at the reunited couple and their son and caught the cook's slight nod towards the hall door. Mumbling excuses, they all left Bert Kelton and his family alone, and went into the living room.

'Well, that's one in the eye for Stan Kelton anyway,' Ford said, with just a hint of satisfied malice in his voice. 'You think Bert will leave now?'

'I shouldn't be surprised,' Jenny answered. 'He's been so miserable without her. And now that they have another place to live, and another business to keep them going, I can't see him letting his father keep them apart for a second time. And neither,' she added thoughtfully, 'can Stan.'

'You caught that look on his face then, eh?' Moulton asked, but without his sergeant's spite. He too could feel sorry for a man who was about to lose, through his own cruelty and injustice, his oldest son and heir.

'Hmm,' Jenny murmured. 'I wonder if Sid's happy — wherever he is.'

'When this is all over,' Ford mused, 'it wouldn't surprise me if our young Delia and big brother Bill also swanned off into the sunset.'

'No,' Jenny agreed thoughtfully. 'It wouldn't surprise me either.' And wondered some more.

* * *

Mrs Jarvis skidded slightly on the last of the rapidly vanishing snow, and looked up as the courtyard of Kelton Farm came into view. She'd had her lunch, settled down to do some knitting and found the afternoon suddenly stretching interminably ahead of her, like a long wet weekend. She'd convinced herself that she really wasn't going to go back to the farm — it wasn't safe. She had common sense enough to know that. And yet here she was. She sighed as she opened the gate and walked in, ignoring the gander, which returned the insult by ignoring her. It was obviously beneath the bird's dignity to terrify such a nonentity as the daily.

Her spine tingled and her steps slowed as she approached the side door, and she knew herself for being all kinds of a fool. None of the Keltons would be surprised if she stopped coming. She was just storing up trouble for herself, and no mistake. But she just had to *know*. What had they learned? It had been three days since Sid had died. If they'd found anything out, it was imperative that she discovered what it was.

She stiffened her backbone, opened the door and breezed in. And stopped dead. There, sat at the kitchen table and as large as life, was Janice Kelton. Moreover, Bert was leaning over her, looking as if he'd just been kissing her, and young Jeremy was grinning from ear to ear. Well!

Janice felt the cold draught and drew away. She glanced across and was immediately relieved to see that it was only the old daily, and not Stan Kelton returning from the sheep pens. 'Oh, hello, Mrs Jarvis. How are you?' she asked brightly.

Mrs Jarvis blinked. 'Eh? Oh, I'm all right. My chilblains are giving me jip again though.'

'Oh, what a nuisance,' Janice said, then added craftily, 'Why don't you go through to the living room, where it's warmer?'

Bert smiled at his wife's genuine kindness and very useful tact, and watched as the old daily, very warily, walked past them, shot them an avidly curious look over her shoulder and disappeared into the hall. Jeremy laughed out loud at the exaggerated theatrics.

Bert, who'd also been watching their unexpected visitor, found his eyes swinging back to his son, and all the laughter in his own face fled. Unknowingly, his hold on his wife's hand tightened. Janice caught the sudden, frightened look on his face, and her own heart leapt as a sudden shaft of panic swept through her. A cold sense of foreboding snaked up her spine and made her shiver.

What was wrong? What could possibly be wrong now, just when they'd got everything sorted out?

She'd told Bert all about how Sid had found her sharing a flat with an old school friend, and how he'd sounded her out about what she'd like to do with the rest of her life. She'd told him, thinking he'd only asked out of friendly curiosity, and had been shocked but delighted when he'd returned a month later with the papers all drawn up that made her the new half-owner of The Old Duke antique shop.

She'd gone on so happily to tell Bert how she'd turned the flat upstairs into a cosy little place for three, always hoping her husband and son would soon join her, and about how well the shop was doing. She'd also told him how Sid had insisted she say nothing to Bert about it all until after Christmas. It was all so totally out of character for Sid, and it had seemed like such a long time for her to wait, but, after all, Sid was giving them the shop. So, reluctantly, she'd agreed.

Then she'd gone on to tell Bert how nice it was to live in town. And just to make sure he was getting the message loud and clear, she'd gone out of her way to stress how much she was looking forward to him travelling the country with her, helping to buy up stock. For good measure, she'd also added how nice it would be to have someone warm beside her in bed again, and Bert had laughed, and kissed her, and his arms had felt so strong and safe and reassuring.

Life, in the last ten minutes, had become wonderful again. Bert had sworn he would leave the farm and join her there, along with Jeremy of course. Janice had been so happy. But now she was suddenly afraid again.

Because Bert was afraid.

'Bert, what is it?' she asked softly, and saw Jeremy's happy face crease into a frown.

Jeremy shifted uneasily on his chair. His father really was looking at him in a most peculiar way. 'Dad?' he said sharply.

Bert dragged his eyes away from his son and returned them to his wife. There could be no dark doubts gnawing at him with her pretty eyes shining on him.

'Bert, what is it?' Janice whispered again. 'You're frightening me.'

'It's nothing,' he said gruffly, wishing it were true.

'It's something,' Janice insisted. She knew her husband well. 'What? Can't you tell me? We shouldn't have secrets from each other, not now. We need to be strong.' Stan, she knew, would not let Bert go without a fight.

Bert sighed. It seemed to come from the depths of his soul. 'It's just that all this talk of the future . . .' he trailed off helplessly.

Janice's heart plummeted. She should have known that it wouldn't be so easy to pry Bert away from this damned farm, and the influence of that malevolent force, his father.

'And none of us even know if we *have* one,' Bert continued, almost in a whisper.

Janice paled even more. 'What do you mean?'

Bert glanced at his son, then quickly looked away again. 'That policeman — Inspector Moulton. He's not going to give up, you know.' Bert's voice had a hard edge to it now, which was strangely at odds with the resignation so apparent in his face. 'He won't let any of us leave here until he knows who killed Sid.'

Janice almost laughed out loud as she wilted in relief. Was that all? For a moment there, she'd thought Bert was having second thoughts about coming back to her.

'But he must find out who did it soon,' Janice said, offering what she thought must be comfort, and saw instead a ripple of some unnamed but terrifying emotion cross her husband's face. It was like watching a dark wave, a sinisterly dangerous current, rushing by beneath an otherwise placid-seeming pond.

Something, Janice thought, her mouth going paper-dry, was terribly wrong with her husband. A dread that she couldn't give name to — or maybe didn't dare give name to — clutched her heart, making her chest ache and sending a violent shiver down her spine.

Again, she noticed Bert's eyes dart across to those of their son and then quickly, painfully, move away again.

And this time, Janice felt the bottom drop out of her world. Every vestige of colour bleached out of her face. She turned wide, panicked eyes towards her son. Jeremy?

Oh no. *NO!*

Jeremy, who'd become more and more fidgety, suddenly found his mother looking at him with stricken eyes. It was more than he could bear. 'What?' he demanded, his face becoming flushed. '*What?*'

Bert shook his head. 'It's no good,' he said finally. 'I know . . . I *know*, son.' His hand left those of his wife, and moved to capture the cold hands of his son. He squeezed them hard. 'It'll be all right,' Bert whispered in encouragement. But he knew, in his heart, that it never would be.

Jeremy transferred his stare to his other parent. 'What? You know what?' he demanded, exasperated and more than a little unnerved now.

Bert gave Janice an utterly despairing look. He shook his head. 'I know Jeremy wasn't in the fields when Sid was killed,' he told her. 'I went down to the lower forty to ask him if he'd noticed any fox tracks coming out of the spinney.'

He turned, finally, to look his son in the eye. 'And you were nowhere to be seen.'

This time it was Jeremy's turn to have his face fade to white. His lips fell apart. His eyes widened to enormous dark pools. 'You think . . . All this time, you've thought that I . . . ?' He swallowed hard, on the verge of tears.

Janice covered her hand with her mouth. Her son had lied to the police. He had no alibi. Sid . . .

'I think I can help out there,' a cool voice suddenly cut into the scene, and Janice almost jumped out of her skin.

Bert swivelled round, his eyes narrowing on the cook. 'You,' he said, but whether it was a curse, a resigned statement or a benediction, she couldn't tell.

'If you ask him,' Jenny said, very patiently, 'I think you'll find that he sneaked off to see Mandy. Her father, apparently, was out of the pub that day and they arranged to snatch some time alone. Isn't that right, Jeremy?'

Jeremy was still staring at his father, his one thought still stuck in the same hideous groove. 'You thought I'd killed Uncle Sid?' he said at last, his young voice suddenly sounding ancient and tight with betrayal and disbelief.

'*No*,' Bert said, the word so full of despair and denial that it penetrated even Jeremy's icy anger. 'I never thought you might have done it!' Bert wailed. But, he thought, pressing his lips tightly together so that he could not possibly speak his thoughts out loud, I was so afraid you might have seen who did . . .

And kept quiet about it.

Jeremy threw himself against his father, burying his face against his shoulder, everything suddenly all too much for him. He was still so young, after all, and had felt so miserable for so long. Bert caught him, his big burly body wilting with the release of tension. Janice gave a dry sob, and rested her hand against her son's shoulder. She gazed at her husband, amazed at all that he must have gone through, since Sid's awful death.

Over the boy's head, Bert met the cook's narrowed thoughtful eyes. And he hoped, oh he so fervently hoped, that she wasn't really the mind-reader she so often seemed to be.

\* \* \*

In the living room, Mrs Jarvis fidgeted on the sofa, and periodically gave the policemen a penetrating gaze.

The cook had just gone to make her some tea, after the inspector had said, rather enigmatically, that he thought 'they' had had enough time. 'They' being Bert and Janice,

Mrs Jarvis surmised accurately. But, enough time for what? Had they arrested Bert of all people? *Bert!* Was that why Janice was there?

Jenny came back five minutes later, tea tray in hand. 'I think Mrs Kelton is about to leave,' she said to Moulton, her voice totally neutral and giving no hint as to what had taken place in the kitchen.

Moulton rose, wandered into the hall, saw Bert kissing his wife on the doorstep, and felt abruptly embarrassed. He half turned his back. Sometimes, although eavesdropping was a vital part of the job, he found it extremely distasteful. Not that people had a right to expect privacy during a murder investigation. But still . . .

'But why can't you stay here?' Bert was wheedling, the longing in his voice carrying clearly across the distance and making Moulton colour slightly. Ford, who'd also risen with his superior, very thoughtfully looked elsewhere. It wouldn't do for Moulton to catch him smiling.

'Because you know what it would be like,' Janice Kelton's pretty, rather lilting voice also carried clearly to the two policemen. 'Stan would . . . well . . . it would be very awkward. No, it's far better if I go back to the flat and get it ready for you. And Jeremy. He will come too, won't he?'

Bert murmured something Moulton didn't quite catch, and a few moments later he heard the front door shut quietly.

Moulton turned, nodded at Bert, and went back into the living room. He glanced at the daily. Now why, he wondered, momentarily distracted, had *she* been in such a hurry to return?

'I think Miss Starling could do with a hand in the kitchen, Mrs Jarvis,' he said, anxious to get her out of the room so that he and Ford could confer. Not that he could see what Janice Kelton's turning up had added to the puzzle, but you never knew.

Jenny easily took the hint, and stood up. 'Come on, Mrs Jarvis, you can bring your tea. I'll cut you a nice piece of my Christmas cake.'

Mrs Jarvis sniffed. 'I've still got plenty of my own cake left,' she pointed out. But, five minutes later, as she took a large bite out of the fancy cook's cake, she had to admit that it really *did* taste very nice. And it *was* so beautifully iced.

* * *

Ford pulled the curtains across the window and sighed. These dark winter days were so depressing. It was only five o'clock, but it was already as dark as midnight outside. He made his way to the kitchen, his spirits soaring as he sniffed the air. 'Lamb,' he murmured, his stomach rumbling. He came up alongside Delia in the hall, who was also making her way down for dinner.

'Hungry?' he asked her cheerfully, and then felt instantly deflated as she gave him a miserable look.

'Hardly,' Delia said coldly, and put a spurt on, no doubt in order to get out of his orbit as quickly as possible. The police, she thought angrily, could be so insensitive at times. As if she was hungry! She wondered, sometimes, if she'd ever feel hungry again.

Moulton was already at the table, Ford noticed a shade sourly, and Jenny checked her watch as she saw Ford and Delia take their own places. Mrs Jarvis, busy scrubbing out the shelves, heard her own stomach rumble, but she knew instinctively that the cook would put out a plate for her, too. Jenny Starling was the kind that would.

'They're late,' Jenny remarked, but no sooner were the words out of her mouth than the door opened and Stan Kelton walked in, a heavily scowling Bill right behind him. Bill shut the door with a nice, reverberating slam.

Upstairs, Bert and Jeremy heard it clearly and made their own way down. They'd packed a lot of their stuff already, anxious to make the move to Woodstock as soon as possible. Bert had felt the need to do something positive, and packing was as positive as it got. He *would* leave the farm and the packed suitcases now lining his bedroom walls proved it.

Jeremy, too, had been more than happy to pack. Although he now had a car, and he'd propose to Mandy at the very next opportunity, he was realistic enough to know that the wedding was still a long way off yet. He'd need to get another job, and would need to find a place to live whilst he did it. And he couldn't see his grandfather letting him stay on living at Kelton Farm once he knew that he had no intention of continuing to work on, or inherit it, in due course.

Besides, the thought of living in a town was exhilarating. Even if it was only good old Woodstock.

Jenny watched the seats around the table steadily fill up and reached for her oven gloves, then found her eyes falling to the wet and muddy floor. She shot a dirty glance at Stan and Bill, who were too busy trying to out-scowl each other to notice the mess they'd made, and reached for the ever-ready mop, throwing the oven gloves back down onto the table.

Jenny resentfully hoped that they all felt starving, and she set to with the mop as slowly as she could possibly manage. It would do them good to sit with empty growling bellies, whilst she was forced, *yet again*, to clean the damned floor!

She continued to mutter darkly under her breath as she worked. Her eyes absently followed the progress of the mop head. It was one of those grey, raggedy sort of mops, and as she slowly swept it rhythmically from side to side, the material absorbing the melted snow and mud on the tiles, her movements began to wind down and, finally, stop altogether.

She felt a tingling start, somewhere deep in the back of her mind. Something . . . something . . . something about that morning, when she'd returned to find Sid stabbed through the chest. Something about the state of the floor.

Moulton, who'd glanced casually her way, suddenly sat bolt upright. Ford, catching the movement, followed the line of his sight, and his own eyes narrowed on the cook.

Jenny Starling had such a tight, strange look on her face that Ford felt his own heartbeat pick up a pace.

Jenny didn't notice their attention. She was too busy going back in time, and was once more coming in from collecting the eggs on that crisp Christmas Eve morning. She took off her hat, coat, scarf and boots in the hall. She came into the kitchen and crossed over the floor . . .

She looked down at the mop, at the dirty and wet footprints. She had crossed over the floor in just her bare socks, to put the kettle on and get the mince pies out of the oven. And Sid was sat there, dead.

Jenny felt herself sway and closed her eyes. 'Of course,' she whispered. *Of course!*

By now, everyone in the room had become aware of the two policemen's sudden taut silence, and now, almost as one body, they too began to stare at the cook. Everyone seemed to hold a collective breath.

And one heart in particular began to pound. Sickeningly. The silence was so complete, even Jenny's whisper reached them all clearly.

Moulton licked his lips. At last. *At last!* It was coming. He could feel it. He felt his body strain, wanting to move, wanting to *dance* with excitement, but he forced himself to be still. Nothing must break her concentration now.

But, for a long moment, the cook did nothing more dramatic than continue to stare at her mop.

Her mind leapt and churned as images, thoughts, conclusions and finally the truth, the so clearly self-evident truth, all tried to cram into her mind at once.

How *stupid* she'd been. It was so blindingly obvious now who had killed Sid. There was only one person it *could* have been. All this time, she'd been on the wrong track, thinking she had to find out *why* Sid had been killed, when the evidence of *who* had killed him had been right under her nose all this time!

She almost groaned out loud.

The Kelton family sat frozen at the table. Each and every one stared at the cook, waiting, waiting, knowing as instinctively as Moulton had known that the moment was now here.

Some of them were surprised that it was the cook, of all people, who had somehow discovered who the killer was. Some, Bert among them, was not surprised at all.

Like racers poised at the starting line, trembling, every nerve straining, waiting for the pistol to fire, the Kelton clan waited for the cook to speak.

Jenny, however, was totally unaware of them. Her mind was whirling like a dervish on ice skates. So, she knew who. But she still didn't know why. It seemed to make no sense at all.

And yet it must. And suddenly, it did.

Once again the images flashed in her head as more of the truth, until now held back, came flooding into her mind in a dizzying deluge. And, once again, once you understood how to look at things, it all became so obvious. There had been so many clues. So many obvious pointers. And she'd been blind to them all. *Blind!*

Because the reason Sid had been killed was just as obvious as the identity of his killer.

Jenny almost smiled. Almost, but not quite.

*Blue eyes crying in the rain.*

Even her subconscious had been trying to get her attention pointed in the right direction.

'Of course,' she said again.

And turned to look straight at Bill Kelton.

# CHAPTER SIXTEEN

Bill went pale.

He held the cook's penetrating gaze for just a few seconds, then turned to look first at Bert, then Jeremy, and finally his father. 'What are you all looking at me for?' he asked aggressively, his chin jutting forward, his skin suddenly filling with colour again.

In her corner, Mrs Jarvis sank down onto the nearest chair, her heart thumping. She felt quite sick.

Moulton stood up. 'Mr William Kelton, I am arresting you for—'

'Inspector, please do stop that,' Jenny said firmly, putting the mop to one side, and walking to the table to slowly pull out her chair.

Moulton blinked at her. 'But . . . I thought you had it all sussed? You looked like you had,' he accused her, his voice almost comically aggrieved.

Jenny sat down briskly, and folded her hands in front of her, laying them on the table and looking at them thoughtfully. 'I do indeed have it all sussed, as you so quaintly put it,' she said shortly. 'But Bill isn't the killer. He's the reason *why* Sid was killed, yes, that I'll grant you,' she carried on, quickly marshalling her thoughts. 'But please don't jump the gun — if you'll pardon the figure of speech.'

'*What?*' Bill roared, his fair brows drawing into a deep frown. 'Now, look here, I don't know who you think you are, or why everyone around here seems to think you're the next best thing since the invention of the wheel all of a sudden, but I never had anything to do with poor old Sid getting killed. So you watch your mouth!'

'You watch yours, my lad,' Moulton snapped grimly, and turned to look at Miss Starling. He only hoped she knew what she was doing.

The cook, he noticed at once, was looking a little paler than usual, but her eyes were steady, as were the hands she held out in front of her. What's more, she appeared to be perfectly calm, Moulton noted with growing relief, and best of all, perfectly rational. But more than all of that, she had a quality of stillness about her, Moulton realized with a little atavistic shiver, that was close to near supernatural composure. She looked somehow immovable, like a mountain.

Moulton, somewhat reassured, sat back down. Bill glowered at him.

'I don't understand.' It was Delia who was the first to admit her ignorance. 'You said Bill was the *reason* why Uncle Sid was killed. But why?'

Jenny lifted her head briefly in Delia's direction, then slowly turned her head a few degrees. She was looking now towards the head of the table. 'Would you like to tell them all why Sid was killed, Stan, or should I?'

It was the first time she'd ever used Stan Kelton's first name to his face, and it would be the last.

Stan Kelton stared at her. 'I don't know what you're talking about,' he said flatly. But his eyes were shifting rapidly from side to side, unable to settle anywhere. And, under the table, Jenny distinctly heard his feet scrape sharply across the floor in agitation. His big body had jerked, on being asked such a simple question, but he'd brought himself rapidly under control and was now sitting quite, quite still.

Moulton and Ford exchanged glances. Neither of them spoke. Bill stared at his father. Delia stared at Bill. Jeremy began to bite his nails. Only Bert, it seemed, stared naturally ahead, looking almost easily from the cook to his father, his expression unreadable.

'I think you know exactly what I'm talking about,' Jenny contradicted him, her voice elevating just a little, her blue eyes becoming almost electric as she continued to meet Stan Kelton's granite-faced gaze. 'You killed your brother, and you killed him because of Bill.'

Bill shifted on his chair. He spared just a single glance for the cook, then kept his eyes fixed on those of his father. Suddenly, he knew he didn't have to defend himself anymore. And it was a hideously wonderful feeling.

Stan Kelton's big hands slowly clenched into fists as he assimilated the cook's inexorable words, but — at the same time — a rather hideous smile began to pull at his lips. It made him look grotesque.

Delia shivered, and looked away. It was her father, and yet it was a stranger. She couldn't, she realized a little wildly, even think of the figure at the head of the table as a 'him' anymore, so inhuman had he suddenly become.

'You killed your brother,' Jenny said again. Her voice was so flat, it was a mere statement of fact, not even an accusation.

'Prove it,' Stan said, equally as flatly.

And something in the room shifted. Until that moment, the Kelton offspring had not *quite* believed it. They'd *wanted* to believe it, yes. He was a tyrant, after all — but a murderer? But when Stan finally uttered those flat two words, which might just as well have been a confession, none of them were able to deny it anymore.

An almost inaudible sound echoed around the kitchen, a communal hiss of reaction. Delia let out her breath on a trembling sigh. Jeremy's teeth miscalculated the length of a thumbnail, and his two sets of molars came together in an audible click. Bert's chair creaked as he slumped against the back of it. Bill made the loudest noise of all — a kind of low, rumbling growl.

Jenny glanced at Moulton, and frowned. Knowing who the killer was and proving it were two very different things, after all. And the only piece of evidence she had was so flimsy as to be a defensive lawyer's dream. But it was not her job to prosecute — merely to uncover. She shrugged the worry off, like a duck shedding water off its back.

'There were so many things that pointed to you, and to the motive, that at first I couldn't see them,' she began — somewhat confusingly. 'Not being able to see the wood for the trees is one of my failings, I'm afraid,' she admitted.

Ford hastily got out his notebook and began to take down every word she said in rapid, precise shorthand. His face was pinched with excitement.

'But all the pointers only came together in my mind just now,' she added, somewhat unnecessarily. 'When I was mopping the floor.'

Moulton glanced briefly at the mop, then away again. He didn't want to miss a single nuance of expression on Stan Kelton's face.

'You see, ever since I came here, I've been mopping that dratted floor,' Jenny continued, her voice almost dream-like now, as her thoughts rallied together. 'The very first thing I did, in fact, on the very first day I came here, was to mop the floor.' She paused and looked up at Delia. 'You probably remember that?'

Delia nodded. 'And when Dad came in, you told him off, and he told you that you'd better get used to it.' She glanced just once at her father as she spoke, then hastily shifted her gaze back to the pepper pot on the table.

Jenny nodded. 'Indeed he did. He told me that the kitchen door led straight out into the courtyard, and that nobody was going to take off their boots outside, getting their socks wet and their feet cold, just so that I wouldn't have to mop the floor. Even I had to admit, he had a point.'

The cook allowed a slight, whimsical smile to cross her face. 'So, every time the men came in from the fields, I had to mop the floor. I mopped it the first day. I mopped it the second day. On Christmas Eve.'

With the last few words, everyone suddenly perked up, and paid greater attention. Even Moulton had been wondering why she was going on about mops. Now his eyes sharpened — but not on Miss Starling. He still had his gaze fixed firmly on Stan Kelton's face, so he didn't miss the sudden shifting in the man's dark brown eyes. Nor did he miss the telltale movement as Stan's jaws clenched tighter together.

She's on to something, he thought, excitedly. By gum, she's actually on to something!

'You probably remember, Bill, Bert, that the floor was clean and dry that morning? The morning Sid had breakfast with us for the last time?'

Bill looked at Bert, who was already nodding his head. 'Yes. I remember,' Bert confirmed simply. 'None of us had been out and brought back any muddy footprints yet.' There was something much stronger about Bert now, she noticed with satisfaction. He was quietly confident and competent.

'But, Inspector Moulton,' Jenny turned to the inspector, forcing him to shift his gaze back to her, 'when you came to the farm for the first time, the floor was once again as muddy and wet as ever.'

Moulton nodded. 'Of course. When I got here, all the Kelton men, and Miss Delia, were already here, having come in from outside.'

'And the floor was wet and dirty because of it,' Jenny confirmed. 'Yes.' She rearranged the salt pot, which slightly out of alignment, and frowned thoughtfully. 'You see, all along I felt that I was missing something. Whenever I thought back to that morning, and went over it, I knew, I just *knew* there was something I had overlooked. And it was only a moment ago, as I was mopping the floor, that I knew what it was.'

She looked straight at Stan Kelton.

'After I'd collected the eggs, and took my coat and boots off in the hall, I came back into the kitchen and walked all over this floor.' For a moment, both of them glanced down at the tiles in question. 'I went to the sink to fill the kettle. I went to the stove to get out the mince pies and finally I went to the table, where Sid was. And that's what I should have remembered,' she finished, as if it must all be perfectly obvious now.

'You walked to the table?' Bill asked, fascinated now in spite of himself. 'I don't get it. What's significant about that?'

Moulton was wondering the same thing, but since he was once more back to watching Stan Kelton like a kestrel hovering over a mouse, he saw at once the expression of rising panic creep into the man's eyes. Whatever the significance was, Stan Kelton understood it only too well.

'What's significant, Bill,' Jenny said, 'is that I was walking about in just my socks. *And my feet didn't get wet.* They stayed perfectly dry.'

Bert slowly leaned forward, a light of understanding dawning in his eyes. He nodded. 'The floor was still dry,' he repeated slowly, turning to stare at his father. 'If one of us had come in from the fields, or Delia from the Brays' place, in order to kill Sid, we'd have left a trail of wet and muddy footprints on the floor. But that day . . . that day . . .' he couldn't go on.

But by now Bill, and both policemen, had also caught on. 'You were in the tack room,' Bill said, taking up the tale, his eyes turned to the door that led off to the corridor that opened out onto the stables. 'You never had to go out in the snow that morning. Your feet would have stayed dry. And yours were the *only* ones that would have.'

'And did,' Jenny confirmed. 'You know the stables well, Bill. Could Stan have seen me pass by on the way to the hen house?'

'Easily,' Bill said quickly.

'Then that's what he did,' Jenny nodded. She turned her chair just enough so that she could face Stan Kelton head on without having to keep on swivelling her head. 'You saw me leave, took your chance and came in through that door.' She pointed to the little-used door.

Everyone else quickly turned to look at it.

'You came in, perhaps said "hello" to Sid, and went across to the knife drawer.' As one, heads swivelled to the knife drawer. They could all see it playing out in front of them. Delia wanted to cry out at her 'stop it, *stop it*,' but her mouth was too dry. Instead, just like all the others, she forced herself to listen in grim, painful silence, as the recital went on.

'Sid wouldn't have thought anything of it,' Jenny speculated. 'You were working on the bridles or what have you. You might have needed a sharp knife, or even one of the skewers that I noticed you keep in there to pierce the leatherwork. I don't suppose he was even alarmed when you turned and came back here, to this table, with the knife in your hand. Was he?'

Stan Kelton said nothing, but his big body began to move forward, towards the edge of the chair. Moulton, too, instinctively moved forward. If the man was going to make a run for it . . . He glanced at Ford, still busily scribbling away in his notebook, and relaxed a little. He was a good man, Ford. Together, they'd keep Stan Kelton in his place.

'The actual stabbing itself didn't take long,' Jenny went on remorselessly. 'The police doctor confirmed that it was a single blow. You're a strong man, Mr Kelton, and Sid . . . well, there wasn't much flesh and blood to Sid,' she said sadly.

Delia gave a trembling sob. Bert reached up a hand and gently stopped his son from nibbling yet more of his nails.

'And that's it, is it?' Stan Kelton asked at last, his voice mocking. 'That's your so-called evidence. Any one of them,' he waved a meaty paw at his tense family, 'could have taken off their boots outside, then put them on again after the killing.'

'And risked wasting all that time?' Jenny asked sceptically. 'I don't think so. They'd want the deed over and done with and to get well away from here in the shortest possible time. Nobody in their right mind would want to dawdle outside, taking off or putting on boots, when they might be seen at any moment either by myself, coming back from the hen house, or any other chance caller or even Mrs Jarvis. Besides, habits are hard things to break. By their very nature, people indulge in them without ever realizing it. It wouldn't have occurred to any of you, yourself included, to stop and take off your boots first, before coming inside. Even if you were coming inside to commit murder. You wouldn't even have given it a thought, you're so used to just coming right on in.'

And everyone at the table knew she was right. But Moulton and Ford knew something else.

It was not enough.

Stan Kelton seemed to know it too. 'You're just whistling in the wind,' he jeered.

Jenny smiled. 'If that was all, perhaps.'

She didn't miss Moulton's look of glee, even seeing it out of the corner of her eye, and Stan, face to face with him, had no chance of ignoring it. His big hands jumped, and he made a great show out of folding his arms arrogantly across his chest.

Not so confident as you'd like to make out, are you, matey? Moulton thought silently. He now had no doubt that Jenny Starling had picked the right man. *Again.* But they needed more evidence. Much more. And he still didn't know why Bill Kelton should have provided the motive. Come to that, he still had no idea what the motive was.

As if he'd somehow plucked the inspector's thought from out of the airwaves, Bert looked across at his father. His face was blank, except for a look of pain, set deep in the back of his eyes.

'Why did you do it, Dad?' he asked simply. And spoke for all of them. For now, nobody in that room doubted that Stan Kelton was a killer. It would take some getting used to — to have a murderer for a father. Bill shuddered; he felt sick to his stomach. Tainted blood. That's what he had. The thought was like a black sucking mud, making him sweat all over.

Stan Kelton blinked at Bert, angry colour rising into his face. He opened his mouth, then quickly closed it again.

'He'd like to tell you,' Jenny said coldly, 'that he did it all for you. Just to see your face.'

And from the fulminating look of loathing Stan gave her, it was obvious that her words were as accurate as hitting a bullseye.

'I thought you said Bill was the reason,' Jeremy, for the first time, spoke. His voice sounded hopelessly young and lost in the tense silence of the room.

Bill frowned, but said nothing.

'And so he is,' the cook said, confusingly. 'Isn't he, Mr Kelton?' she goaded softly.

Stan gave her a look filled with fear and hate, but he was not so far gone that he didn't know enough to keep quiet. She didn't have enough to convict him and they both knew it. So the less he said, the better.

But Jenny was relentless. 'At first, I was totally puzzled by the lack of motive in this case,' she mused, sounding so police-man-like that Ford smiled over his notes. 'Everybody hated Stan, but everyone loved Sid. Yet it was Sid who was killed. It made no sense. It made me feel, and continued to make me feel for a long time, as if I was investigating the wrong murder.'

Moulton gave a slight nod. He remembered saying the same thing to her, not so long ago.

'But all the time the clues were right under my nose,' the cook continued, her self-disgust plainly evident.

'If they were under your nose all the time, Miss Starling,' Bert said gently, 'they were under ours as well. But I never saw them. And I still don't.'

'Me neither,' Bill said. 'I wish you'd get on with it,' he added, but not harshly. The truth was, the strain was begin-ning to tell on his nerves.

Jenny sighed. She was feeling tired now. 'Yes. Of course. Well, the first thing that struck me as odd was the way that Stan was treating his two sons so strangely. From what Mrs Jarvis said,' Jenny glanced in the daily's direction, only to see the old woman glance back at her. She had an ugly look of glee and triumph on her face as she contemplated her hated enemy's downfall, and Jenny looked quickly away. 'Yes. Er . . . Mrs Jarvis told me that Stan had previously been all for Bill, and all against Bert. And that made sense.'

She paused, glanced apologetically at Bert, but carried on. 'It was obvious to me that Bill was the dominant brother, and that Bert was much more easygoing. I could quite see why a man like Stan Kelton would be proud of Bill, a go-getter, and rather scornful of Bert, who seemed rather placid by nature. But now, suddenly, things had turned full circle. It was Bill who was the despised one, and Bert who'd become all important, in Stan's eyes, at least. In fact, Bert was so important that Stan even destroyed Janice Kelton's letters to him. It was obvious he was determined to keep them apart, and make sure that Bert stayed here. And it was just as obvious that he wanted Bill out. Now that just didn't make sense.'

'I told you,' Mrs Jarvis piped up, her voice as full of terrible glee as her face. 'I told you he always kept the boys at loggerheads. Now he'll pay.' She all but cackled.

'Yes, you did,' Jenny agreed, her voice cold. 'But I never accepted that as a reasonable explanation. If Stan had wanted to keep his sons arguing amongst themselves, he would have been all for Bill one week, then all for Bert the next. Little and often is the only way to sow real contention in a family, a fact that a man of Stan Kelton's character would be only too well aware of. But for all of his life, Bill had been the favourite. No. This was something else. Something specific must have happened to change the way that Stan Kelton saw his sons. That was the first thing that set me thinking.'

Now that she explained it to him, it set Moulton thinking too. But, try as he might, he was damned if he could see where she was heading with all of this.

'Then we had the surprise of Sid's Christmas presents to the family,' Jenny carried on. 'And I had to ask myself, what was Sid up to?'

Stan Kelton snarled. There was no other word to describe the noise that rumbled from his throat. 'He was up to no good, that's what he was up to,' he rasped.

'He certainly had something on his mind,' she agreed, not allowing him to rile her. 'And the only conclusion that I could come up with was that Sid wanted Bert out, and Bill in, as much as you wanted it the other way around. Why else would he ensure Bert and Janice had a new place to live, and a new business to keep them going, if he didn't want Bert to leave? He had already arranged for Delia to have some money to get away, and for Jeremy to have a new car. He didn't want to leave anyone out. But the main beneficiary of Sid's generosity was Bert, which would have put him, Sid, directly at loggerheads with Stan, his younger brother. And that worried me — because always before, Sid had let Stan have his own way, in order to live a quiet life and keep the peace in the family.'

'But Sid didn't give me a spectacular present,' Bill felt compelled to point out. It was ridiculous, he thought, how much that still hurt him. Even now, amidst all of this.

'Ah,' Jenny said. 'But he never intended to leave you out, Bill,' she said softly. 'He intended you to have the biggest prize of all. Isn't that right, Mr Kelton?' She turned once more to Stan, who was going an acid shade of puce.

'The *stupid old sod*,' Stan sneered. 'As if I'd let him.'

Moulton glanced quickly at Bill, just long enough to see that the young man was as puzzled as himself.

'Let him do what?' It was Bert who asked the million-dollar question.

'Why, let him have the farm, of course,' Jenny said.

There was a long, long moment of silence, during which Stan Kelton's eyes became murderous as he stared at the cook. Moulton moved another notch forward on his chair. Stan looked like he was getting ready to throttle her.

'But only the oldest son can inherit the farm,' Delia said, puzzled.

'Yes, I know,' Jenny Starling said. 'Bill is the oldest.'

Bert shifted on his seat. 'I'm afraid you're wrong there, Miss Starling,' he said. 'I'm the oldest.'

'You're the oldest son of *Stanley* Kelton, yes. Or, rather I should say, you're the *only* son of Stanley Kelton. Bill,' Jenny said, and looked across at him, 'is the only son of *Sidney* Kelton. And since Sid was the oldest son, Bill is the rightful heir.'

Bill stood up abruptly. He stared first at the cook, then at the man at the head of the table that he'd always called Father, opened his mouth to say something — he wasn't sure what — and felt himself sway.

Just as abruptly, he sat back down again.

'Just like an old woman. Coming over all wobbly,' Stan Kelton sneered, causing a dull, ugly flush to rise up over Bill's face. 'Just like Sid, in fact,' he spat, loathing and hate spewing from him like venom from a snake's fang. 'No damned backbone.'

'You thought he had plenty of good stuff in him when you thought he was *your* son,' Jenny shot back promptly, and didn't so much as flinch when he turned his venomous stare on her. Instead she stared steadily back at him, completely armoured against his evil.

'I'm not your son,' Bill breathed, as if unable to take it in. 'I'm not your son,' he repeated, more strongly, and suddenly began to laugh. If there was just a little hysteria in it, nobody in that room (with the exception of Stan Kelton) begrudged it him.

He *was* going through the grinder, after all.

Then, suddenly, Bill stopped laughing. He said just one word: 'Sid.'

Jenny looked at him sympathetically. 'Yes. I'm so sorry you lost him, before you ever had the chance to understand. Sid was your father.'

Bill looked at Miss Starling, his face slack with shock, his eyes round. 'But . . . how?'

Stan snarled and sneered again, and Moulton said sharply, 'Shut up, you, if you know what's good for you.' And there was something so surprisingly sharp and *hard* about the inspector's voice that Stan found himself instinctively obeying. It was probably a novel experience for him.

Jenny reached out to take Bill's cold hand in her own, then glanced across at Bert. 'Do you know about your mother, Eloise, and Sid being in love before she ever met Stan Kelton?'

It was Bert who nodded. 'I heard some women gossiping once, at the church fete, oh, years ago. You were only about fifteen.' Bert looked at his brother, who was now only his half-brother, his eyes troubled. 'I heard them say how Mum and Sid should have been the ones to marry. That Dad had split them up on purpose.'

Bill swallowed hard. It was a lot to take in all at once.

'Even then,' Jenny said, 'Stan Kelton was determined at all costs to have the farm. He was willing to do anything to get it. Including breaking his brother's heart, stealing the girl he loved and marrying a woman that he himself felt nothing for, just to sire sons that would one day take over the farm.'

She leaned back in her chair, her smile wry. 'I was very dim, there,' she admitted. 'I thought it might be interesting to find out if Sid had had any children on the wrong side of the blanket, and even asked around the village. But it should have been quite obvious to anyone with any brains,' she grimaced at her own stupidity, 'that no two people who were in love could live together in the same house and not turn to one another for solace. Eloise and Sid would have to have been made of stone *not* to have had an affair. I should have realized that fact, right from the start.'

She gave another sigh at her own dimness, and turned once more to Stan Kelton. 'It must have been quite a blow when Sid told you that Bill was really his, and must inherit.'

Abruptly, the entire colour fled from Stan's face.

'I imagine you must have rallied quickly though,' she added sadly. 'Janice tells me that Sid asked her not to tell Bert about the antique shop until Christmas, so it gave you some leeway. What did you do?' she asked Stan, without expecting an answer. 'I imagine, when you realized that there would be no deterring him, that you asked Sid not to say anything to the others until after Christmas as well? Put on a bit of a production, did you? Tell him how much Bert would be upset? No doubt you asked him for some time to prepare him for all this? Time to get used to the idea of no longer inheriting? Time to get used to losing Bill as a son? And Sid . . .' Jenny shook her head. 'Sid would have been kind-hearted enough to agree, wouldn't he? I can almost hear him saying it. "All right, Stan, we'll have one last family Christmas together, just as we are. But after that . . . I'm talking to Bill." It would have gone something like that, wouldn't it.'

Stan Kelton was amazed at her powers of deduction. It had, in fact, gone very much like that. Sid had been a sentimental old fool. But Stan was hardly about to say so.

'It was that stupid old magazine article that did it, you know,' Jenny said, once again setting everyone else all at sea. 'I don't think Eloise ever told Sid that Bill might be his son. I think, even then, she would have been afraid of what would happen. And she certainly wasn't about to tell you,' she met Stan's eyes, doing nothing to try and hide her own contempt. 'No, if she had told him Bill was probably his son, Sid would have made his stand a long time ago. Who knows, Eloise might have given the man she really loved one last blessing in keeping the truth from him. After all, it ensured that he lived, in relative peace at least, for another thirty years or so.'

And nobody doubted her wisdom, because nobody doubted that a younger Stan Kelton would have been any less murderous than a middle-aged Stan Kelton.

'Old magazine article?' Delia finally said, remembering that day they'd cleared out Sid's room. 'He was always reading them,' she added wistfully. 'He'd even liked going through really old ones people were throwing out for recycling. He was a great reader of bits and bobs, but it did mean that he wasn't often up-to-date in what was what. But what have they got to do with all this?'

'One of them,' Jenny explained patiently, 'was tucked out of sight, away from all the others, hidden under the mattress. That alone should have told me,' she added exasperatedly, 'that there was something that set it apart from the rest. Why else would Sid carefully hide it under the mattress? I should have immediately read it from cover to cover. As it was, luck was on my side. I read enough to make it clear to me now what must have happened.'

'But what was in it that was so important?' Bert asked raggedly.

Jenny shrugged. 'An old and not up-to-date article on genetics, about the blue eye/brown eye gene, and which was dominant,' she said drolly, and took pity on his blank stare. 'Never mind the statistics, since they can be confusing. The upshot was, Sid got it into his head that since both Stan and his wife had brown eyes, the fact that Bill had blue eyes — like his own — meant that Bill must be his son.'

Everyone looked at Bill. Strange how they had never taken any notice of his eyes before. But Sid and Bill had been the only blue-eyed ones amongst them all. Funny, how you took things for granted, and never questioned them.

'I remembered thinking what beautiful brown eyes Eloise had when Stan Kelton showed us all the family album,' Jenny continued. 'I couldn't figure out why I kept thinking back to Sid, sat at that chair, his eyes open even in death, as if he was trying to tell me something.'

Delia shivered. 'Oh, don't.'

'But he was trying to tell you something,' Bert said, his voice little more than a whisper.

Yes,' Jenny said. 'His blue eyes were definitely trying to tell me something. To make matters worse, even that dratted song about blue eyes crying in the rain kept playing in my head. But still I was too dim to see it. But you can see why Sid thought the way he did — and why he decided he needed to act the way he did. And the real tragedy is, a simple DNA test would have proved it one way or another. But, ironically — and in a way — it doesn't really matter which one was the father — only that both brothers believed Bill was Sid's. And that provided ample motive for murder. Luckily for us all, Stan Kelton made mistakes.'

'Such as?' Moulton asked.

'Telling Bill to pack his bags and get out was the worst. Stan was a man who liked to keep his family around him, and very much under his thumb. Giving Bill his freedom was just so out of character. And then, when he realized that I had experience in murder investigations, he tried to throw me off the scent by asking me to give him the name of the killer first, in order to exact retribution, he'd have had me believe.'

Jenny straightened and turned to give Stan Kelton a final, level gaze. 'But I told him then that the murderer of Sid Kelton would spend the rest of his life in prison.' Her own lovely blue eyes suddenly lost all their contempt and became, instead, rather flat. 'And so he will,' she added.

'So he will,' Moulton agreed. 'Since you're the only one with a motive, Mr Kelton, and we have the evidence of the kitchen floor, no jury in the world will let you off. You can—'

Bert gave a cry of warning as Stan, with shocking quickness, launched himself from the table. But he wasn't interested in the door, or in a bolt for freedom. He only wanted to get his hands on his cook.

'*You bitch,*' he roared, knocking over his chair and grabbing her by the throat before she had a chance to rear back. Ford dropped his notebook and sprang to his feet. Bill and Bert did the same, but someone else was quicker by far.

A black and white flash shot out from under the table as the sheepdog, with a hair-raising snarl, sank his teeth firmly into Stan Kelton's backside.

The dog had waited such a long time to do it.

In an instant Jenny was free as Stan Kelton roared in pain, and in the next instant, Moulton and Ford were all over the furiously cursing farmer, handcuffs at the ready.

'Remind me to give that dog some of the best steak I can find,' Jenny said, to no one in particular, as she rubbed her sore throat.

# EPILOGUE

Jenny hefted her holdall out onto the landing floor, then turned for a final glance around her room. The bed was made, the fire was safely out and the fireguard was back in place. She hoped Bill would have central heating put in soon. If he didn't, any wife he might take most definitely would!

She nodded once and shut the door firmly behind her. As she turned and bent once more to her holdall, a door further down the landing opened and Bert Kelton stepped out. She straightened up and glanced at her watch. It was barely eight o'clock.

Moulton and Ford had taken Stan away yesterday afternoon, after cautioning him. Jenny, who had been very much aware that the remaining Keltons badly needed time, space and, above all, *privacy* in which to sort themselves out and do some serious talking, had pleaded tiredness and the desire for an early night.

But only after serving dinner, of course. Everything stopped for food, in Jenny Starling's book.

Now, Bert watched her coming towards him and his eyes dropped to the holdall. 'I didn't realize you were going to leave today, Miss Starling,' he said, his voice as warm as she'd ever heard it.

She was glad that the 'real' Bert was at last emerging from the former shadow that had been Bert Kelton when she'd first arrived. Now he walked upright and lightly, and his face had lost its haggard and haunted expression, making him look years younger.

'I think it's probably best,' Jenny said primly. She had no desire to remain at the Kelton residence after delivering up one of their members to the police, even if the rest of the Kelton family were happy that she had done so. 'Besides,' she added, 'I was only hired for the Christmas season.'

'There's still New Year,' Bert said. 'I know Bill wouldn't mind if you stayed on a bit longer.'

Jenny smiled. 'I think, you know, that he might. Anyway, I want to be off before it starts snowing again. Have you seen the weather outside?'

Bert had, and he agreed with her. Another blizzard seemed to be on its way, and who could blame her for not wanting to get snowed in at Kelton Farm for a second time?

'I see. Well . . .' He held out his hand, a little awkwardly, and Jenny promptly took it and gave it a firm shake. 'I'm really glad you came to us, Miss Starling,' Bert said earnestly, and even as he said it, he realized what a massive understatement it was, and laughed.

Jenny met his sincere gaze, but her own was shrewd. 'Truly? I thought, once or twice you know, that I had you worried.' Her eyes twinkled.

Bert had the grace to blush, even as he shrugged it all off. 'I know. It was because of Jeremy, you see.'

'But you never really suspected him?'

'Oh no. No, but I thought he might have seen who had done it.'

Jenny nodded. 'And you suspected Bill?'

Bert gaped at her. 'How did you know?'

Jenny smiled. 'You were rather quick, that morning when I came back with the police, to confirm both Jeremy's and Bill's story about the order in which you all came back. It made me wonder why.'

Bert laughed. 'Bill's temper has always worried me,' he admitted wryly. 'There's just no fooling you, is there?' he said, then murmured a heartfelt, 'Which is just as well!' under his breath.

Jenny pretended not to hear. 'Well, goodbye, Mr Kelton. I take it you'll be joining your wife in Woodstock soon?'

Bert nodded happily. 'But Jeremy's agreed to stay on here for a few weeks, just until Bill's had the chance to hire some more locals. That'll be a popular move, at any rate. A good thing too. We Keltons have got some fence-mending to do. Not that anybody will care about Dad being . . . well . . . Let's face it, nobody will care about Dad,' he said simply.

'Quite,' Jenny said, briskly. Useless platitudes never had been her forte. 'I hope you enjoy the antique business, Mr Kelton,' she said, and smiled and turned for the stairs.

Halfway up, she met Delia. The girl gave her a beatific smile. 'Me and Sissy are going to move into Woodstock. Bert and Janice have promised to help us find a flat. And now that I have Uncle Sid's money to get us started, it doesn't matter that that old bag, Cordelia, stole Sissy's, does it?' she chirruped happily.

Jenny smiled. Indeed it didn't. And she approved of Delia staying well within range of her family. Some girls matured more quickly than others, after all, and she could well imagine that Janice would keep a motherly eye on her young sister-in-law — at a distance, of course.

'I'm very glad to hear it, Delia,' Jenny said, and moved to one side as the teenager shot past her, all restless, happy energy. How fast the young healed, the cook mused, setting down her holdall beside the front door and making her way into the kitchen. There she paused on the threshold, pensively observing Bill Kelton's back as he stood at the sink.

She must have made a slight noise, for he turned, saw her, and hesitated. Although his look was friendly enough, it was also strained, and Jenny smiled slightly.

'I have my bag outside,' she said straight away. 'I thought, under the circumstances, it would be best if I didn't stay for the New Year.'

Bill smiled in obvious relief. And immediately felt guilty. 'Miss Starling,' he said, taking a deep breath. 'I owe a lot to you. We all do, of course. Nobody likes being under suspicion of murder. But I owe you more than most — and I have the farm now. Bert's leaving for good, did he tell you? Him and Jeremy both.'

Jenny nodded.

'Bert said he never really wanted to inherit the farm anyway, and especially not now that he's back with his wife and has a whole new life to look forward to. He just wants to forget about this place,' he waved a hand vaguely around to encompass their surroundings.

'Does that mean he think's Sid's your father? Do you? Are you going to have a DNA test?' Jenny asked, with pardonable curiosity.

Bill shrugged. 'No, I'm not getting tested. Why bother? I prefer to think of Sid as my father. So Bert and me, we're going to go to a solicitor and get it all sorted, legal-like. Bert will sign some papers saying I'm the eldest son of the eldest son, so it's all official.'

'Well, that's what Sid would have wanted,' Jenny agreed softly.

'Yes. Anyway,' Bill said gruffly. 'I wouldn't want you to leave thinking that I'm not grateful.'

Jenny smiled. 'It never crossed my mind, Mr Kelton.'

Bill smiled in relief, his tense shoulders relaxing. 'Good, and if there's anything I can ever do for you, just let me know.'

'Well, as a matter of fact,' she said, hesitating, unsure how to be tactful about it, and saw Bill immediately tense up again.

'Yes?'

Jenny coughed. 'Well, er, there is a question of . . . well, my wages.'

Bill gaped at her, and then began to laugh. 'You mean you haven't been paid in advance?' he asked. 'Isn't that just like the miserly old sod.'

He left the room for a few minutes, and then returned with a gratifying number of twenty-pound notes. And although they amounted to far more than she had agreed to be paid in her letter to Stan Kelton, Jenny promptly put them away in her purse.

Waste not, want not!

'Well, goodbye, Mr Kelton. I want to drop in at Kidlington before going back to Oxford. I never got the chance yesterday to say goodbye to Inspector Moulton and Sergeant Ford.'

'Oh, of course,' Bill said, following her out into the hall. Jenny shook his hand briefly, and firmly waved away his offer to walk her to the bus stop in the village, where the buses were once again running.

But, from the look of the sky, not for much longer, she mused. She'd better put her best foot forward. As the door closed behind her, Jenny took a deep breath, hefted her hold-all over one shoulder, and set off. Never had she been so glad to leave a place behind!

She had covered no more than half a dozen yards when the gander spotted her. His beady eye alighted on the holdall, and he gave an avian hiss of triumph. He couldn't, of course, let her go without one last attempt at showing her just who was boss.

Jenny, who'd been keeping an anxious eye on the iron-grey snow clouds above her, heard the hiss just in time. She turned and deftly lifted one ankle out of the firing line of an extended beak. The bird, massive wings still extended, executed a perfect Charlie Chaplin-like turn on one webbed foot, and came back for a second try.

A cold wind, full of snow and ice, suddenly gusted across the yard, and Jenny shivered.

'You know,' she said thoughtfully, and loudly, 'I really could do with some goose feathers to make myself a nice warm quilt — especially in this weather.' And she took a quick step forward, as if she fully intended to start chasing *him*.

Just passing the kitchen window, Bill Kelton heard a fearsome honking, and looked up just in time to see his gander head for the barn as if all the foxes in Hades were after him.

### THE END

# THE JOFFE BOOKS STORY

We began in 2014 when Jasper agreed to publish his mum's much-rejected romance novel and it became a bestseller.

Since then we've grown into the largest independent publisher in the UK. We're extremely proud to publish some of the very best writers in the world, including Joy Ellis, Faith Martin, Caro Ramsay, Helen Forrester, Simon Brett and Robert Goddard. Everyone at Joffe Books loves reading and we never forget that it all begins with the magic of an author telling a story.

We are proud to publish talented first-time authors, as well as established writers whose books we love introducing to a new generation of readers.

We won Trade Publisher of the Year at the Independent Publishing Awards in 2023. We have been shortlisted for Independent Publisher of the Year at the British Book Awards for the last four years, and were shortlisted for the Diversity and Inclusivity Award at the 2022 Independent Publishing Awards. In 2023 we were shortlisted for Publisher of the Year at the RNA Industry Awards.

We built this company with your help, and we love to hear from you, so please email us about absolutely anything bookish at feedback@joffebooks.com

If you want to receive free books every Friday and hear about all our new releases, join our mailing list: www.joffebooks.com/contact

And when you tell your friends about us, just remember: it's pronounced Joffe as in coffee or toffee!

## ALSO BY FAITH MARTIN

### DI HILLARY GREENE SERIES
Book 1: MURDER ON THE OXFORD CANAL
Book 2: MURDER AT THE UNIVERSITY
Book 3: MURDER OF THE BRIDE
Book 4: MURDER IN THE VILLAGE
Book 5: MURDER IN THE FAMILY
Book 6: MURDER AT HOME
Book 7: MURDER IN THE MEADOW
Book 8: MURDER IN THE MANSION
Book 9: MURDER IN THE GARDEN
Book 10: MURDER BY FIRE
Book 11: MURDER AT WORK
Book 12: MURDER NEVER RETIRES
Book 13: MURDER OF A LOVER
Book 14: MURDER NEVER MISSES
Book 15: MURDER AT MIDNIGHT
Book 16: MURDER IN MIND
Book 17: HILLARY'S FINAL CASE
Book 18: HILLARY'S BACK
Book 19: MURDER NOW AND THEN
Book 20: MURDER IN THE PARISH

### MONICA NOBLE MYSTERIES
Book 1: THE VICARAGE MURDER
Book 2: THE FLOWER SHOW MURDER
Book 3: THE MANOR HOUSE MURDER

### TRAVELLING COOK MYSTERIES
Book 1: THE BIRTHDAY MYSTERY
Book 2: THE WINTER MYSTERY
Book 3: THE RIVERBOAT MYSTERY
Book 4: THE CASTLE MYSTERY
Book 5: THE OXFORD MYSTERY
Book 6: THE TEATIME MYSTERY
Book 7: THE COUNTRY INN MYSTERY